Pillow Stalk

Pillow Stalk
A Mad for Mod Mystery

diane vallere

Polyester Press
www.polyesterpress.com

Acknowledgments

A large thank you is owed to the many people who set this project into motion (whether they knew what they were doing or not!). To my parents, Mary and Don Vallere, for finding that jewel of an apartment while I was busy at work. To Debbie Hargrove, who gave me a copy of *Pillow Talk* as a going away present when I left Texas. And to Josh Hickman, who did the impossible and introduced me to a part of Dallas that I fell in love with.

I want to thank the many readers and writers who gave me feedback on opening pages and early drafts: Susan Chalfin, Jennifer Gates, Katherine Grey, Polly Iyer, Susie Klein, Andrew MacRae, Mannid Pock, Kellie Rix, Barb Schlichting, Susan Schreyer, and Steve Shrott. And to Gigi Pandian, who not only helped with feedback, but liked Madison enough to encourage me to revisit her in our joint novella project.

To my editor, Ramona DeFelice Long, who asks the questions that need to be asked and makes my writing better, and to Richard Goodman, who showed the appropriate amount of enthusiasm while still challenging plot points. Thanks to Kendel Lynn, my fellow Capricorn, whose friendship encompasses far more than the world of writing. And, of course, to Mary Ann Kappelhoff, for being exactly who she is.

Dedication

For Josh

One

"Mr. Johnson, I'm calling to discuss the disposition of your mother's estate," I said into the yellow donut phone.

"Are you a lawyer?" asked a gruff voice on the other end of a crackly line.

"No, sir, I'm an interior decorator. Madison Night. I own Mad for Mod, on Greenville Avenue," I paused, giving him time to react. When he didn't, I continued. "I assure you I mean no disrespect. In my experience, you are about to be faced with the time consuming challenge of handling your mother's affairs, and I am in a position to take a portion of that challenge off your to-do list." Internally, I cringed at the holier-than-thou tone that had crept into my voice. It was an oral knee-jerk reaction to people not taking me seriously. "Mad for Mod specializes in mid-century modern design. Your mother's house was—"

"What was your name again? Madison?" he snapped. "What are you, twenty?"

"Madison was my grandmother's maiden name," I offered. I pushed my long hair away from my face, then used my index finger to free a couple of strands that were stuck to my hairline, thanks to the Dallas-in-May humidity. "I'm forty-seven, and I've been in this industry for over twenty years." The man was obviously more distraught over the death of his mother than the fact that my grandmother's surname had come into fashion sometime in the nineties, but at times like these, minor details could change the course of our conversation.

"My mom didn't have anything valuable. Her whole house was insured for fifteen thousand dollars, and I'd be better off if it had burned down and I got the check. Now I'm stuck with a bunch of junk I could never convince her to throw away."

I wrote *$15,000?* on the side of a real estate flyer that sat on my desk and put on my best can-do attitude. "Mr. Johnson, I'm prepared to make an offer on the entire estate. If you accept it, I can bring you a check tomorrow, and you can be on your way back to Cincinnati as soon as tomorrow night."

"Let me get this straight. You're offering to write me a check for stuff you haven't even seen?"

"That's correct."

"Lady, if this is a joke, you have a lousy sense of humor." He hung up on me.

I drummed my fingers against the top of my desk and stared at the flyer, temporarily distracted by the overdone graphics and the photo of the listing agent.

Pamela Ritter, a recently licensed realtor, stared back at me, a picture of blond hair and blue eyes not all that different from my own, though she was half my age. *Blast from the Past!* screamed the heading, above listings for a string of ranch houses on Mockingbird. *Live like a Mad Man!* promised the copy on the side. Turquoise bubbles filled the background of the paper, and starbursts, outlined in red, gave it a comic book *Pow! Bam! Bop!* feel.

Pamela had jumped on the new movement to capitalize on all things fifties, thanks to a recent pop culture focus on the Eisenhower era. I'd been nurturing my passion for mid-century decorating since I was a teenager, since I first watched *Pillow Talk* after learning that I shared a birthday with an actress named Doris Day. I had surrounded myself with items from the atomic age long before Pamela was born, and thanks to my business, I'd found a community of others who shared my interest and appreciated my knowledge. I crumpled up the flyer and tossed it at the trash bin. It bounced off the rim and landed on the carpet.

I glanced at the brushed gold starburst clock mounted close to the ceiling. Photos of rooms, stills from Doris Day movies, swatches of fabric and paint chips from the hardware store covered the bottom two thirds of the wall, thumb-tacked to cork squares I'd glued on top of the paint. Arrows and notes connected a couple of the inspiration points and identified those ideas that I had earmarked for a specific client. Merchandise and props to make an authentic mid-century room were not cheap or easy to come by, and I depended on the obituaries to identify estates that might be rich in the era's style. Thelma Johnson, age seventy-nine, lifetime resident of a two bedroom split level in the M streets, had that kind of estate, but her son wasn't interested in my sales pitch.

I twisted my blond hair back into a chignon, then secured it with a vintage hairpin. It was ten minutes to six. I could leave early. Nothing was going to happen in ten minutes. I flipped the open sign to closed, locked the doors, and carried the small bag of trash out the back door, swatting the light switch on the way. I emptied the trash into the dumpster and rummaged through my handbag for my keys before noticing the flat tire on my powder blue Alfa Romeo.

I bent next to the tire and a slash of pain shot through my left knee. After a skiing accident two years ago, I had been left with a reminder that I had to look out for myself, because no one else would. The chronic pain forced me to acknowledge my limitations. It kept me from doing the kind of things that independent women knew how to do for themselves and Texas

3

women took for granted that someone else would do for them. And today, it would keep me from getting home ten minutes early.

I went back inside the studio and called Hudson James, my handyman. "What are the chances you're up for rescuing a damsel in distress?" I asked.

"Depends on the damsel."

"Thanks to a flat tire, I'm stranded at the studio. I'd try to change it myself," I said, but stopped when the humiliating reality of me calling a man to ask for help resonated in my ears. I never thought I'd be that kind of woman.

"Madison, it's no problem. I'm in the neighborhood and I'll be there in a couple of minutes."

Hudson's blue pickup truck pulled into the alley by my studio and parked next to the dumpster. His longish black hair had curled with the humidity, the front pushed to the side, behind his ear, the back flipping up against the collar of his black t-shirt. "I thought you were calling because you had a job for me," he said.

I flushed. "I might," I said, "I'm still working it out. A woman died—"

He held up a hand. "I don't want to know the details."

"It's just business."

"I look at you and I see sweetness and innocence, not a ruthless business woman."

"Don't let the blond hair and blue eyes fool you."

"Honey, they had me fooled me the first time I laid eyes on you." He winked and took the keys from my hand. Before he turned back to the car, his eyes swept over my body. "Is that a new dress?"

I looked down at my dress, a light blue fitted sheath that was significantly more wrinkled than it had been when I left the house hours ago. A series of circles in gingham, stripe, and polka dot had been appliquéd to the neckline and hem.

4

"It's a new-old dress. Early sixties. From an estate sale in Pennsylvania, before I moved here. The woman died in a car accident—"

"Enough! I like the dress. I like the dress on you. But I don't need to hear the obituary of the woman who owned it first." He disappeared next to the tire.

"It's good for business," I said.

"The dress or the estate sales?"

"Well, both. But the only client I talked to today was over the phone, thank you very much." Maybe things would have gone differently if I had met Steve Johnson face to face. Not because of the dress, but because he'd see that I was legitimate.

Inside the studio, the phone jangled. Technically, Mad for Mod was still open, and every phone call was prospective business. "Do you mind if I get that?"

"Nah, go ahead. This'll take a couple of minutes."

I picked up the ball of paper by the wastepaper basket and set it on the corner of my one-of-a-kind desk, then reached for the phone.

"Mad for Mod, Madison Night speaking," I answered. I heard a click, then a dial tone. I sank into the chair and batted the crumpled-up flyer back and forth across the slick surface of the desk.

The desk was a gift from Hudson, a hodgepodge of parts from items too damaged to repair. It had cost him more in time and vision than materials, and I wouldn't trade it for anything. More than once I'd asked him to be a partner in my business, and every time he declined. He was reliable, artistic, genuine, and best of all, smelled like wood shavings. In a parallel universe, I might have entertained romantic thoughts of us, but life as it was for a single, forty-seven year old businesswoman with trust issues didn't allow for fantasies like that. And even if I was capable of giving in to attraction, I had long learned one lesson: men may come and go but good handymen last forever.

5

I closed up the studio for the second time. The phone mocked me from the other side of the back door. I ran back in and answered on the third ring, slightly out of breath.

"Ms. Night, this is Steve Johnson. You called me about my mother's estate?" His voice had changed. The gruff had been traded for something else. Either way, I launched into my spiel.

"Mr. Johnson, I know it's unorthodox for me to have made an offer over the phone, but if you have time available tomorrow, I'd be more than happy to meet with you in person."

"That's not necessary. I changed my mind and I'm willing to sell. Take this number down and call me in the morning."

I grabbed a thick black marker out of the orange Tiki mug on the desk, flattened out Pamela's real estate flyer, and scrawled the number across her bright white smile.

"Perfect," I said, too eagerly, considering the circumstances. And then, for the second time that day, Steve Johnson hung up on me, leaving me to wonder what exactly had happened to change his mind.

Two

"We got a problem," Hudson said, startling me. He leaned against the white doorframe of my office and rubbed at his hands with a neon yellow terrycloth towel. "Your trunk is stuck, and I can't get to the spare."

"I bet it's caught on a pillow." He raised his eyebrows. "I know, I know, I have to stop driving around with inventory in my trunk, especially when I have a perfectly good storage unit."

"How about this. You take my truck home. I'll see what I can do about the trunk and the tire."

"What if you can't fix it?"

He looked at me as though that wasn't a possibility and I smiled. Since we first started working together, I consistently challenged him with items either bought for pennies or rescued from the trash. Chipped wood chairs, broken clock radios, and the occasional portable bar, all so in need of repair others had thrown them away. But Hudson saw the same potential in the discarded objects that I did, and had never failed at a job. I liked to think his skills gave new life to items owned by people who were now in a place that needed no decoration. Inanimate reincarnation, if you will.

7

"I'll bring your car by tonight and you'll be ready to go in the morning."

I tipped my head to the side and considered his offer. "Okay, but no joy rides."

"You got it." We worked out a plan for retrieving each other's keys and he turned back to the car. I didn't gather my things right away, guilt over leaving him with my problem weighing heavy.

As if reading my mind, Hudson looked up at me. He had one knee on the gravel, one foot planted on the ground, as though he were about to propose to my car. "You better get moving. Rock's gonna be hopping mad if you're not home on time."

"I was just thinking that."

"I'll take care of the car, you take care of him." He stood up and slapped his hands against his black denim jeans. A lock of hair had fallen forward and when he pushed it away, his fingers left a dusty streak on his forehead. He walked over to me and put a hand on each of my upper arms. "Madison, it's okay." The light caught in his clear amber eyes, highlighting flecks of gold. With his hands gently resting on my arms, he turned me around. "Don't worry so much," he whispered and gave me a slight push toward his truck.

I climbed into the cab, easily four feet higher than my sporty blue coupe and started the engine. The Rolling Stones poured out of the stereo, and for a second I smiled, picturing Hudson's six foot frame folded up in my little blue Alfa Romeo, listening to the Doris Day CD I'd left in the player. He smiled back even though he wasn't in on the joke, at least not yet, and waved while I drove away.

It didn't take long to get from the studio to my apartment building. On a good day, with Advil, I could walk it, but today was trash day, and I'd taken the opportunity to drive around Lakewood in search of castaway treasures that had since been moved to the storage unit behind my studio. I groped in the

8

dark for the chain to the pink and brass floor lamp that sat inside the front door.

"Rock? I'm home!"

Soft rose light bathed the room, washing over a small caramel-colored Shih Tzu puppy in his crate, on his hind legs, barking short, hyper yaps.

"I'm sorry I'm late, Rocky," I said while he showered me with affection. "I got a flat tire and Hudson came over to help."

His obvious enthusiasm had nothing to do with the mention of Hudson or the flat tire, but when it's late and you live alone, you talk to your puppy and pretend he understands. I clipped on his light blue leash and grabbed my cell phone, then took him out front for a walk.

Rocky sniffed at a patch of dandelions, then pulled me along the sidewalk. He was named after the *other* star of *Pillow Talk,* but it had morphed into Rocky because you can't have a Shih Tzu without a perky name. And since I'm originally from Philadelphia, most people assumed I'd named him after the boxer, which might have made more sense if he actually *was* a Boxer.

We returned to the apartment building, where I showered off the remains of the day, including two smudges of dirt on my upper arms left behind when Hudson had spun me around. I changed into white silk pajamas and Rocky followed me to the kitchen. One of us chewed on a slipper and one of us ate a bowl of ice cream. Just another day in the life of an independent, opportunistic, midcentury-modern interior decorator with a Doris Day obsession.

Or so I thought.

True to his word, Hudson had my car neatly parked in my space the following morning, in time for me to go to Crestwood. Newer, more social swimming pools existed in Dallas, but they weren't for me. What had started as the only form of exercise my knee could handle had become my escape.

The ladies of Crestwood, mostly octogenarians, had long given up trying to fix me up with their sons and accepted me as one of their own. The old men eyed me with a different agenda, one that usually held steady at winks and stares. The more daring were not above an occasional pinch. Occasionally we dealt with a couple of newcomers who wanted to check out the novelty of the outdoor pool, but mostly it was just us. Swimming side by side the retired set fit my lifestyle.

I tied Rocky to the lifeguard chair and dove into the cool water. My mind focused on the estate of Thelma Johnson. *Just a bunch of junk she would never get rid of,* her son had said. If I was right, that junk would be right up my alley.

Between sets, I stood in the shallow end, stretching my shoulders. A motorcycle grumbled from the parking lot. I tugged on my white rubber swim cap, too hard, and the rubber split. I pulled the cap off, tucked my goggles under the right leg of my bathing suit, and climbed out of the water. Mr. Popov, one of the occasional pinchers, sat next to my straw tote bag, the flyer with Steve Johnson's number on top. The old man dangled a white terrycloth robe with pink and blue appliqué flowers from his hand. It was my favorite vintage cover-up, despite the unfortunate grape jelly stain at the hem.

He looked away as Pamela Ritter walked in, holding a helmet in one hand. She shook her long hair to the side. Mr. Popov let out a low whistle as she strode past us, a far cry from the retro image she used for her promotional real estate flyer. I folded the piece of paper in half and shoved it into the pocket of my robe, not wanting her to see that I carried it with me. When I turned around, Mr. Popov's hand connected with my behind. I quickly pulled on the robe and tossed the torn swim cap in the trash. I followed Pamela into the locker room, leaving him behind, snickering about, well, my behind.

She changed into her bathing suit while I dressed in an early sixties pale pink double-breasted sleeveless tunic and matching pants. What was a costume to her was my regular style.

"I don't get it, Madison. You could do so much more business if you branched out into different eras. I mean, right now the fifties thing is hot, but trends like this don't last forever. I mean, most people like big houses with central air."

"I'm curious. How can you sell them, when you don't even like them?"

"You saw my flyer. Great! What did you think of the graphics?"

I thought it best not to answer that honestly. "Eye-catching."

"Did you like my picture? Can you tell I was copying you? Well, you and that old actress?"

Despite the fact that she had worn a dress that I saw last week in an Old Navy ad, it should have pleased me that she had used me as her role model. Truth is, I don't look my age. The blond hair, blue eyes and vintage clothes don't hurt. Neither does the swimmer's body. But my real secret weapon is the sunscreen I've applied every day since college. You can buy five hundred dollar moisturizer at the makeup counter at Macy's, but you can't buy long-term foresight. I had a feeling that concept would be lost on Pamela.

Alice Sweet, a petite eighty-something, arranged her gray hair into a neat row of pin curls. "I saw the picture, Pamela, and I thought you looked darling. You and Madison could be mistaken for twins." She continued to get ready, the clink of hairbrushes and bobby pins on the counter filling the room.

"We don't look *that* much alike," Pamela said. She shut her locker and spun the lock, then slipped on a pair of white flip-flops with fluffy flowers on top, probably the only common items in our closets. Seconds after she left us behind she returned, rummaging between Alice's and my bags in search of something.

"Did you see my cap and goggles?" She knocked my wicker basket over and my robe fell out. "I can't swim without them."

"I have an extra cap in the trunk of my car," I said, and held out my keys. "But if you're going to go out there wear this. Mr. Popov is in rare form today, and you'll need protection." I offered my robe with the other hand, a terrycloth olive branch to show I wasn't offended by her earlier attitude.

"This isn't a photo shoot. I wouldn't be caught dead in that robe."

"Madison," Alice interrupted, "Andy Popov is my friend. You know you hurt his feelings when you don't call him by his first name. It makes him feel old."

"Take the robe, Pamela." I paused for emphasis. "*Andy* just slapped me, which means he saved the pinch for you." I glanced at Alice to show her that I was trying, and kept the vintage cover-up extended.

Pamela pulled on the robe and held the two sides together with her fist while the belt dragged behind her through dingy puddles of water. Her blond hair hung in soft waves around her face, a far better look than the teased and sprayed style she favored when not playing the retro card. The irony was that I wanted to make her over as badly as she wanted to me.

I finished buttoning the front of my pink vest and dotted on minimal makeup. "I'll get the robe back tomorrow," I called to her back as I wrapped my bathing suit in a towel and tucked it inside the bottom of my straw tote. I realized she had the flyer with Steve Johnson's phone number in the pocket of the robe and hurried to collect Rocky before catching up with her.

I walked quickly thought the entranceway, down three concrete steps to the unpaved parking lot, and shielded my eyes while I scanned the parking lot for her. My car sat where I'd left it, the closest space to the entrance, facing the tennis courts. A chain link fence, ten feet tall, separated the lot from the pool property; nothing a couple of teenagers interested in a midnight swim couldn't overcome. Blocks of wood marked off each space, a smattering of bluebonnets and dandelions decorating the fringe of the property. Rocky ran along faster than I moved, exploding with barking as we approached the car.

And that's when I saw the body. A body wearing a pink, blue, and white terrycloth robe with fluffy floral appliqués and an unfortunate grape jelly stain. A body with tanned legs that stuck out from behind the rear wheels, wearing flip-flops with daisies on the top.

Three

I scooped up Rocky and held him close while I stared at Pamela's body. Only minutes ago, we were talking in the locker room, her full of life. She said she wouldn't be caught dead in my robe. And now here she was...dead. In my robe. Despite the already warm temperature, goose bumps sprung over my flesh and I shivered.

"Help!" I yelled. "Someone call 9-1-1!" Mr. Popov looked out of the entrance. "Call the cops!"

He turned inside and repeated my instructions to someone I couldn't see. Rocky yelped madly and I failed at trying to shush him. Mr. Popov came down the stairs as fast as his old legs could carry him. For the first time since I'd met him, the look on his face showed nothing but concern. It wasn't long before the peaceful poolside scene turned into a menagerie of cop cars, an ambulance, pulsating lights, and swarms of people. Yellow crime scene tape appeared. A man in a tight white t-shirt snapped pictures of Pamela, the parking lot, the tracks in the dirt. Probably a lot more than that, I couldn't tell. I had a hard time focusing on anything except Pamela's body. The rest of the world was out of focus, like someone had slipped an experimental filter over my eyes.

"Excuse me, are you Madison Night?" asked a pretty female cop, the first officer to arrive on the scene.

"Yes, that's me."

"I'm Officer Donna Nast, with the Dallas Police Department. You found her?"

I nodded.

"What can you tell me?" she asked. Her dark hair was pulled back in a low ponytail under her hat. Green eyes, high cheekbones, and full lips cast a contrast to the standard issue uniform she wore. I vaguely remembered what it was like to be her age, when being in charge felt the same as being in control.

"I finished getting dressed and came out here after her. My dog started barking like crazy. That's when I saw her—her legs, sticking out behind my car." My stomach turned. "She's...she is dead, right? Do you know what killed—do you know how?"

"Not sure. The ME determines that." She shielded her eyes and looked across the parking lot.

"But..." I thought about Pamela's body lying under my rear wheels. "If she was alive and I backed over her..." I hugged Rock so tight he yelped. I couldn't believe what someone had done. "Did someone do that on purpose? To make it look like an accident?"

"Could be." Officer Nast watched my expression closely. "How well did you know her?"

"Not that well."

"You said you came out here after her?"

"I loaned her my robe. I left something in the pocket. Can I get it?"

"No."

Several cars drove down the gravelly driveway of the pool, stopping by the uniformed officer who stood in the middle of the road. The first three turned around and drove away. The fourth, a Jeep, stopped. The driver exchanged words with the officer then continued past him and parked next to the shrubs across from the entrance.

"I got a crime scene here. Can somebody please take responsibility for keeping the riffraff out of it?" Officer Nast called behind her. Nobody answered.

"Did someone get your contact information?" she said to me.

"Yes."

"Okay. Don't go away yet." She walked away. I was still standing next to my car, next to Pamela's legs, and despite the fact that I was already outside, I needed fresh air.

The Jeep's driver walked toward me. Even from a distance I knew I had never seen him around Crestwood before. Thanks in part to the bent and worn straw cowboy hat on his head, the only hair I could see were his long, light brown sideburns. He had a boy's expression on a man's face. Laugh lines were etched onto tanned skin that set off glowing blue eyes. His square jaw clenched a few times while he took in the pool, the car, the body. Eventually his sweeping gaze connected with mine and his jaw relaxed.

Rocky wriggled in my arms, and I knew what that meant. I set him down on the ground and let him pull me toward the sparse row of trees at the far end of the parking lot. Behind us, cops stood in a group by the snack bar; swimmers huddled together under the awning. Rock sniffed a beam of concrete that marked the end of a parking space, then lifted a leg and peed on it. *Please don't make him have to poo,* I thought to myself. *I don't have a plastic bag and I don't want to be seen carrying a turd around a crime scene.* Then instantly I thought I was going straight to hell. What kind of a person thinks about dog turds when a woman just died?

When Rocky finished his business I tugged his leash back the way we'd come. He pulled further the opposite direction.

"Rocky! Not now." I tugged him back. He pulled more of the slack from the leash. *"Rocky! No!"* I said in my bad-dog voice.

"Excuse me, ma'am, is everything okay over here?" asked a casual drawl behind me. I turned around, and the man in the cowboy hat approached us.

My pulse quickened and I wished I hadn't strayed so far from the group of people clustered together by the chain link fence.

"I'm fine, we're fine. I mean, we're not fine, but I'd rather not talk about it," I said. For a second I wondered if he knew Pamela, if that was why he was here.

He looked across the lot at Officer Nast. "Is she the one in charge?"

I nodded. Involuntarily I looked past his shoulder to my car, to Pamela's legs. I felt dizzy and reached a hand out to steady myself with a tree branch. The branch snapped off in my grip.

Cowboy hat's blue eyes bored into me. They were the color of soft, bleached denim but as penetrating as steel. He was older than I'd originally thought, and something about the way he looked at me made me wonder if, as inappropriate as it would have been, his interest in me was because I was a pretty blonde standing alone by the edge of the pool's parking lot. I tugged Rocky's leash so we could rejoin the others.

"You sure you're okay?" he asked.

"I had to get away from—my puppy wanted to investigate the trees," I offered.

"Investigate? You training him to be a police dog?" he asked. He smiled, and the boyish charm took over his face, putting me at ease. He stooped and petted Rock's head. Rock put his front paws on the worn knee of Cowboy's jeans, feeding off the attention. "He looks like a real killer."

My eyes flickered again from the man's beat-up straw hat to the yellow crime scene tape in the parking lot behind him, to

17

the image of the body of Pamela wearing my robe. Again, I shivered.

Cowboy stood back up. "I didn't catch your name, ma'am,"

"Madison. Madison Night," I said.

He tipped his head and flicked the brim of the straw hat so it popped up a bit on his head. "I think that's pretty near impossible for me to believe."

"Why's that?"

He jerked a thumb over his shoulder toward the crowd. "I've just been told by a couple of folks over there that Madison Night is dead."

"No," I said, shaking from his statement despite its obvious untruth. The greens of the trees went flat in my line of vision, like a black and white movie.

"Ma'am?" he prompted, and put a hand on my elbow. "You okay?"

"I prefer Madison to ma'am, thank you very much," I said, struggling to regain composure. "And as you can see I'm not dead. I've spent more time here than I'd planned and I'd like to be on my way, if you don't mind."

"I'm going to stick around a little, but I'd like to get your number, so we can talk more later," he called from behind me.

The nerve of that guy! "Sure," I replied without looking. "I gave it to the police when they arrived. I'm sure they'd be happy to share it." I expected the sarcasm in my voice to deliver the message in my head. Even Rocky seemed to understand it was time to storm away.

While Rocky had been peeing, paramedics had moved Pamela's body from behind my car. I rooted around in my canvas bag for my keys, then remembered I'd given them to Pamela.

"What do you think you're doing?" asked Officer Nast.

"I'm leaving. You said you had my information."

"Yeah, sure. You can leave, but your car can't."

"Why not?" I asked.

"It's part of the crime scene."

I searched her face for signs of a joke. "You're going to impound my car?" My voice had risen.

Cowboy stood off to the side, talking to Alice and Mr. Popov. The three of them turned to face me. And that's the first time I noticed the small shield clipped to the waistband of Cowboy's jeans.

Officer Nast noticed him looking at us. "Wait here. Do *not* move." She pointed a square French-manicured fingernail directly at me.

The slack on the leash pulled every couple of seconds, but I let Rocky do whatever it was he wanted to do under the car. Officer Nast approached Cowboy. The look on her face was one of recognition, not annoyance. Maybe a little of both. He smiled a half-smile at her, that she didn't return. I recognized the wordless communication, the body language. There was history there. Personal history. And the pretty officer was not happy to have Cowboy at her crime scene. The group pulled apart and the two of them strode toward me.

"You really are Madison Night? This is your car?" Cowboy asked.

"I'm exactly who I said I was," I answered.

He held out a hand. "Sorry about that back there. Lieutenant Allen."

I shook his hand firmly. Always good to show a sense of confidence and power, especially when you're wearing a powder pink pantsuit. "Madison Night," I said again.

"Didn't mean to shake you up any more than you already were. The old guy didn't have his glasses on when he ID'd the body, and apparently she's wearing your robe?"

"Mr. Popov's eyesight might be poor but his pinching fingers work just fine, especially when a woman walks past him in a bathing suit. I loaned Pamela my robe for protection."

"I see." An inappropriate half-smile cloaked his face.

"May I leave?" I asked.

19

"You can leave. Your car can't," he said, corroborating what Officer Nast had told me.

"Why not?"

"It's part of the crime scene. This whole area is. Everything stays, until we have a chance to go over it, get some kind of clue to what happened here."

"Lieutenant, my puppy has been destroying your crime scene for the past ten minutes, and you're not going to find any clues in front of, behind, or under my car."

We all looked down to where the leash had disappeared. Rock chose that moment to come out from underneath, covered in dirt and gravel, with a round aqua velvet pillow between his teeth.

"What were you saying?" asked the lieutenant.

Four

"Rock! Give me that!" I said, stooping down get the pillow from his teeth.

"Don't!" Lieutenant Allen commanded. He padded his pockets, looking for something. "Nasty? You got a spare set of gloves?"

The pretty brunette officer scowled at him. "I'm guessing last night's bed didn't have a homicide kit next to it?"

She tossed a plastic package at him, which he easily caught with his left hand. He pulled a glove over his right hand and grabbed the side of the pillow. Rocky sensed that they were playing the same tug of war that I played with his stuffed lion at home and pulled away, placing tension on the delicate velvet fabric.

"Rocky!" I admonished. When the tone of my voice changed to all business, he released his bite and cowered. I scooped him up and held him close. The lieutenant shook his head at our display, then handed the pillow to another officer who placed it in an evidence bag.

"Have you seen that pillow before? Is it yours?" asked Officer Nast.

"I'm a decorator. I have lots of pillows. There are about three dozen in my trunk right now."

"Open it," she instructed.

The keys dangled from the lock on the trunk. I turned them, but the trunk didn't open at first. I shot a quick glance at the officer and the lieutenant. They looked impatient. "The lock's been giving me trouble lately."

Lieutenant Allen pulled off his hat and put his fist inside it, then gave the lock a swift, sideways punch. The trunk popped open. He inserted the bent straw brim of the hat in the opening and eased the trunk open without making contact. A couple of pillows in pink, yellow, and aqua were nestled inside the gray cavern next to unopened packages of matching velvet curtains.

"I thought you said you had three dozen pillows in there?" Officer Nast interjected.

"I did." I bent over the trunk and looked around.

"Don't." Her hand clamped onto my upper arm and pushed me upright.

"That's quite a color palette," said Tex. "Where do you find stuff like that?"

"My store, for one."

"And where do you get this stuff? You make it?"

"Those pillows are from 1959," I declared.

"And that's a good thing?" he asked.

"Do you have any honest to goodness questions for me? Or can I go now?"

Lieutenant Allen slammed the trunk of my car shut. "You can't take your car, if that's what you're asking."

"May I have my keys?"

"No," said Officer Nast.

"Sure," said the lieutenant. The two of them exchanged looks. "I'll have a duplicate set made up for you," said the lieutenant.

I turned around and stepped away. It was still early by most people's standards, seven forty-five. I could call Hudson and ask for another favor. I flipped through the contacts on my cell phone and hovered over his name, but yesterday's favor made me hesitate before making the call.

"You calling a friend?" Lieutenant Allen said, from over my shoulder.

Startled, I whirled around and dropped the phone. He picked it up and looked at the screen before handing it back to me. I took a step backward to put a normal amount of space between us.

"I'll call a cab."

"Nonsense. I'll give you a lift somewhere." He shielded his eyes with the straw hat and scanned the parking lot. "Nasty! Take it from here. I'll be back."

"You? Don't you have to stay here?" asked Officer Nast.

"You've got it under control," he said, exchanging a heated gaze with her. He put a hand on my elbow and steered me toward the Jeep. I shook off his touch. Rocky bounded ahead of me, expanding his leash, eager to get into the car. At least one of us would enjoy the ride.

"Where to, Ms. Night?"

I weighed my options. Without my keys, I couldn't get into my studio or the storage unit. I couldn't call Steve Johnson, because his number was in the pocket of my robe. That left one place. I scooped up Rocky and took a step backward, looking away from the emergency vehicles and cop cars. I shivered, even though the hot Dallas sun was already threatening to turn the air into a thick veil of humidity. I needed to get out of there, to get away from the image of this morning. "Give me a ride to the Mummy."

"Where's that?" he asked once we were buckled inside.

"The Mummy Theater at the end of Lakewood Drive?" He didn't react. "Used to be the Casa Linda? Sat vacant for years?"

He kept up his blank stare.

"It's across the street from the topless bar, Jumbo's Playhouse?"

"Oh, that place. Didn't realize they'd reopened."

The sound of the wind whooshing around our exposed heads replaced conversation until he pulled into the theater's lot. "You work here?" he asked.

"Sort of," I answered. It dawned on me that he wasn't just making conversation but trying to casually find out about me. Some things he'd discover pretty easily with a Google search. Others not. I decided to save him some time.

"I own a mid-century modern decorating business called Mad for Mod." I slid a business card out of a small silver cigarette case that I'd scored at one of my buying excursions and handed it to him. "I volunteer here. I spend my mornings swimming laps at Crestwood just like today. I live on Gaston Avenue, and if you do some digging, you'll discover that I own the building, though my tenants don't know that and I'd kind of like to leave it that way."

He held my card out in front of him. "Madison Night. Mad for mod. Cute." He reached two fingers into the ashtray and slid out a card of his own. "In case you want to talk."

"About what?" I asked.

"About anything."

"I told Officer Nast everything I know."

"I don't want to get the info from Nasty. I want to get it from you."

That was the third time he'd called her that, and although it offended my feminist sensibilities, I chose not to comment.

"If you have no other questions for me, I'm going to go." I fought the door for a couple of seconds, which put a damper on my take control attitude. Rocky put his paws on the door and stood on his hind legs looking outside and when I finally got the door opened, his little body stretched for a wild second until I cupped his belly and scooped him close to my chest.

24

"Goodbye, Lieutenant," I said, shutting the door behind me.

"It's Lieutenant Tex to you," he said back with a smile. "And Ms. Night? I'll be in touch. You can count on that."

He let the engine idle while I found the spare keys in the mailbox out front and unlocked the doors. I scooped up the junk mail and promotional flyers someone had fed under the door. The rest of the team, paid employees and volunteers, liked coming at night to take care of business, but with my morning habits and flexible schedule, I preferred to handle small projects during the day.

Rocky led me down the hallway to the makeshift manager's office behind the concession stand. I clicked on the overhead light and turned on the computer. The room was a box of stale air, like it always was when I first walked in. Trace scents of stale popcorn and soda lingered from last Saturday night's box office. I popped the window lock and cranked the small metal wand in a circle to tilt the glass at an angle and allow either fresh air in or stale air out. Either would be an improvement.

A yellow post-it was stuck to the monitor screen. *Madison, Emergency meeting tonight. 7:00. See you then.* The note was signed by Richard Goode, the film school graduate who ran the newly renovated classic theater. I dialed the number below his name.

"Richard, it's Madison. I can't make the meeting tonight. What's the emergency? I'm at the theater now. Is there anything I can do?"

"Madison, we've got a big problem. Cancellation for the fourth of July. That's two months away, and we got nothing."

Richard's idea of an emergency paled drastically in comparison to what I'd seen that very morning.

"Now's not really the best time for me to brainstorm, Richard."

"C'mon, Madison. I need something. Anything. You've got the best contacts of everybody on the staff."

Richard had been pushing Russian space movies, his idea of ironic highbrow on the anniversary of the moon landing, for months. Richard was the only one of us making any money at the theater, his salary paid by the owners, and thus the only one with something to lose if we failed to bring in viewers. I scanned the piles of paper on his desk and felt a shock of pain through my chest when I found myself looking at Pamela's flyer. She must have delivered them everywhere. Where yesterday her smiling fake-fifties image had bothered me, today it touched a nerve. I wanted to remember her like the picture on the flyer, not the picture in my memory.

"What about Doris Day?" I asked.

"For the anniversary of the moon landing? Those movies are hardly cinematic history, and you're probably the only person who would show up to see it. I don't think the owners will go for that. Give me something else."

But as soon as I'd said it, I knew it would be the perfect project to take my mind off of the murder at the pool. "I can fill your theater for you, if you give me a chance. We can show *The Glass Bottom Boat*. Rod Taylor plays an astronaut and there's a special featurette with Doris at NASA."

"That's not the direction I want to go."

"Good luck telling the owners that you'd rather be closed on a major holiday weekend than pack the house with a retrospective of a well-known American actress."

"Madison—"

"Richard, I can make this happen. Quickly. It's good idea, and I know you have the authority to give me the green light." Tires on gravel sounded outside. "I gotta go."

I hung up and tiptoed to the open window, looking out at an angle. The Lieutenant's Jeep sat idling by the side of the building. I leaned backward, not sure I wanted him to know I was there, and regretted opening that window. If he wanted to come investigate, he'd literally be able to reach right in and touch me.

The Jeep drove away. Outside of Rocky, occupied in the corner with an old shoe from the lost and found, I was alone. I spun through the Rolodex, looking for other volunteers. If I were going to do this, I'd need help convincing Richard. Ruth Coburn, mother of three, would be a great place to start. She answered halfway through the fourth ring and hollered something at someone before saying hello. After identifying myself, I went straight into my sales pitch.

"Ruth, would you support the idea of a Doris Day film festival over the Fourth of July weekend?"

"I would support anything that would give me a chance to get out of this house and leave the kids with my husband. Doris Day would be perfect."

"Great. I can't make the meeting tonight, but I've already told Richard my idea. I'm going to start working on it, so will you push the idea tonight?"

"Absolutely. You know, my daughter is the spitting image of Doris in *Pajama Game*. She's been acting in her school play."

"You have a daughter in high school?"

"Put down the grape jelly!"

"Excuse me?"

"Madison, you're lucky you don't have kids. I gotta go."

I spun the old Rolodex to the S's and found the number for Susan from American Film Rentals, or AFFER, as we'd come to call them. I'd met Susan exactly once, three weeks after moving from Philadelphia to Dallas. She'd flown from Los Angeles to help host a Rat Pack themed weekend. She was the quintessential party girl, out until two every night, stretching the limits of my lifestyle. Thanks to AFFER's ongoing long distance relationship with the Mummy, we'd stayed friends ever since.

AFFER was one of two major rental companies that we worked with to secure the best copies of films to show in our theater. There existed a unique crowd of people interested in seeing old classics on the big screen, people willing to trade the comfort of their living room sofas and the convenience of the pause button for the movie going experience. That was the audience we catered to. Local film buffs made our reopening a possibility and they wouldn't appreciate if we simply hooked a projector up to a DVD player. They wanted the reel thing, honest-to-goodness 35mm film that spun on metal reels, scratches and all. I fired off an email to Susan.

Dear Susan,

I'm trying to sell Richard on a Doris Day film festival for July. Tight schedule! I'm curious what films AFFER has available? Initial idea is for six different features to show over three nights as double features. Obvoiusly would prefer to rent all movies from one house. Richard's not a fan, so let me know what's in your inventory and we'll go from there.

I ran a spell check, fixed "obviously", and sent the note.

The phone rang but I let it go to the recording. Most of the mid-day calls were for show times and addresses. Only in my early days did I make the mistake of answering, and that time I'd ended up defending John Hughes' movies for close to an hour. A bell sounded from the computer and an instant chat window appeared. It was Susan from AFFER. "Answer your phone!"

I picked up the jangling receiver. "Susan?"

"I thought Richard wanted you guys to answer the phone with 'Dig Movies at the Mummy'?" said her bubbly voice. "He's not there, right? He can't be there. He'd never allow you to answer like that."

"Why the call? Did something happen?"

"I got your email. Are you really talking Doris Day?" she said. Even the crackling of the old phone line couldn't hide her obvious enthusiasm. I couldn't keep up with her, not now, not today. My world was still in slow motion, my interest in mounting a Doris Day film festival unfairly unimportant regardless of how much I wanted to sink my teeth into it. I looked at the computer screen at a movie poster of *Pillow Talk* and concentrated on the simplicity of what it promised. "Yes, I'm talking Doris Day. Are *you* talking Doris Day? You sound a little too excited to be on the same page as me."

"No way. I've been waiting for the right person to pitch this idea for years!"

"I didn't know you were such a fan," I said.

"I'm not. But I've been sitting on some Doris Day dirt, and if you're willing to use it, your film festival will turn into one hell of a seat filler."

Five

"You've got dirt on Doris Day?" I asked, immediately sucked into the moment.

"Here comes the manager." Her voice dropped to a whisper. "I'll call you later."

If there was dirt, and I mean good dirt on Doris Day, I would have known about it. Even though we were literally Night and Day, from the moment I'd discovered that we shared a birthday, I felt a connection to the actress.

I called up Google and typed *"dirt on Doris Day."* Nothing. I tried other phrases, ones that felt wrong to type, but found no scoop. The woman, at least on the Internet, was still as squeaky clean as she'd been her whole career. It only piqued my interest more.

I was pulled from my internet research by the phone. "DIG Movies at the Mummy," I answered, cringing at the phrase the Dallas Independent Group wanted to use.

"I called Richard about the film festival. You're right, he's not into it," said Ruth.

"What did he say?"

"He's going to take some convincing. But this could be very good for my daughter. She's looking for something special to put on her college applications and this could be perfect."

"What could be perfect?" I asked, not sure what she was suggesting.

"She can work the lobby as a lookalike. I mean, no offense, Madison, but she's seventeen and you're my age."

"Richard said yes to this?"

"Like I said, he's going to take some convincing."

Finally, after a bowl of very stale popcorn from a bin in the stockroom and an exhaustive search that involved quotes, image searches, and more than one porn site, I closed the Internet. Susan hadn't called or emailed me back, and I had to keep myself busy if I wanted to keep the images of the morning at bay. I was on foot, and that made getting from here to there, here to anywhere, harder than the turn of a car key and the press of a pedal.

I felt around the bottom of my wicker handbag and pulled out a stretchy brown bandage and wrapped my knee. I'd learned to take precautions, to protect my injury so it wouldn't get worse. High heels were a thing of the past, and I'd probably never learn to dance the jive, but I could deal with the damage. I had to. If I wanted to keep moving forward, there wasn't any other choice.

I picked up the composition book that the staff used to track our daily box office intake, tucked last month's calendar of events into the middle of it, and placed it in the bottom of my tote bag so I could analyze it later. Dirt or no dirt, I was going to make sure this thing happened, and whatever arguments Richard used to go highbrow in the middle of a hundred degree summer instead of allowing me to organize three days of sex comedies, I was going to swat away like a cloud of mosquitoes. In a confusing bit of rationalization, I felt I owed it to Pamela.

Rocky followed me out the front door and sniffed a discarded concrete block while I locked up. Several hours had passed while I'd been inside. The bright Dallas sun had hit its peak, creating oppressively thick air that I now passed through on my way down the street. Walking anywhere was going to feel like a marathon through an oven with a roasting pan of water surrounding me like a portable sweatshop. Call a cab, or walk the five blocks to Hudson's house and ask for another favor. Hudson, I knew, had a set of keys to my apartment, from the frequent times I'd hired him to go in and fix something. The company of a friend trumped the company of a stranger, and I started the hike to his small house by White Rock Lake.

Twenty minutes later I stood on the curb in front of a modest white ranch. A trickle of perspiration ran down the back of my shirt. Hudson worked in his garage, in worn jeans and safety goggles. His hair was messy from the humidity and his bare chest was coated with a thin film of sawdust. A portable CD player played the Ramones. Hudson didn't move to the music, or mouth the words, but I sensed that he knew them as well as anybody, to be able to play this in the background while he worked the kind of magic on damaged materials that brought them back to life.

The man was too modest. In another man's hands, the table legs would be sanded, patched with wood putty, and painted, or even scrapped and replaced with a prefab part from Home Depot. Hudson understood the grain of the wood, the process of the repair, and the importance of being true to the integrity of the mid-century design. I didn't have to tell him what I expected; his work surpassed my expectations every single time.

A three-legged table sat on its end along the wall behind him. I knew the table. It was a job I'd hired him to do between whatever other jobs he took that paid his bills. No deadline. But still, he had made my job a priority. The first time we met,

I'd noticed the deep lines around his eyes, etched into place with the life he'd lived. They made it difficult to place his age. Not knowing made me curious, but not wanting to offend kept me from asking.

He maneuvered one of my table legs under a sander, stopping occasionally to stroke the shavings off one of the curves, to polish the wood with the palm of his hand. I walked to the garage slowly, wanting to watch the process up close. Soft green grass silenced my footsteps. As I closed in on the garage, the noise of the sander filled the air, drowning out the radio. Rocky barked, but I couldn't hear him. Wood shavings spun through the air, landing on Hudson's biceps.

I caught my reflection in one of the windows of the house, immediately self-conscious about my appearance. My hands flew to my head to smooth down the flyaway hairs that had sprung loose from my chignon. I'd picked up a layer of dirt and grime from the hot, humid walk and I didn't want him to see me like this.

He turned off the sander. The Ramones filled the quiet and Rocky caught me off guard, bolting toward the garage like he'd been fired from a canon. The slackened leash pulled from my hand. For a moment I froze, uncomfortable with my surprise visit and my second request for help in as many days.

Hudson set his equipment aside, pulled on a black t-shirt, and knelt down to play with my dog. Rocky stood on his hind legs, front paws on the contractor's dusty knees, while Hudson's fingers got lost in the long fur that framed Rocky's face. The warmth I felt had nothing to do with the temperature. Rocky hopped back and forth through the wood shavings. After today, that dog was in serious need of a bath.

After today. This morning. Pamela. Dead.

I was assaulted by images. Rocky carting a pillow out from under my Alfa Romeo. Flashing lights. Emergency Technicians. Cops. And Pamela, wrapped in my daisy robe, lying dead in the parking lot under my back wheels. The

33

reality—no, finality—of her death slammed into me like a category five hurricane. I'd tried to block it all, push it away, hide it under layers of soft pink and yellow and aqua pillows and Doris Day film fluff but in one moment triggered by a hyper puppy and a half-naked man, the fluff cleared like feathers in front of a fan.

I stumbled into the garage, more interested in not being alone than self-conscious about my appearance. They both turned and looked at me.

"Madison, I figured you were close," Hudson said.

"Somebody killed her," I answered. The room spun. I put a hand on a white plastic lawn chair to steady myself but it didn't really help. My knee buckled and I dropped into the chair. "She's dead. For good." I squished my eyes shut to try to block out her image.

When I opened my eyes, Hudson knelt in front of me. His brows pulled together, not following my outburst. The oscillating fan blew past my left cheek then my right. Hudson held out a glass of water. Without speaking I took it and sipped, then held the cool glass against my forehead. The condensation felt good against my flushed skin.

"Where's Rocky?" I asked when I realized the two of us were alone.

"I put him inside," he said.

"He can be a terror."

He cut me off with the wave of a hand. "The worst he can do right now is annoy my cat."

It surprised me to learn that Hudson had a cat, though somehow it fit. Cats were private, self-contained, independent animals, just like he was. They held their affection in check, but when they trusted you and chose to share that affection, it tugged on your heartstrings like nothing else.

Hudson took the glass from my hand and set it on the workbench. Instinctively I put my hand on his wrist and held on to him while our eyes connected. He knelt down on the ground in front of me. I wanted to apologize for my behavior or explain what had happened or just ask him to hug me for comfort but I couldn't find my tongue. We stayed like that, me in the plastic white lawn chair and him kneeling in front of me with my grip on his wrist, for longer than I would have thought possible. We were interrupted by a hissing sound followed by a whimper followed by a throaty growl.

Hudson stood up and opened the door that separated the garage form the house. A large black cat stood, tail fat with fighting instincts, crouched low to the ground in warrior stance, facing Rocky. In addition to the dirt and wood shavings, there was a small dot of blood on his nose.

Rocky, it seemed, had just lost his first fight.

"Mortiboy! Stop it," Hudson said, stepping between the two animals. The cat's stare didn't waver. Hudson scooped up Rocky and inspected his small light brown face. Rocky licked the tip of Hudson's nose.

"You okay, boy?"

"Give him to me," I said. He handed me the puppy and I finally got my hug.

Where ten minutes ago I had blurted out the words "she's dead," now, holding a scared and shivering caramel puppy in my arms while Hudson calmed his black panther of terror down in his, I felt pulled in two directions—literally between a Rock and a hard place. I wanted to get Rocky home and give him a bath and restore him to the once-clean condition he'd been in before today had started. I wanted to shower off what was left of the day, change into cool silk pajamas and put on one of my favorite movies. But I didn't want to be alone, not yet, and despite the your-pet-can-beat-up-my-pet scenario we'd experienced, Hudson's company felt right.

"What brings you here?" Hudson asked.

"I might have a job for you," I said. "Thelma Johnson's estate. She lived in the M streets. I haven't worked out the details yet."

Hudson's face grew dark and he turned his back on me.

"Hudson, wait." I reached a hand out and placed it on his back. He didn't step away. "We can talk about this later. Can I give you a ride home?"

"I can walk," I said, though I'm not sure it sounded very convincing.

"This little guy has had enough action for the moment. How about you cut him some slack and accept my offer?" He bent down and ruffed Rocky's fur while he spoke, swapping the tension in our conversation with tenderness.

My knee throbbed, more than I wanted to admit. Painkillers would have done their job but I avoided them as much as I could. The dull ache I'd grown accustomed to was a constant reminder to look out for myself. I didn't want to be seen as a victim, but I didn't know how much more I could take.

"Madison, it's not a problem. Let me get my keys." He disappeared down the hall. His cat had lowered himself to a sitting position on top of the workbench and tucked his front feet underneath his body. I ran my hand over the top of his head. His yellow eyes turned to me, and he pulled away. He didn't trust me and there was nothing I could do about it.

Hudson and I walked to his truck, where he opened the door for me, a chivalrous gesture that wasn't uncommon in Texas. It tended to make me uncomfortable since I'd been opening my own doors my whole life. Instead of pointing out my equal rights and ability to do such mundane things on my own like I sometimes did with other men, I thanked him and stepped inside, letting Rocky jump in by my feet then up to my lap, where he hung his head out the window. While I was happy for the company, I was surprised that Hudson didn't ask me about my outburst, or why I'd collapsed. Six blocks later, we were in front of my apartment. The ride had been all too short, and barely any words had been exchanged.

I thanked him and walked to the front of my building. Inside, I checked the mail and tucked the newspaper under my arm before turning around. He was still at the curb, watching me. I waved, he waved back, and he pulled away.

First things first. Someone was getting a bath.

Giving Rocky a bath quickly turned into me needing a bath and my entire bathroom needing a thorough going-over. By the time I was done with the process, Rocky had air-dried and three towels were damp from absorbing the spray of water that had shot off his fur when he'd shaken his head. I went from my pink pantsuit to the shower to a pair of pale blue silk short-sleeved Chinese pajamas. The sun was just starting to drop but there was no break in the temperature. Dallas was like that. In the hot summer there was little more than a five-degree variance in the temperature from morning to night. During those early hours when I swam I got the chance to exist without the oppressive heat and humidity. It was a time just for me.

I poured a generous glass of wine. Today had been a humble-jumble of a day and I wanted a distraction from Pamela's murder. I dug through my bag for the notebook from The Mummy and carried it to the sofa, where I got comfortable, prepared to work on the Doris Day Film Festival. Doris would get me through the night. Rocky snuggled next to me, and I nuzzled his head for a few minutes before turning back to the notebook in my lap. I pulled the calendar out and set it on my low wood coffee table, then flipped through the pages until I found the most recent entries. That's when I saw the scrap of paper, pressed between the pages. Written on it, in a messy scrawl that tilted backwards were the words: *YOUR DAY WILL COME.*

Six

It wasn't meant for me. It couldn't be. But it was unnerving to see. My pen rolled off my lap and Rocky chewed on it while I stared at the torn piece of notebook paper. The simplicity of aqua blue lines on the clean white paper did little to block the message. And on a day where someone's days really *had* been numbered, I was calling this day as over. I tucked Lieutenant Allen's card between the pages. I'd tell him about it tomorrow.

I let the empty wine glass sit on the coffee table and walked into the bedroom. That was a risk, I knew, because Rocky didn't understand about breakable items, but I wanted to crawl into my bed with him curled up at my side, and somehow move from the awake world where people were murdered at swimming pools to dreamland, where murders and threatening notes didn't exist.

The next morning, like every morning, I woke up at the crack of dawn, though this time with a sense of dread. The threat from last night lay on my desk, closed in a notebook, but regardless of whether or not it was intended for me, it was there. Routine dictated that I pull on a bathing suit, pack a bag filled with clothes, underwear, and general what-nots, and drive to the pool. But I couldn't swim; the pool was closed. I had no car; it was at the—somewhere, I didn't really know where. At the police impound? Still at Crestwood? Driven on a joy ride around Dallas by a couple of cops who'd never been inside a powder blue Alfa Romeo with whitewall tires and white leather interior? Thinking about my car brought back images I didn't want to face. I pulled the covers up to my chin and slept for an extra forty-seven minutes.

Rocky woke me the second time, wriggling next to my arm, fishing for attention. I scratched his head and organized my thoughts. It would be another day on foot. Better wear comfortable shoes and pack the bottle of anti-inflammatories.

Just to be certain that yesterday hadn't been a nightmare I peeked out the window at the parking lot. Parked neatly in my space, which must have taken a bit of effort considering the size of my space, was a Jeep. And leaning against the front of the Jeep was Lieutenant Allen.

He was wearing a white T-shirt and blue jeans that hinted at a once-fit body that had softened with age. Sandy brown hair, partially wet, had been pushed away from his face, but a couple of locks had air dried and dusted his forehead. His arms were crossed over his chest like every man on the planet who finds himself waiting around for a woman. Only, if he was waiting around for me, nobody had told me that we'd had a date. I didn't know what he was doing at my building. And that made me a little angry.

I looked around for my pink and white terrycloth robe, until I remembered I'd loaned it to Pamela and now it was part of a crime scene. I belted a flimsy cotton duster over my PJs and padded down the stairs to the back of the building. It was going on seven o'clock and I knew from history that most of my tenants weren't even up yet. Not the best time to make a scene.

"What are you doing here?" I asked, crossing the parking lot to Lieutenant Allen.

"I'm afraid we got off on the wrong foot yesterday."

"Am I under some kind of surveillance?" I asked angrily. "Is this your way of keeping an eye on me?"

"You're not a suspect. Too many credible people saw you swimming and a couple of them know you offered Pamela your robe." His eyes jumped to my chest and back to my face.

"So you've been sitting around my parking lot hoping to run in to me to tell me that?" I asked.

"Consider me your personal escort for the day." He flashed me a mouthful of pearly whites that hit me like a two-gallon drum of unmixed plaster.

"Let me get this straight. You, a lieutenant, are offering to drive me, a non-suspect around for the day?"

"Your car'll be released soon. I thought it best not to keep you under house arrest. Not having a car must've been nightmarish."

I shrugged. "It wasn't so bad. I walked to-" I stopped. I wasn't sure how to describe my relationship with Hudson. Until yesterday, it would have been easy, but something had changed and I didn't know what. "a colleague's house," I finished lamely.

"I thought you were in business for yourself?"

"I'm smart enough to recognize when I can use a little help." *Smart enough to recognize a chauffeur, too,* I thought. "Are you seriously offering to drive me around for the day?"

"I'm here, aren't I?" he answered.

All of a sudden I realized I was standing in the parking lot in my very sheer pajamas and robe. I knew how transparent one layer was, that's why I'd pulled on the robe. But I'd never looked in the mirror. Instinctively I balled up my fists and brought my arms in front of me, pretending that I was cold so I could cover my chest. In the middle of a Dallas summer heat wave, where it already felt like we'd hit the eighties, it was a wasted gesture.

"Nothing I haven't seen before, Night. Go get dressed and meet me out here. I'll wait."

I wanted to say something brilliant and snappy. I wanted to tell him he'd better have appreciated anything that he did see because he'd never see it again. But I wanted to get back inside the building more. So I did. But I did make him wait another half-hour while I showered, dressed, made coffee, and took Rocky out the front door for a quick piddle.

Somewhere after the shower and before the coffee I admitted to myself that it's not every day that a private citizen gets the opportunity to be driven around by an attractive cop, even if he did seem to be overly aware of his charms, so it was my civic duty to take it. When I finally returned to the parking lot it was in a white cotton v-neck dress with a full skirt, carrying two mugs of iced coffee.

"Peace offering?" I said, extending one of the mugs toward him.

He eyed me up and down before taking the offered blue metallic mug. He took a long drink without asking what it was, and the sun sparkled against the blond hairs on his tanned forearm.

"I almost called you last night," I said while he was drinking. He pulled the mug away from his mouth.

"I almost called you, too."

"Why did you almost call me?"

"You first."

I set my mug on the hood of his Jeep and pulled the notebook out from under my arm. "I borrowed a couple of files from the Mummy and when I got home I found this." I opened the notebook to the page that had the threatening message. Last night it had really bothered me. Today I felt a little like maybe it was nothing. It wasn't even my notebook.

His eyes scanned the page, then he flipped the notebook closed and looked at the cover, then opened it again and thumbed through the pages. "What is this?"

"Box office tallies, mostly. I was working on a film festival and wanted to do some research, see if I could determine some patterns to help my proposal."

"What are you proposing?"

"A Doris Day weekend. It's all very last minute and I have to convince a lot of people that it's a good idea."

"Why don't people think it's a good idea?"

"Do *you* think a Doris Day film festival is a good idea?" I asked.

His head tipped to one side then another. I was curious to hear his answer. Most men acted like a close proximity to Doris Day would threaten their masculinity.

"It has its high points," he started. "Be good for your business, I bet. People seeing those sets, right?" He reached past me and opened the door to the Jeep. When I didn't move, he put his hand on the small of my back and directed me into the seat. I gathered up the white eyelet fabric of my skirt and stepped onto the floorboards, then sat down. He shut the door behind me and walked around the car to the driver's side.

"Are you saying you would attend? Maybe even bring a date?" I challenged, when he was in the car.

"Are you asking me?"

"If you'll come?"

"If I'll be your date."

I felt the heat rush to my face. "That's not what I meant."

"So you *don't* want me to be your date."

"Can you be serious for a second, Lieutenant?"

He leaned back in the driver's seat. "You don't have to keep calling me Lieutenant, you know," he said.

"What do you want me to call you?

"You can call me Tex." By now there was a full on smile on his face.

"Is that your name?"

"First name's Tom. Middle name's Rex. Most people who know me call me Tex."

"Why don't they call you T. Rex? Or Trex?"

"Because I tell them not to."

"Do people always do what you tell them to?"

He didn't answer, and it occurred to me that maybe the answer was yes.

"Where's your hat?" I asked suddenly.

He put a hand on the top of his head for a moment, like he was going to demonstrate that he could rub his tummy at the same time. "I just got this Jeep. Not used to driving a convertible around in the Dallas sun. Yesterday morning when I got the call I was. . . I wasn't at home. The only thing I could do was grab that hat to wear, or burn the shit out of my head. Seemed lesser of two evils."

There was so much in that statement for me to think about at another time, things that told me how vastly different the lieutenant's and my lifestyles were, but right now, the only thing that mattered was the full tank of gas in his car.

"Hey, where's the little fella?" he asked.

In order to make up for yesterday I had to make a decision about Rocky, and that decision involved leaving him at home for the day. He was in his large cage, easily big enough that he probably wouldn't notice that he was inside. The interior was filled with plush animals that he would chew on for hours at a time, along with food, water, and the ever-important pee pad. I'd asked one of my neighbors to check in on him in later. Her husband was allergic to dogs so she couldn't have one of her own. I knew she enjoyed the moments she shared with mine.

I explained about the dog sitter and justified it with a quick recap of my need to be productive. I didn't spell out our agenda because I wasn't sure how long I'd be willing or able to accept his oddly generous chivalry.

"Okay, fair lady, where to?" he asked.

I scooped the full skirt of my white cotton sundress under my thighs and tucked my feet onto the floorboards. Even though I'd agreed to this chauffeur routine, I'd worn

43

comfortable Keds in the event that something—I still wasn't sure if it would be his attitude or mine—interrupted the convenience of his offer and I ended up on foot. I was nothing if not prepared.

"I want to go back to the Mummy, do some work on the film festival. Do you know how to get there?"

"I took you yesterday, didn't I?"

Tex drove to the theater. He pulled into the lot and parked out front. We both got out and a small puff of dust swelled up from under my white sneakers when they hit the ground.

"You're coming in?" I asked.

"That okay?"

"Sure." The truth was, after the note I'd found in the middle of the box office tallies, I was a little wary of entering myself. I didn't really believe that someone was out to get me, but it seemed the company of a police officer wasn't so bad as far as security blankets went. I unlocked the front door and he followed me inside.

"So what are you going to be doing in here?" he asked.

"Office work, mostly. On the computer." I was hoping to reach Susan for that Doris Day dirt, and if I did, that would require a bit of privacy. I crossed the room to the desk, and flipped through a couple of calendars Richard had left scattered on top of his inbox. "You can walk around if you want. Go upstairs and see the projection booth. Not many people get a chance to see that."

"Sounds good," he said from right behind me. "If you need me, will I hear you?"

"Why would I need you?" I turned around. I didn't realize that he'd followed me. He stood close. Too close. His face was inches from mine and he smelled like powdered sugar. It was so unexpectedly charming that I resisted the predictable donut jokes.

"If you don't need me now, you will soon enough." His eyes jumped from mine to my lips, where they lingered for a moment, then back to my eyes. He stepped backward and looked me up and down. I stayed where I was, leaning against the desk. The bodice of my white cotton dress hid anything that he might have seen that morning yet still I felt exposed. I didn't move or reply. He turned away and walked to the door. Once he reached the hallway, without turning around to face me, he said, "By the way, Night, that's a hell of a dress." Then he disappeared in the hallway.

There was no time to waste questioning the lack of "Ms" or applauding my choice of outfits for the day. The Rolodex was still open to the AFFER listing and I dialed the number.

"I can't believe you never called me back!" Susan answered.

"I thought you were going to call me?"

"Whatever. Listen, I don't have a lot of time—"

"Neither do I," I interjected, glancing at the doorway. Thanks to the old building I could hear Tex's footsteps in the room above me, but I wasn't sure how well my voice traveled so I kept it low. "What's this dirt you want to tell me?"

"It happened about ten years ago. Before my time. It was crazy, at least it sounded crazy. Someone wrote to the president of the company about destroying all of Doris Day's movies. He said it was the only responsible thing to do, to 'protect the landscape of American Cinema'. He outlined every movie that AFFER had in the vaults. The staff at the time thought it was some kind of a joke. Then there was a break in. The only thing missing was the second reel of *Pillow Talk*."

"Did it ever turn up?

"Well, something turned up but it wasn't a reel of *Pillow Talk*."

"Don't hold out on me now. What was it?"

She lowered her voice to barely a whisper. "Rumor has it the second reel of *Pillow Talk* was replaced with a home movie starring a certain blonde in a compromising position."

Seven

"*What?*" I exclaimed.

"Madison?" yelled Tex. His feet thundered down the stairs.

"What?" I hissed into the phone. "Are you kidding me?"

"Madison? What's wrong?" asked Tex from the hallway.

"Nothing. I just heard some good gossip about a coworker, that's all." I smiled sweetly, wondering if he'd buy it.

"Madison? Who's there?" said Susan through the receiver. "Madison!"

"Hold on, Susan." I covered the receiver and stared at Tex. "Sorry if I scared you. I forgot you were here."

He shook his head. "I'm going back up there. You guys might want to clean that room every once in awhile. Looks like a couple of transients have taken up residency." He turned his back on me and reclimbed the stairs.

"The manager is a slob. Not my job to clean up after him," I called to his back. "Okay, I'm back," I said to Susan.

"Who was that?" she asked. "Nobody knows I know this and I don't want to get in trouble."

"That was the cop who's driving me around for the day," I said.

"Who is this and what have you done with Madison?" she asked abruptly.

"Susan," I started.

"What are you wearing?"

"A white cotton sundress with a fitted bodice, full skirt. Very Liz Taylor in *A Place in the Sun*."

"Shoes?"

"White Keds." The modern-retro footwear of choice for the vintage-wearing injured.

"Okay, it's you. Should I be worried? Why is a cop driving you around?"

"Long story. I'm not sure it was a good idea to accept."

"Is he cute?"

I paused for a second before answering, a flash of Tex's boyish smile, long sideburns, and ice-blue eyes in my head. "You could say that."

"Madison, it's time you had some fun. A cute bad-boy cop could be just what the doctor ordered."

The image of Tex was quickly replaced with Pamela Ritter's lifeless body in my terrycloth robe. "Nobody said this was any fun."

"Then you're not doing something right." She laughed.

"What else can you tell me about this Doris Day thing?" I said, bringing the conversation back to where it should have been all along.

"Not much. A couple of people were testing a print of ours and found it mixed in with the inventory. Nobody talks about it and none of those people are still here."

"So how can I find out more about it?"

"John Phillips was the director, but he retired a couple of years ago."

"I thought nobody knew about it?"

"Nobody outside of AFFER. We kept it on the down-low. But John took a special interest in the whole thing, as you can imagine. I have his number at home. Let me call him and see if he remembers the details."

"Promise you'll keep me in the loop, right?"

"Absolutely. This is the kind of thing that could really put the Mummy on the map."

She disconnected and I jotted some notes on a piece of paper lying on the desk. *Dirty Doris Day footage?* It felt naughty just to write it down. I folded the paper into a small square and put it in my handbag.

I spent the next couple of hours working on research. Lists of Doris Day's extensive filmography, maps of run times, combinations of movies to pair up for double features. Comparative schedules to determine if it would be better to run them chronologically or thematically. Whether to lump Rock Hudson into one night, Cary Grant and James Garner into another, and whether we'd get a better draw with David Niven, Keith David, or Rod Taylor.

Knowing Tex was meandering around the theater probably getting bored while I worked had kept me busy for longer than I needed to work. My cell phone rang, interrupting my productive streak.

"Ms. Night? This is Steve Johnson."

It took a couple of seconds for me to place the name.

"Mr. Johnson! Thank you for returning my call." I paused for a moment, not sure what direction our conversation was going to turn. The pause extended too long. "I'm sorry I didn't call you yesterday. Something came up—"

He cut me off. "Ms. Night, are you still interested in my mother's estate?"

"Yes. And call me Madison."

"I wish you'd called yesterday like I asked you to. When I didn't hear from you I made arrangements to donate the whole estate to charity."

I didn't like going head to head with a charitable donation. I'd lay odds that Thelma Johnson's estate was filled with the kind of mid-century modern style that had been untouched for decades, but I knew a charity would benefit from the donation more than I would.

"Circumstances kept me from calling you back." I felt Tex's presence before I saw him, but looked at the doorway to confirm what I felt. I was right.

He leaned against the doorframe, not bothering to hide the fact that he was listening in on my conversation.

"But I understand your decision. Again, I'm sorry for your loss," I finished, and hung up.

Tex crossed the office, finally settling his muscular frame into the seat in front of the desk. His gaze was less flirtatious than direct.

"What was that about?" he asked.

"If I tell you, you're going to think less of me," I said.

"How so?"

"It involves my opportunistic business side."

"I didn't know you had one of those."

"The decorating business I mentioned? I told you I specialize in mid-century modern. I've discovered the best way to get authentic inventory is from the original owners. And the best way to find the original owners is to read the obituaries, and contact their next-of-kin before they hold a yard sale."

"Thelma Johnson," he said.

I nodded.

He stood up and paced back and forth inside the small office. My cell rang again before I could ask what he was thinking.

"Take the call."

"Madison Night," I spoke into the phone, with my eyes trained on Tex.

"Ms. Night, it's Steve Johnson again. Listen, I had a thought. My mom had a lot of stuff. If you can come by now, we can talk about what you're interested in."

I'd overestimated Mr. Johnson's charitable impulse. It appeared as though his interest in my cash offer was now equal to my interest in his mother's kitsch and had trumped any karmic points he thought he'd get by giving it all away.

"I can be there in twenty minutes," I said, studying the expression in Tex's eyes.

The drive to the Johnson estate was in silence.

I got the feeling that Tex was used to figuring women out quickly, but I knew I wasn't so easy to read. The outside package—vintage clothes, blond hair, and Doris Day obsession—all said Time Warp. The business savvy and independence said Modern Woman. I knew it all added up to me, a single woman who had learned, through a series of false starts and dead ends, to take care of herself. Everything about me said Madison Night, but Tex's listening skills might have been a little rusty.

"You mind explaining why we're here?" he asked after pulling the Jeep alongside a curb in front of the Johnson house.

"I told you already."

"This time I want details."

I took a deep breath. I wasn't used to explaining my actions, and no matter what words I chose, there was a pretty strong chance that I'd look heartless.

"I read the obituaries every night. Thelma Johnson died on Saturday. She was born in 1928. I've found that women born in the twenties and thirties tend to own the kinds of items I use when doing a house in a mid-century theme. Usually these women are the original owners. The furniture is generally pretty worn, lived in, and needs a fair amount of TLC to bring it back to its original state, but I'm lucky. I've got help with that—I've got that covered."

"The colleague you mentioned earlier. What's his name again?"

"Hudson James. Why?" I asked.

He nodded. I couldn't explain what I felt at the moment, or why it felt like talking to Tex about Hudson suddenly felt like I was talking about a secret I wanted to keep to myself. True, Hudson did work for me. Good work, good enough that once I'd found him, or he'd found me, I'd let my other freelance contacts fall by the wayside. Still, I wanted the lieutenant to see me as an equal, not someone who needed help to run her own life. Something made me want to not attach myself to anyone at the moment.

"You have his card?"

"Not on me."

"So...Thelma Johnson," he said. "What's your connection to her?"

"She fit the profile. Nothing more to it."

I got out of the Jeep and so did Tex. Our doors slammed at the same time. He walked around the front and stood in my path.

"So now you know what I'm doing here. Just consider this: it's not easy to have the conversation that I'm about to have without insulting the people who just experienced a loss. I'd really prefer if you'd wait in the Jeep while I go in there and talk to her son."

He aimed his keys at the car and a double beep sounded. Pretty sure that meant, despite my request, he was coming in with me.

"Fine. Then please remember, this is my business, and I have a few ground rules. If you're going in with me, you have to act like you work for me. Can you do that? Or would it be too much of a threat to your masculinity?"

"Hand me that scarf," he said and pointed to my handbag.

I looked at the paisley silk square knotted on the handle, then back at him, then back at the scarf. I untied it and held it out. He tied it around his neck, tucking the ends into his shirt like an ascot. Then he walked around the back of the Jeep, pulled off his cowboy boots and replaced them with brown wing-tipped oxfords that had been tucked behind his seat. Last, he replaced his aviator frames with a pair of square black plastic reading glasses from the glove box.

"Now I look like I work for you."

I shook my head at the transformation.

"What can I say? I'm adaptable."

He followed me up the steps to the front door where I rang the bell. A man with little more than a fringe of hair circling the rest of his bald head answered. He wore a white polo shirt, curls of chest hair peeking out at the open collar, khakis, and an expensive-looking silver tank watch strapped to his wrist.

"Mr. Johnson? I'm Madison Night."

"Call me Steve," he said, looking past me, to Tex.

"This is my assistant," I said, and let the sentence hang in the air, unfinished, not sure if Tex expected me to provide a full introduction.

"Come on in," Steve said, holding the door open for us to enter. I stepped past him into the small foyer that separated the front door and the kitchen. Tex followed. I would have paid good money to have seen Tex's reaction when I called him my assistant but at the moment all of my good money was going toward Thelma Johnson's belongings.

The kitchen was small but efficient. A laminate table sat under the picture window, the sill lined with a neat row of African violets in white ceramic pots. A corner display shelf filled the space between the cabinets and the window held a collection of Eva Zeisel china in hues of white, aqua, and pink. With just a glance, I could tell she had almost the entire set.

My eyes swept the room and took in the Danish modern chairs neatly tucked beneath the table. Yellow curtains, faded with fifty years of sunlight, showed off an atomic print of dingbats and daisies.

"So, how do you do this? You'll be quick, right?" said Steve Johnson.

"I'd like to walk through the house first, then make you an offer, if that works for you."

"Sure, but you won't take too long, right? I think I can catch an earlier flight."

"You're not a fan of Dallas, are you?" I asked.

"I want to get out of this godforsaken city," he answered. "I can't believe Mom stayed here."

"Didn't she live here her whole life?" I asked. My initial assessment of the furniture was that these belongings hadn't seen a moving truck or the critical eye that accompanies a major move from city to city. They looked lived in and loved, and like they'd been where they were for a very long time.

"Yeah, but some people try to move on after tragedy. Not Mom. I offered to move her to Cincinnati to live with me but she wouldn't hear of it."

"So you were close?"

" 'Were' being the operative word. We lost touch when she started dating."

I gave him some time to continue if he wanted. Experience had taught me sometimes people needed an outlet—a stranger like me—to listen to them unburden themselves of complaints, frustrations, or just memories they were left with after their loved one had moved on. I wondered briefly about Pamela's family and what stories they would tell about her. But Steve Johnson didn't continue and I didn't push. It felt more respectful that way.

"Do you mind if I start? And if I make notes and take pictures?"

He shrugged. "Do what you have to do. I'll be in the garage if you need me."

I pulled a small digital camera from my handbag and handed it to Tex. "Photograph the kitchen. I'm going to the living room."

He hadn't expected me to put him to work. His eyes widened and I smiled.

I'd been right. After a thorough walk through, the living room, sitting room, and the upstairs two bedrooms, I knew what kind of offer to make. It would take more than Hudson's pickup truck to clear out the loot, but I could try to make arrangements with Steve before he left. I found him in the garage rooting through a pile of movie reels.

"Steve?"

He straightened. His white polo shirt had errant cobwebs stuck to the front.

"Are you done?" he asked.

"Not quite, but I know you're pressed for time."

I made my offer, and after mild negotiations that seemed more inappropriate on the part of the grieving son than on mine, he accepted. I wrote out a check.

"There is one potential problem," he said before taking the check.

"Actually, there's two. Can I talk to you for a second?" said Tex from just outside of the garage.

"Excuse me," I said to Steve. "What?" I asked, closing the gap between the garage and the Jeep.

"I can't stick around any longer. I got a call." He held up his cell, "I have to split."

"That's okay, I can get home by myself."

"I don't think you should stick around here by yourself."

"I do things by myself all the time," I said, with just a little annoyance.

"Call a cab." He pulled a twenty from his worn leather wallet.

"I have cab money." We stared at each other for a couple of seconds. "I might dress like it's the fifties but I don't act like it."

He didn't pull the money back right away, but finally, when I didn't take it, it went back in his wallet which went back into his pocket. He pulled the scarf from around his neck in one quick motion but walked away with it in his hand.

I turned to face the house. Steve Johnson stood inside the garage, watching us. Behind me, Tex drove away.

"Ms. Night, I need a couple of days alone here, to make peace with her death."

"I understand. I'd like a chance to go through the house, make some notes, before I come back with a truck. Is that okay?"

He rubbed his hand over the bald top of his head and stared at the small brick residence. "Take all the pictures you want tonight. Put the keys in the mail slot when you're done."

At this point it seemed easier to spend my time figuring out what I didn't want than what I did. By the time I left the house, it was after six, but the time had been time well spent.

Thelma Johnson was a classic example of a woman who hasn't redecorated in fifty years, but also of one who was quite stylish in her day. A closet filled with double-knit polyester pantsuits, cotton dresses, smart skirt suits that would have made an Avon lady proud, and a collection of hats in pristine round boxes were just the tip of the iceberg. There would be no resale value on the clothing because I'd have it all cleaned, tailored to my frame, and adopted as my own. It was like being a walking business card for Mad for Mod.

Hours later, I locked the door behind me and fed the keys through the mail slot. I rooted around in my handbag for my cell phone. It was time to figure out how I was getting home. Only, the phone wasn't here. I moved toward the front steps and sat down, emptying the handbag. Definitely not inside. Had I used it at all today? Did I leave it at home?

The Johnson house was locked up and the keys were inside the mail slot. It was a good thing I had on sneakers. I started walking. Fortunately I'd paid attention while Tex drove, and knew that Thelma Johnson's house was two blocks from White Rock Lake, and if I followed the path around the lake I'd get to Buckner. A right on Buckner would take me to Gaston, which would take me home.

But a left on Buckner would take me past Hudson's house, where I could take him up on his standing offer.

My knee pulsed with pain. Two days of unexpected travel on foot was doing a number on the injured joint. If Crestwood wasn't open tomorrow morning, I was going to have to find another place to swim. It was the only thing that helped.

It was slow going, slower than if Rocky had been pulling me along with his leash. I made it halfway around the lake when I spied Hudson's truck parked on the side of the street. When I reached it, I cupped my hands around my eyes and stared at the interior.

"What are you doing?" I heard behind me.

"Hudson!" I whirled around and faced him.

He took a step backwards, into the shadow of a dogwood tree.

"I know I've been taking advantage of your generosity, but I still don't have a car, and my ride bailed on me, and I don't have my phone to call a cab. Can I borrow your phone? Or better yet, can you give me a ride home again?" I stepped forward to see him more clearly.

His mouth turned down, and his eyes were narrow. I moved back, away from him, scared by his expression.

He stepped out of the shadows, and the closer he got, the more clearly I could see anger on his face. I'd overstepped my boundaries. I'd known him for close to a year but this was now the third time in three days I'd asked for a personal favor. He didn't look happy about it, but he strode toward the car door all the same.

"Nothing good ever comes from rescuing women stranded on the side of the road," he said. He got into the truck, gunned the engine, and drove away.

Eight

Hudson's tires kicked up a spray of gravel and dust that swirled around my ankles. My white sneakers had turned the color of powdered Ovaltine and the hem of my dress matched. Sweat trickled between my breasts. I looked down at my knee, now the size of a grapefruit ready to be juiced. And the worst thing was I was still over a mile away from my apartment.

I started walking, slowly. The sun had dropped below the horizon and it was starting to get dark, yet the needle hadn't moved on the temperature and there was no rain in sight. While I walked, I thought about Hudson. No matter from what angle I approached his reaction, it didn't make sense. Despite our professional relationship, there had been moments, flashes of something more, I didn't think I'd imagined. Even if my request had inconvenienced him, it didn't warrant the hostility he'd flung at me.

As an indication that my luck was turning, a cab drove down the street in my direction. I flagged him down and rested against the sticky vinyl seat while the driver looped around the lake, Buckner, and Gaston. I re-ponytailed my long blond hair and ran a tube of tinted lip balm over my lips. I was far from fresh but close to home. After close to two hours of walking, the cab delivered me to my front door in seven minutes. I would have been happy about that if it weren't for the fact that Tex was sitting on my front steps playing with Rocky. I paid the cabbie and did my best to walk without favoring my knee.

"Before you say anything, your neighbor had to leave and didn't know what to do with your dog. I happened to be waiting here for you. I showed her my badge and she let me in."

"What exactly is going on here?" I asked angrily, even though Rocky was hopping around my feet waiting for a kiss.

"I wanted to make sure you got home safely after I bailed on you," he said.

"I am continually shocked by what you claim falls under the title of normal cop behavior."

"Maybe it's not cop behavior. Maybe it's nice guy behavior. Does that shock you, too?" he asked.

Rocky, frustrated by the lack of affection from me, had returned to the ankles of his new friend, who instinctively ran his fingers through Rocky's long fur.

"Officer Nast didn't seem to think you were a 'nice guy.'"

"I'm not going to talk about her."

"Okay, so talk about me. I'm not a suspect, but all of a sudden I've got a lieutenant showing up at my door offering to drive me around, checking to see that I made it home safely?"

"Madison. I told you you're not a suspect and I meant it. But I think do you're tied to the murder of Pamela Ritter."

"Do you have any news on the-that?"

"On the murder? No, not much more than a hunch at this point."

"So why do you think I'm tied to it?"

"Well, there is one other thing. Remember the pillows, the pillow your dog pulled out from under the car?"

"The pillows? From my trunk?" I looked away from Tex to a brown patch of grass on the front yard, trying to process

58

what he said. "They're not that hard to come by, if you know where to look—"

"Madison, listen to me. That pillow was the murder weapon. That's what was used to kill her."

Tex's words bit into my mind. I wanted to tell him not to talk about her, but it was too late. "She was suffocated. Our team found a death mask on it."

"Those pillows were new old stock. There shouldn't have been anything on them."

"A death mask is an impression left behind on the fabric. It's made by her nose, mouth, eye sockets. . ."

I lowered myself onto the step next to him as his voice trailed off. I wasn't used to hearing the technical terms associated with a murder and I started to shake, even though it wasn't cold. Tex put his hand on my knee, not knowing how badly it throbbed. I flinched and he pulled it away, mistaking my reaction. I looked at him, searching his face for something comforting. He kept it unreadable.

"Who else knew those pillows were there? Who else had access to your car?"

"I don't know. It wasn't a secret. I gave Pamela my keys so she could get a swim cap out of the trunk. The keys were in the lock when I found her. Those pillows have been in there for a week. Anybody who walked past while the trunk was open would see them."

"When's the last time you saw them?"

"I don't remember. I was planning to put them in my storage unit soon, but the trunk of my car has been giving me trouble. Remember? You had to hit it to get it to open at the pool. What does it mean?"

"I don't know what it means yet, but one thing seems for sure. Someone broke into your trunk and stole the pillows, then used one to murder Miss Ritter."

After Tex's news I wanted little more than to collapse inside my apartment. Tex ruffled Rocky's fur then stood up and said goodnight. I entered the building. The mailbox overflowed with colored circulars from the local grocery stores that I tossed directly into the recycle bin in the foyer. Rocky pulled me up the stairs and stood on hind legs, paws on the door of our apartment. I turned the two locks mechanically and pushed the door open.

Unclipped from his leash, Rocky ran into the bedroom and returned with one of my terrycloth slippers in his mouth. I let him play while I swallowed a prescription strength anti-inflammatory then kicked off my white canvas sneakers and left them in a pile covered with my dirty dress. I took a long shower, ridding my body of dust, dirt, dried sweat, and tense muscles. After drying off, I dressed in a fresh pair of yellow pajamas with white flowers and searched the freezer for a quick dinner option. There was a small Tupperware of frozen jambalaya left over from a big batch I'd made last month. I pulled the lid off and nuked it.

I carried the hot Tupperware to the table and set it down next to the newspaper. While the rice, sausage, and chicken concoction cooled, I unfolded the paper. I was so hungry that I scooped a forkful of jambalaya into my mouth, only to burn my tongue. I ran to the refrigerator and chugged milk directly from the carton.

I turned back to the table. The Tupperware had fallen to the floor and Rocky was lapping up the spilled jambalaya. "Rocky! *No!*" He froze. I crossed the small room, and with a wad of paper towels in my hand, cleaned up the mess that was left. I wasn't looking forward to finding out what jambalaya did to a puppy's intestinal tract.

"Go to your crate," I commanded.

He stared at me with soulful brown eyes that looked like a melted Hershey's Special Dark and my heart broke a little. But he was still a puppy and puppies have to learn.

I won the standoff and he walked, both tail and head down, to the metal cage that sat along the east wall of the apartment. I pushed the door shut but didn't bother to lock it.

When I returned to the table it was with a torn off piece of bread that had been sliced open and slathered with butter. I sat in front of the newspaper and smoothed my hand over the creases.

That's when I saw the headline.

Unsolved Twenty-Year-Old Homicide in Lakewood Back in Public Eye

I scanned the article. Twenty years ago a woman had been left for dead by the side of White Rock Lake. Her body had been found dressed only in white cotton panties and a man's denim shirt. There was no evidence of sexual assault. Details indicated she'd been killed in a different location from where she'd been discovered, her body moved after the crime was committed. Eyewitnesses saw a stranger drive her to her apartment building that night, providing the only substantial lead.

The reporter had written a piece heavy on nostalgia that begged for the reader's attention. Attractive, blond, Sheila Murphy smiled at me from the photo they ran next to the story, side by side the promotional photo Pamela Ritter had used on her real estate flyers. Two blond women, murdered, twenty years apart from each other. Oddly, both women bore a striking resemblance to Doris Day, but that wasn't the strangest part of the article. It was the ending.

Hudson James, longtime Lakewood resident, was taken into custody for the murder of Sheila Murphy, but was not charged with the crime. He declined comment for this article.

Both murders remain unsolved.

Nine

The heat left my body, and I felt like my bones had been dipped in ice water. It was about eighty degrees in the apartment, yet my hands went white and rattling teeth shook my jaw. Somehow I reached Rocky's crate and opened the door. He bounded out and I scooped him up and held him close. It wasn't until I felt his wet fur against my cheek that I realized I was crying.

"How can that be?" I whispered. I carried him past the bathroom to my bedroom and set him on the purple and white polka-dotted comforter. In lieu of a headboard, I had a skyline jigsawed out of particleboard, painted lilac, and mounted on the wall behind the bed, backlit with soft twinkling Christmas lights. The glow from the cutout windows illuminated the room. I looked out the back window, half-expecting to see the lieutenant's Jeep in the parking lot. Instead, a blue pick-up truck patched with primer circled past the parked cars.

Instinctively I backed away from the window, realizing too late that Hudson had seen me. I stood in the shadows with Rocky clutched close to my chest until the truck pulled out of the lot moments later. There was no doubt in my mind that

Hudson had been watching my windows to see when I'd arrived home.

Hudson, who had refused to give me a ride.

Hudson, who had a deep, dark secret that had just been exposed.

Hudson, who'd had access to my trunk the day before Pamela was murdered.

I turned off all of the lights except the tall pink and white striped floor lamp that sat inside the front door. I sank to the floor and cradled Rocky close to my chest. I'd been alone so many nights before and it had never felt like this. My loneliness was splintered by fear and distrust. I went to bed with more questions than answers and more doubts than confidence, staring at the early sixties pattern of circles on the ceiling long after I'd turned off the lights.

A week ago, my life had been business as usual. Swim in the morning, open the studio afterwards. Shop estate sales, flea markets, and second hand stores for inventory, and take Rocky for a walk, two times a day. In the wake of my last relationship, a shook-me-to-my-core affair that had ended abruptly, I'd given up on love. The day-in, day-out life I'd designed had been enough. I had my own business, I had my own building, I had my own life. I was independent. Like Doris Day's character in Pillow Talk. But the biggest problems she had were a playboy neighbor and an overly-forward client. I was in the middle of something horrific—a murder investigation—and I was very much alone.

Doris Day movies had taught me how to recognize a womanizer. She had shown me, time and time again, how to stand up for myself and resist the advances of single men who were interested in one thing. Fifty years had passed since she'd made those movies, but the messages were still viable. Protect yourself. Spot a wolf in sheep's clothing, and treat him like a wolf. And when all else fails, storm out of a room and slam the door behind you.

But there were no Doris Day precedents for homicide. When one of her leading men turned out to be someone other than who he pretended to be, she one-upped him and proved her worth. When one of them threatened her idyllic lifestyle, she stood up for herself. No matter how attractive they were, she took care of herself, first. That's what I had done when I moved to Texas. I pushed painful memories deep down inside and moved on without looking back. It was time to do that again. I would take care of myself and move on. That was the only option.

It was a fitful night of sleep, peppered with knee pain and nightmares. I woke at four-thirty, barely rested. I showered and booted up the computer. It sat on a Danish modern sideboard that had been beyond repair when I found it. The top was in good condition, but the sliding panels in the front were severely splintered. I had removed them, allowing room for my knees when I sat in my molded fiberglass desk chair. I loved this office, unconventional as it might seem to many people. But unlike most nights, tonight it didn't comfort me. Too many things were spinning out of control. A murder investigation. An old unsolved murder. A suspect who I'd trusted like a friend and business partner for a year. Tex had cautioned me, told me to be careful, but I hadn't wanted to think about his warning. I didn't want to think that I was connected.

I had to find something to take my mind off the murders. I had to take control of something. I opened my Doris Day files and started working on the proposal. There was peace with Doris Day. I understood her, recognized her in me. Nothing bad could happen while I remained focused on Doris. My knee was stiff and swollen despite the anti-inflammatories. I bent it a few times to loosen it up, with only limited success.

I fleshed out the details of the film festival and wrote blurbs for the movies that I'd selected, formatted the bones of the thing, and emailed it off to Richard sometime around six.

The sun was coming up and I was stiff in twenty places other than my knee. I needed to work out. Badly. And with Crestwood still closed, there was only one other option. The Gaston Swim Club.

I changed into a bathing suit and stepped into a white polyester dress that zipped up the front. I slid my feet into red patent leather flats and took Rocky out for a quick sprinkle on the front lawn, then set him up inside his crate.

"I'm sorry, honey, I can't take you to the Swim Club. Not today." I kissed the top of his head and bribed him for forgiveness with a dog biscuit.

It was darn close to ridiculous to call a cab to take me to the Gaston Swim Club, less than a mile from my apartment, but the pain in my knee didn't leave me with much of a choice. I waited out front for the driver who arrived within minutes and shook his head in disgust when I told him my destination. I tipped him too much to make up for my embarrassment.

When I arrived at the Gaston Swim Club, the sharp pinch of chlorine stung my nose. I wasn't surprised to find a couple of the Crestwood regulars already in the lanes. Their familiar presence comforted me. Old habits die hard, and for some of these folks, this was a routine so set in stone, to break it would be to give up the will to live. True to form, aside from a wave hello, we each concentrated on the reason we were there.

The pool felt like bathwater, too warm for lap swimming. The Crestwood pool was kept at a steady seventy-eight degrees, refreshing but not too hot. It would be hard to complete three miles here. But each time I reached the wall and somersaulted into a flip to turn around, my knee became a little more limber. Pushing off the wall gave me the chance to stretch. By the second mile, my mind was clearing.

By the third mile, my mind was alert.

I stopped at the end of the pool to catch my breath and think. Something from yesterday hadn't been right. Something Tex had said in the car.

When I was sitting in the Jeep in front of the Johnson estate talking to Tex, he'd tried to get me to talk about Hudson. *That colleague you mentioned yesterday, what's his name?* He had known about my connection with Hudson long before we'd gotten to Thelma Johnson's house. And the article in the newspaper, the twenty-year old murder, I was willing to bet Tex knew about that, too. *That's* why he was spending valuable time with me, driving me around Dallas and flattering me with his attention. He was using me to get info on Hudson.

Anger bubbled up inside me. I wanted to find him, to confront him, to ask what he was really doing hanging around my building, following me around Dallas, acting like—what did he call it—a nice guy?

But aside from the anger, I was scared. Tex had told me he thought I was connected to Pamela's murder, and I hadn't wanted to see the obvious. Pamela had been wearing my robe. She was by my car. She looked just like me. Was it possible, could it be, that someone had wanted to kill me instead of Pamela?

I felt sick. Tex must have thought as much, that's why he said we were connected. But by not coming out and saying it, he was checking to see if I'd figured it out for myself.

I dove deep into the water and swam below the other swimmers next to me until I reached the wall. The water's buoyancy lifted me to the surface with barely any effort. Before getting out I checked the thermometer. Eighty-four degrees. No wonder my energy felt sapped. I climbed out using the silver metal ladder and crossed the deck to my things.

"Too bad there aren't any other options around here for us morning birds, right, Madison?" said a familiar voice. Alice sat on the bottom bleacher, tucking her short white curls under her swim cap. Her radiant smile stripped ten years from her wrinkled face.

"I tried to take a couple of days off but couldn't do it," I said. "Don't overexert yourself in there. It's pretty warm for lap swimming."

"When we didn't see you here we all wondered if you knew about some secret swimming hole."

"All?"

"Sure. Jessica is here, so is Mary. Andy, too. It's a reunion party!"

I looked at the shallow end, where an energetic woman conducted a water aerobics class. Seven women and one man held colored foam noodles over their heads and moved to one of the lesser known Madonna songs. In the deep end young kids did cannonballs even though the lifeguard had whistled at them to stop. All this before seven o'clock.

"I hate the Swim Club," I said, towel-drying my arms and legs.

"It's better than nothing," Alice replied.

"Have you heard anything about Crestwood?"

"No, but Jessica said she calls the cops every day and they said they should allow the pool to reopen soon. By the end of the week, we're hoping."

I held up crossed fingers, smiled, and stepped into my polyester dress. I'd worked a lot of last night's tension out of my body, but what I'd realized about Tex had brought on a whole other source of stress. On top of everything else, I was exhausted from not sleeping. No matter how in shape a body is, it refuses to function like a teenager's once it's well past that age.

There was little I wanted more than to go home and sleep, but first things first. I instructed the cab driver to take me to Budget Rent-A-Car on Ross, and twenty-five minutes later I drove away in a midnight blue Ford Explorer. It was the biggest thing they had. After what I'd learned about Hudson, after how he'd left me on the side of the road, I wasn't comfortable asking him for help, on Thelma Johnson's estate or anything else, and this was the next best plan I had.

I made it home and unlocked Rocky's crate. His puppy affection warmed me in a way that the showers at the Swim Club would never be able to do. After a quick shower, I dressed in a smocked white cotton tunic and yellow gingham pants, stuck my feet into pink ballerina flats and ponytailed my long blond hair. I dug through a bin of crocheted handbags until I found a pink one with a silk cord that could be worn across my chest. Inside I put my wallet, lip balm, tape measure and scissors, a small notepad and a tube of SPF 50. The sun was bright, already, and I suspected it was going to be another hot one.

Before I had a chance to head out to Thelma Johnson's house, my phone jangled. The only reason I kept a land line was because I needed it to provide an Internet connection. The second of a pair of working yellow donut phones sat on the Danish modern hutch-turned-desk, ringing infrequently with calls from the few people who had my home number.

"Hello?"

"Madison, it's Richard."

"Hey, Richard. Did you get my email?"

"Forget the Doris Day thing. It's not going to happen."

No. The idea had started as a tribute to Pamela but had turned into the thing I needed to cling to, the one normal thing I could focus on while surrounded with homicide. I wasn't giving it up.

"You don't make all the decisions for the theater. I've done a lot of work on this and I think you should see my proposal before you kill the whole project. In two short days I've uncovered some very valuable contacts related to this film festival, contacts that I think you should know about. You at least owe me time at the Tuesday meeting to make my pitch to the committee."

"Madison, listen. It's not me, it's the cops."

"The cops? Why? What do they have to do with Doris Day?" I asked on high alert.

"They shut down the theater indefinitely."

Only yesterday I had told Lieutenant Tex Allen about the film festival and he acted like he thought it was a good idea. It infuriated me to recognize the lengths of his manipulation, and I wouldn't let him take the project away from me. I needed it more than he knew.

"Let me handle the Lieutenant."

"Madison, you don't understand. There's been a murder at the theater."

"What?" I asked. Other questions tried to formulate in my head but they all started with *what,* and I couldn't make sense of the rest of the sentences. Richard's voice sounded hollow through the vintage receiver. I held my free hand over my right ear so I could hear him better even though there was no other noise in the apartment.

"The cops found a body at the theater this morning. I don't even know what they were doing there, but they came around and there was a dead woman in the parking lot. It gets worse, too."

How could it get worse?

"Who was she?" My voice cracked as I asked the question.

"Ruth Coburn's daughter. The one who's the spitting image of Doris Day."

Ten

wanted—no, needed—to get to the Mummy. I grabbed the
new set of rental car keys and opened the door. Rocky
whimpered by my feet, staring up with bulging round eyes
like Dr. Pepper-colored shooter marbles.

"Fine. You better behave," I said, clipping the leash on his
collar. I locked the door behind me and we took the back steps
down to the parking lot.

I wasn't accustomed to driving such a big truck. The
urgency of getting to the theater kept my heart pounding in my
chest while we made the trip. Even Rocky, who normally
would have hung his head out the window, sat silently on the
passenger seat, staring at me. It was as though he knew this
wasn't a simple pleasure ride.

I pulled the truck into the Mummy parking lot and parked
next to Richard's VW Bus. Cop cars swarmed the lot close to
the front door, where blue and red lights whipped around,
bathing us in light at pulsating intervals. Several uniformed
cops talked to Richard by the front door. A body lay face down
in the dirt.

Numbered yellow plastic tent cards sat by her head and
handbag. More were scattered through the parking lot. There

were bags over her hands and feet. A dusty round pillow that used to be aqua but was now a dingy greenish-blue sat, discarded, a few feet away. I felt the recognition of the pillow more than I saw it. It was one of the missing pillows from my trunk. My hands started to shake and my stomach turned as I suspected what the pillow was doing here. I gulped three deep breaths but no air reached my lungs.

Rocky and I got out of the car. I approached Richard and the officers but stopped when Tex materialized from the side of the building. He pulled a cell phone away from his head and held it in his hand.

"What are you doing here? And where have you been?" he yelled at me.

"What happened here?" I asked. Rocky barked wildly at my feet, adding to the melee. Three uniforms turned to face us. One was Officer Nast.

"Allen? Get her out of here!" she yelled.

Tex put his hand on my elbow and steered me away from the theater.

"Madison, you scared the shit out of me. I've been calling you for the past two hours—your calls started going to voice mail around ten. I sent a car to your place but you haven't been there. Why didn't you answer your phone?"

"I don't *have* my phone."

"Where is it?" he asked.

"I don't know. I looked everywhere else and I can't find it."

"Come with me." He crossed the parking lot to his car.

I called out to Richard. He waved me away and resumed his conversation with Officer Nast. I wound Rocky's leash around my right wrist.

"We have to get you away from here. Hop in," Tex said, holding the jeep's door open for me.

I swatted the door shut. "Stop pretending you're looking out for me. You don't care about me, you're not concerned about me one bit. You're using me to find out about Hudson," I

71

said angrily. "You tried to trick me." A numbness radiated out from my chest. My fingertips tingled and I balled my fingers into fists repeatedly. Like that day at Crestwood, when I found Pamela's body, a haze clouded my ability to focus. I needed a release and even though rational thought would have redirected my anger, I wasn't thinking straight. Fair or not, Tex was my target.

"You read the newspaper?" he asked.

"I don't believe everything I read."

"There are worse sources for information."

"And there are probably better ones, too. What happened here today?"

"This isn't the time or the place for that conversation."

"Okay, then tell me what you know about the murder in the newspaper."

"Madison, I like you. But I'm a cop. Telling a civilian about a confidential police investigation does not rank high on my list of things to do."

"I'm not asking for your secret handshake. You're the one who keeps saying I'm connected. I want to know what happened here, and why you're using me to get to my friend. I have questions."

"You'll have to figure out another way to get your answers. I'm not getting into this with you." He took a couple of steps away from me and held out his hand. "Now come on."

"Tex, if I'm connected, then I want to know what is going on. If you won't tell me, I know someone who's probably all too happy to tell his side of the story," I said loud enough for the entire group of cops to hear.

Through the crowd, Ruth Coburn materialized, hysteria and shock evident in her expression and stance. She pointed a finger directly at me.

"You! You did this to her! She came to see you!"

"Ruth, I'm so sorry," I offered. I stepped forward and reached my arms out, wanting to console her.

"She wasn't supposed to be here! She only came here to impress you!" One of the cops put an arm around her waist and kept her from attacking me. "It's your fault!"

My breath caught in my throat. Tex turned back to face me.

"Madison, I'm telling you, stay out of it. Don't do anything stupid."

"This is my life, Tex. Do *not* tell me what to do." I turned around in a huff and stormed away from the theater. Rocky followed reluctantly, yapping wildly at the chaotic scene in the background.

Anger propelled me away from the Mummy to the Explorer and out of the parking lot. The venom in Ruth's words didn't hit until I was a few blocks away. The trembling in my fingers took over again as her voice echoed through my mind, making it increasingly difficult to keep the large SUV on the road. I pulled over and gulped at the air in an effort to calm down. I punched on the hazard lights. Cars whizzed past me, a few swerving dangerously close to the side of the truck.

Once I'd gotten the shaking under control, I turned off the hazards and moved the truck back onto Garland Road. If I could go home, go to bed, to go sleep and wake up with this as nothing more than a nightmare, I would. But it wasn't. It was all too real. Ruth's words hung in my head, repeating over and over like a record with the needle stuck. *It's your fault.* I didn't know how or why. I couldn't begin to understand how a mother feels after losing a daughter. I knew it was her grief, her hysteria, that had caused her to lash out at me. Unless she knew something else. Why had her daughter gone to the Mummy? I didn't want to think about it. I didn't want to go home. I wanted to go someplace idyllic, to a world where murders didn't exist. Slowly I drove to Thelma Johnson's house.

Seventy-five percent of the population keeps a spare key hidden within three feet of the entrance. I found Thelma Johnson's under a blue ceramic pot that sat to the left of the front door. I unlocked it and called hello to the empty house. My missing cell phone sat on the dining room table, the battery dead. There was no sign of Steve Johnson, and perhaps he'd made his peace with his mother's death faster than he'd anticipated. Rocky followed me into the house. It was as I'd left it, like a time warp. The world outside of this house may have held murderers, but inside it was 1960.

The charity truck had picked up the eighties velour sofa and the matching La-Z-Boy chair. Rectangles marked off the rug where furniture had once sat. I walked up the stairs and sat in the middle of her bedroom floor where the four-poster bed had anchored the room. The yellow and white wallpaper bathed me in calm. The chandelier, a white dome of iron decorated with sage green and ochre flowers, cast shadows of distorted daisies on the walls. Frilly yellow gingham curtains hung from a whitewashed wooden rod accented with white metal finials. The fabric tinted the natural light that filtered into the room. It softened the environment more than a Calgon Take-Me-Away moment ever could. I wanted to stay there, to sit in the middle of that room for the rest of my life. In that room, protected by the golden glow of sunshine and daisies, I felt like nothing bad could get to me.

Rocky sniffed the baseboards, the closet, and the feet of the long, low walnut wardrobe. His leash trailed behind him. He disappeared inside the closet for a few minutes and returned with a white leather shoe between his teeth. He carried it to me to play with. Instead, I pulled it out of his mouth and picked him up, cradling his body close to me. He fought my affection, not understanding I needed his comfort more than he needed to play.

We sat that way for a while, until he finally wriggled free. While this stranger's house felt safe, it felt unfamiliar. These weren't my things. They weren't arranged the way I would have arranged them. As long as they sat in this house, they were Thelma Johnson's, a declaration of who she was. Once they left, wrapped in newspaper, nestled in a box, packed away in my storage room or displayed in my studio, a digital picture of them printed out and pinned to my wall of ideas, they would cease to be hers and become available to one of my clients.

Rocky followed me down the stairs to the living room where I began collecting small items that I could carry and fit in the back of the truck. It would take two people to carry out the wardrobe, the sideboard, and the dining room table. When I'd first embarked on this project I thought I could count on Hudson. Today, I wasn't sure. The more I thought about his reaction last night, and what I'd read in the article, the more I wanted to hear his side of the story. Hudson wasn't a killer. Not the Hudson I knew. He was more to me than a friend. Aside from the fact that he didn't know my own deep, dark secrets, he was the closest thing I had to a confidant, and until last night, I had trusted him completely.

I looped Rocky's leash to the white wrought iron banister and began a series of trips in and out of the house, starting with the contents of her closet, then her vast hat collection, finally emptying out her wardrobe. I rolled knickknacks in newspaper and cradled them in empty cardboard crates that had been left propped inside the front door. The logo on the crates were for mangoes; I kept similar crates at the studio. They were lighter than most boxes, easy to carry, and best of all, free.

Exhaustion and a full SUV dictated when I was done for the day. The house was nowhere near empty; aside from the closet, I hadn't even started on the bedroom. But there was something so peaceful about that room, even with the bed missing, that I didn't want to disrupt it. I angled one last dining room chair into the back seat, collected Rocky and left.

Thelma Johnson's house was in the M-streets, a highly coveted area of real estate despite the difficult housing market. Across the street, children lobbed a rubber ball back and forth while a man washed his car. Rocky barked out the window at them. The children waved and smiled. Their world was so serene compared to mine.

I drove down Monticello to Greenville and turned right, following it until I reached the cross street that led to my parking space behind the studio. I set Rocky up in my office and continued on to my storage unit out back.

Within months of moving to Texas, it had been filled with mid-century objects d'art and my design studio had become a stunning testament to what I was capable of doing with a small budget and a passionate client. I advertised with the local realtors who specialized in fifties and sixties ranches before people like Pamela had jumped onto the trend. Those contacts had led me to buying the small twelve-unit apartment building where I lived. Thanks to the crash of the real estate market my bid had been accepted. Thanks to the other tenants who lived in my building, I could pay the bills and worry less about getting my design business off the ground. When I first moved here it was with a door slammed on my past, a busted-up knee, and a fresh new life in front of me. Now, that fresh new life was at stake.

A hodgepodge of items filled the interior. Bookcases, shelves, armoires, tables, all covered with framed paintings, glassware, clocks, candles, lamps, wall hangings. I made several trips from the truck to the storage unit, transferring as many of Thelma Johnson's newspaper-wrapped belongings as I could, until my knee threatened to give out and my energy level threatened to expire.

I collected Rocky, who jumped around my legs as though he'd been kept captive for a week. I looped his leash around my wrist and we ducked out the back door. Hours had passed since I left Tex at the Mummy, and the day had turned to dusk.

In an odd way, my productivity had been doubly successful; I'd kept myself from thinking about the murders. But now, with no more distractions, questions trickled into the back of my mind. Questions that needed answers. Explanations for things I needed to understand.

Foolishly, I drove to Hudson's house.

Hudson was in his garage like he'd been two days earlier. I parked across the street and watched without letting him know I was there. Clear safety glasses covered half his face. His T-shirt and jeans were once again covered in wood shavings, and the buzz of a sander filled the air. A single light bulb illuminated the garage, enough to cast light on his workbench but not enough to let me see what he was working on. The sun had dropped and I was thankful for the cloak of the dark SUV.

Rocky sat on my lap, watching him with the same interest as I did. Hudson lifted the piece of wood he sanded. Against the light, I recognized a table leg I'd given him a week ago. Gently his hand rubbed over the curve, smoothing away shards or splinters of wood that remained from the sanding. He pulled off the safety glasses and breathed onto the wood, then polished it with a discolored rag that sat on the workbench. There was a gentleness to his movements. At that moment, I wanted to talk to him, to tell him I'd read the papers, and that I didn't believe he had anything to do with a murder twenty years ago. I hopped out of the truck and waited while Rocky climbed down the sideboard. Gently I shut the door behind me.

Hudson stopped working. I crossed the street and he squinted my direction. The darkness made it hard for me to see. I held up a hand in what should have been a wave but looked more like an Indian How.

"Madison," he said, and raised his hand too, then dropped it suddenly. He crossed the garage and slammed the door down, putting a hinged metal barrier between us. A few seconds later a second door slammed from somewhere inside his house.

Being here, alone, was dangerous. I stopped, halfway across the quiet street, my feet rooted to the ground. I shouldn't have come, but now I was afraid to leave.

He'd been so angry yesterday when I asked him for a ride. I thought there must be some explanation, but maybe there wasn't. I turned around and willed myself back to the Explorer with Rock's leash in my hand. As my hand reached out for the door handle, a sudden force slammed my body against the truck. Rocky broke away and took off into the darkness as I struggled for balance.

Eleven

"Ungh," I grunted. My palms slammed into the side of the midnight blue Explorer.

The attacker grabbed my ponytail and yanked me backward, then pulled my head from side to side.

I lost my balance and fell. I powered my good leg underneath me and rose again, twisting side to side, trying to shake free, but couldn't. My feet searched the ground for footing. I started to fall a second time. Our feet scuffled on the side of the road, kicking up dirt and loose gravel. Birds flew out of a nearby tree, the flapping of their wings echoing the sound of my Keds smacking the street.

The man pulled me up by my hair and thrust me forward and I fell again. My kneecap crashed against the asphalt. My palms scraped the street. I powered my good leg underneath me and stood. "*Vola j'shiva*," he grunted, and pushed my face into the side of the truck. I turned my head and my cheekbone slammed against the metal door. I felt for the bag still slung across my chest. My fingers closed on the scissors. I threaded my fingers through the handle and reached behind me, stabbing wildly at nothing. I tried to scream but no sound came out.

I twisted my wrist and hacked at my ponytail, chopping at clumps of hair haphazardly. The man let go. I turned around with the scissors in my hand, but he was gone, vanished as quickly as he had appeared.

I wanted to leave. I yanked at the door handle, repeatedly. I pulled on it over and over, so frantic I couldn't concentrate on the simple task of unlocking the door.

Two strong arms encircled me, pinning my own arms to my sides. I screamed and lifted my legs and pushed against the door but I couldn't win. I wasn't strong enough.

"Madison, it's Hudson, relax, it's okay. He's gone. I've got you now."

"Let go of me!" I screamed and writhed in his arms. I gulped the air, panting loud, almost animalistic breaths.

"Shhhhhh. He's gone," he whispered in my ear. My hacked off hair flew into my face, covering my eyes. I struggled again, trying to get free.

"It's okay," he repeated. "Stop fighting me. Shhhhh," he said. "I'm going to let you go. You can leave if you want." His voice was a calm note to my hysteria. He relaxed his arms and placed a hand on each of my biceps, then slowly turned me around so I faced him.

"No," I said, and pushed my fists into his broad chest. I leaned against the truck and searched his face for answers, signals, indications that these were about to be my last minutes alive. Instead of the threat I'd felt out front of his house, he looked as scared as I felt.

"It's over. He's gone." He reached a hand out and pushed my now-freed hair out of my eyes. "I'm sorry I didn't come out sooner. I should have known."

"Who's 'he'?" I asked. As the fight or flight adrenaline wore off, it was replaced with an off-the-charts throbbing in my knee. My mind pulsed with questions. "What happened? Where's Rocky?"

"He ran into the house when I came outside."

"Can we go look for him?" My voice shook with the question and the implied companionship.

"Your knee. You're hurt." He bent down as though he were going to carry me.

"I want to walk," I said, pushing him away. Slowly, gingerly, I advanced toward his house.

He slung an arm around my waist and guided me to the front door. Rocky sat on one side of the screen, Hudson's black cat Mortiboy sat on the other, hissing at him. There was a small pile of puppy poo on the welcome mat.

"I thought I was the one who had the crap scared out of them," I said to Hudson, trying, and failing, to make light of the attack.

He held the front door open. "Go inside. I'll take care of this. There's a bathroom at the end of the hallway. I called the cops, they should be here soon." Sirens wailed in the distance, almost on cue, as if to prove he was telling the truth.

I scooped up Rocky and walked through the house. Mortiboy crossed my path and jumped onto the sofa. Good thing I'm not superstitious. I shut the bathroom door behind me and set Rocky on the toilet. He watched with eyes that trusted me, that knew I was the person to keep him safe. But who was the person to keep me safe?

I looked at my reflection. My blonde hair hung in dirty, sweaty jagged clumps around my face. I hadn't put on much makeup that morning and dark circles under my eyes aged me considerably. A three-inch long scratch and a purple bruise already showed on my cheek. I started to cry, my already red face turning crimson. I muffled sobs and splashed cool water over my face, my hands, my wrists. It revived me temporarily. I raked wet fingers through what remained of my hair to keep it back. My shirt had torn during the fight, exposing part of my bra. The knee of my Capri pants was shredded and blood had caked to the frayed edge. I looked more punk rock than sixties sex comedy, like I was wearing a makeshift Halloween costume. I blew my nose three times, picked up Rocky from the toilet, and flushed the tissues.

There was a tap on the door. "Madison? You okay in there?" asked Hudson.

I opened the door. He held a wine glass in one hand and a plastic bag filled with ice in the other. I took the wine glass and gulped it too fast. Almost immediately my muscles felt sluggish, like a paper towel that's been used to mop up a spill. When I pulled the glass away from my lips he gently pressed the ice against my cheekbone. "There are a couple of officers out here that want to talk to you."

I looked past Hudson and saw Officer Nast and a short, squat male officer standing in Hudson's living room. I ran my fingers through my hair again and hobbled down the hallway to meet them. Halfway there I stumbled and bumped into the wall, knocking an abstract painting askew. When I righted it, I noticed a small HJ in the corner.

"Ms. Night, this is Officer Clark. Can you tell us what happened out there?" Officer Nast said. With the hand not holding her notepad, she fed her hand between her neck and her long unbound brunette hair, and flipped it out, away from her collar.

"I didn't think it would be you."

"Who'd you expect?" Officer Nast said, obviously annoyed.

"I-I don't know." That was a lie. Tex hadn't made a secret of the fact he thought Hudson was guilty of something. I'd been certain he'd grab the opportunity to come, invited, into Hudson's house.

I relayed the little that I could remember. "He came from behind, he knocked me around, and he ran away. I don't know where he came from, and I don't know where he went. I don't know what he wanted."

Officer Nast jotted some notes into a small spiral top notepad. "You didn't see anything but you keep saying 'he'. Why?"

"He was a man, Officer. I'm sure of that."

"But you can't tell us anything about him?"

"No, I can't. I felt him. I smelled him. I heard him. But I didn't see him."

"What do you mean, you heard him? Did he say something?"

"He said—he said sounds. Not words. I don't know." I stopped talking, and closed my eyes, trying to remember. "I think he said my name. I'm not sure. It could have been another language, maybe German, or Japanese," I said, cradling my cheek with the plastic bag of ice.

"Ms. Night, don't play dumb. I'm sure you can tell the difference between German and Japanese."

I slammed the ice bag down on the coffee table. "It could have been Esperanto for all I know. Everything happened too fast. I couldn't understand him."

Officer Nast stared at me for a couple of seconds. Officer Clark stood behind her. "Let's go outside," she said, and led the way to my truck. I looked at Hudson, in the corner of his living room. His hands were deep inside the front pockets of his jeans. He had been listening, I could tell, but not interrupting. It had to be hard, having these cops here, having this attack happen in front of his house. I tightened a blanket around my shoulders even though it was warm, and followed the officers out front, leaving Hudson inside with the animals.

Officer Clark shined a flashlight around the ground, looking for evidence to corroborate my claims. There was nothing.

"Ms. Night, let me ask you this. Why would someone want to attack you?" asked Officer Nast.

"I don't know."

She watched me closely. I felt she wanted me to say something specific, but didn't know what it was.

Someone knew something I didn't, and until I figured out what it was, I was in danger. A killer had gotten away with murder twenty years ago and for some reason they were killing again. Something had shaken up a homicidal maniac and he was threatened. And what did I have to do with it? What had I done to threaten a murderer? I'd done nothing. My life was as innocent and dull as it ever had been, just the way I wanted it. Swim in the morning. Work at Mad for Mod in the afternoon. Volunteer at the theater at night. How had a part of that put me in danger?

"If you think of anything, you call me, Ms. Night. Me. Nobody else." She handed me her card. I didn't look at it. "I think we have all we need. I don't know what happened here, but be careful, ma'am."

"Call me Madison," I said, bristling at the condescension I detected in her tone. While Tex had made 'ma'am' sound like a cowboy's come-on, Officer Nast managed to made it sound old. I walked the two officers halfway down the sidewalk and turned back to face Hudson.

"Can we sit down somewhere?" I asked.

"Sure." Hudson had been quiet during my conversation, standing a few feet away from the officers and me. I met him on the sidewalk and together we walked back into the living room. Rocky trotted by my side.

I collapsed onto the sofa and Hudson took an armchair. I winced when my knee bent. he pain shot through me like two knitting needles shoved under the kneecap. I hid it as best as I could and settled down into the plush cushions.

"I'm sorry I brought the police to your house," I said quietly.

"I'm the one who's sorry. Last night—I should have given you a ride."

I shook my head. "It's not important."

"Yes, it is. I was in a bad place and you caught me off guard."

"I didn't know about Sheila Murphy then," I said.

"But you do now."

"I read the article after I got home last night."

"Madison," he started, "it wasn't me."

I didn't say anything at first, though I knew I'd already reached that conclusion. "I believe you," I said after a long pause.

"Why?" he asked. It wasn't the response I expected.

"What do you mean, why?"

"Why do you believe me? Some of my friends didn't believe me. I almost went to jail. I'd like to know why you do."

I reached out and picked a smooth table leg off the coffee table. It was the one he'd been working on in the garage the day I'd first come over to his house.

"Because of the table legs."

"What?"

"What you did with that old table was art. It wasn't show-offy. It was completely in sync with the existing nature of the piece. You put yourself, your personality, aside and became one with the project."

"That's my job."

I held up a hand to shut him up. "I'm not done. When Rocky came in, you didn't get mad at him. You stopped your work and played with him. I watched. Your phone was ringing and I know you need the jobs and money but you just stopped what you were doing and played with my dog."

"That's why I should have given you a ride home yesterday. You're not like everybody else."

I thought for a second about Pamela Ritter, and about Ruth Coburn's daughter. I could have been either one of them, if I'd been at the wrong place at the wrong time. "I think I'm more common than you think."

"No, you're not. You're different. You look at the world differently than other people. You look at *me* differently than other people do." He leaned forward and rested his forearms on his thighs, cupping his wine glass with both hands. His eyes focused on the table leg on the coffee table between us. I wanted him to keep talking. I wanted to know what he was thinking. "I like who I am when I see myself through your eyes."

I didn't speak for a long time. I understood him completely. This man in front of me had been in a dark place, a place that I couldn't even imagine being in. Yesterday's article had brought twenty years worth of history back to his doorstep. History that was repeating.

"Do you want to talk about it?" I asked gently.

He looked up at my face. This time his eyes sought the answers. "How much time do you have?"

Twelve

Hudson was quiet for close to a minute after he agreed to tell the story. His attention went back to the coffee table, though I could tell his mind was far away from the cozy living room where we sat.

"You're taught, when you're growing up, to be a gentleman. Be polite, offer a helping hand when you can, put women first. I'm not saying that women can't take care of themselves, that's not the kind of guy I am, but I'm not too self-centered to be able to offer someone help when they need it. That's the only reason I gave Sheila Murphy a ride that night."

Rocky jumped up on the sofa and wedged himself between my hip and the green velvet cushions behind me. I sat sideways and propped my leg on the length of sofa to take the pressure off my knee.

"I was driving home from—from somewhere I had to be. It was late and dark and I was the only car driving around White Rock Lake. She was running down the road in her underwear. At first I was going to drive past, I thought she was there with her boyfriend or something, like a midnight rendezvous that I interrupted. Then she ran in front of my car and held up her hands. Her face was a mess. She'd been at a costume party and must have been wearing a lot of makeup, and it was smudged and smeared around her eyes like she'd been hit, or crying or something. I pulled over and offered her a ride. She got in and I gave her my shirt to wear, so she wasn't sitting there exposed."

I kept my hand on Rocky's head, gently massaging my fingers over his scalp, while Hudson told his story.

"She wouldn't tell me what happened. She wouldn't go to the cops, either, said it would cause more trouble than she wanted. I took her to her apartment and dropped her off. A Korean couple in her building was out front, saw us. That's the last time anybody remembers seeing her alive."

"I don't understand."

"Her body was found the next day at White Rock Lake. She was still wearing my shirt."

"But—"

"There was a cleaning label inside with my name on it. The neighbors described my truck and said they'd never seen it around the building before. The police matched tire tracks from the lake to my tires. They found evidence she'd been in my truck, blond hairs on the headrest of the passenger seat. They went by the book, and the story they figured out was that I killed Sheila Murphy."

"But then why. . .?" I let my voice trail off. I'd been ready to ask why he wasn't convicted, but I didn't want to finish the question out loud.

"The cops weren't convinced. They couldn't find a link between us. The press tried to make me out as a—they didn't think I needed much more motive than wanting to kill a young blonde. They said if I wasn't arrested, I'd kill again."

"Hudson," I said softly, but no other words followed. I didn't know how to react, what was appropriate. Mortiboy slunk into the room, looking only at the carpet in front of him. When he reached Hudson's chair he hopped up effortlessly and turned himself around, then sat down on his lap, facing Rocky and me. Within seconds I could hear him purring.

We sat like that in his living room for a while, no words spoken. Even Rocky and Mortiboy co-existed, neither challenging the other's space. A quiet peacefulness I hadn't felt in days filled the room.

"How old are you?" I finally asked.

"Thirty-nine."

"You're younger than I am."

"Does that matter?"

"How come you seem to know so much more than I do?"

"While my friends were worrying about where to score their next joint I was forced to grow up fast."

"Did that make you bitter? Mad?"

"Everybody has to grow up sometime. That's the hand I was dealt."

I wasn't sure that I'd have accepted things so easily. "Why did you stay in Dallas?"

"What do you mean?"

"When it ended. You could have moved away, started over. Fresh."

It's what I'd done. After graduating from college I'd bounced around from one furniture store to another. I could tell eight different types of wood on an armoire from a fifteen-foot distance. I'd gotten my real estate license and sold a couple of houses between two separate bad markets. Eventually I interned for a decorator in Philadelphia who forever altered the things I wanted out of life.

Brad Turlington. We first met in my late twenties, at Pierot's Interiors. Half a lifetime ago. He was more than a boss and mentor, and I was more than an employee. We fit together like the right angles on a house designed by Richard Neutra. It was a job in California that ultimately dictated our break up. And after a series of relationships that never quite worked out, I wasn't prepared for him to come back into my life in my forties, when the owner of Pierot's passed away and left the store to him. Maturity had led me to want different things in a relationship: compatibility, companionship. But with Brad I had it all. I thought we had the kind of magic that lead to happily ever after, until the day I discovered that happily ever after was only in the movies. That was the day when we'd stood together at the top of a ski slope in the Poconos, when he told me he was already married.

Sitting around Philly pining away for a married man wasn't Doris Day's style, and if ever I was to tear a page out of her playbook, it was at that moment. I broke off all contact with him, figuratively slamming the door in his face. Smart businesswoman that I was, I had a tidy little sum of savings, and thanks to reading *Atomic Ranch* magazine religiously, I knew that Dallas had some of the most well-priced mid-century ranches in the country. So I negotiated my way out of my lease, donated my belongings to a local woman's shelter, and moved to the Lone Star state. Land of chain restaurants, big hair, and luxury cars leased to anyone who could make the monthly payments.

In my early-sixties suits and powder blue Alfa Romeo, I stood out like a sore thumb.

But the plan was to start over. Who moves to a city where summers consist of over a hundred consecutive days over a hundred degrees? Where the air is so thick with humidity that it's practically a rainforest? Where the main attractions are the mega-malls? I did. Because Texas was one place that would never, ever remind me of Brad.

It had been lonely at first. I never told my tenants I owned the building. I rented the studio on Greenville Avenue, with a storage unit in back. Regular trips to dumpsters, flea markets, and estate sales begot me inventory, word of mouth begot me customers, and Mad for Mod begot me a future.

I made friends with contractors and handymen who could restore items I found discarded in the trash or bought cheap at flea markets. Hudson was the third. He resuscitated a Barcelona chair, built me a Vittorio-inspired wall unit made from hand-molded plywood, wired my studio for surround sound, and asked me if I knew anyone who wanted to adopt a stray Shih Tzu puppy. Thanks to him, my business took off and my life changed almost overnight. Around that time I erased any romantic thoughts I'd entertained and considered myself lucky to have found something close to a partner.

"About yesterday, Madison, I'm sorry. I thought I'd gotten past it all, the rumors and the gossip, but that article brought it all back. And when you asked me for help, it was too familiar."

"Why did you stay?" I asked again. "You could have moved. Given yourself a fresh start."

"It would never have been fresh," Hudson said, pulling me out of my thoughts. "People would have thought I was running away. The rumors would have followed me. Besides this is where I'm from. This is my home."

"But you were just out of high school, right? You couldn't have had this house," I said, looking around at the comfortable retro-interior.

"This was my grandmother's house. She raised me. When she passed away I inherited it. It's the only thing I feel connected to. I wasn't going to leave that feeling behind."

"It's a nice house. It feels like a home."

"It's mostly what she had, what she left behind. I've fixed up a few things, reupholstered the sofa, painted here and there, but I still feel her. That's how I wanted it to be."

The room fell quiet again. I could feel his internal struggle with what had happened and how he'd adapted. I knew, no matter where he went or what he tried to do that a background check would turn up the details of his past. The murder of Sheila Murphy would follow him for the rest of his life. It angered me how his life was different because of one night when he'd tried to do something for someone in trouble. It wasn't right. He was so talented and he'd been robbed of the opportunities he should have had. What I wanted to say but couldn't, was that he could have been so much more.

"I had a choice. Hold on to the past or move forward. It wasn't a hard decision to make."

I thought about Brad. The romantic weekend getaway to the Poconos Mountain resort when he said he would love me forever. The view from the peak of Big Boulder, covered in a fresh dusting of fairy tale snow that cast the world in innocence. And the look in his eyes when he told me, at the top of that mountain, that he was married. He said he would leave her for me.

I thought about the accident, where I blew out my knee skiing away from him; I thought about the doctors and the pain. And the two dozen roses that were delivered to my hospital room while I recovered, pink and yellow, with a note on stationery from Pierot's Interiors, that simply said, "I'm sorry. I need more time."

What Hudson said was true. We all make choices. My choice to leave Pennsylvania with a torn kneecap and a map to Texas had delivered my new beginning. I'd run from my past while Hudson had accepted his.

Que Sera, Sera.

"Madison, Madison..." Hudson's voice sounded hollow, far away.

I took a deep breath and exhaled, repeated the process, and opened my eyes.

He stood next to the sofa with a green blanket in one hand and a white pillow in the other. "It's late. You can stay here if you'd like. Take the bed. I'll take the sofa."

"Mmmmmmm," was the best I could manage as conversation.

"Come on." He lifted me to a sitting position.

I tipped my sleepy head against his shoulder and breathed in the smoky, woody scent of his shirt. After another labored breath I blinked a few times to wake up, then stood. A bolt of pain shot through my knee. Hudson put a hand on each side of my waist to steady me. We were close. I could feel his breath and smell the wood shavings, and something else, soap? I closed my eyes another time and buried my face in his chest, absorbing the scent. When I opened them and tipped my face up, his face was closer to mine than before.

The wine had dulled my senses as well as my judgment. We kissed. It was long, soft, and urgent. His hands encircled my back and held me against his body. It was an escapist moment that, for a second, pulled me away from reality. When our lips parted, reality crashed into me like a forceful wave.

"You can stay here tonight," he said again, in a soft voice, his warm hand cradling my bruised face. His fingertips lightly traced my cheekbone, where I'd hit the ground. I tipped my head into his warm, calloused palm, and stared into his amber eyes. Rocky was out cold on the bottom of the sofa, his belly exposed, his paws spread out above his head and below his feet. Hudson's offer was tempting, but I couldn't accept it.

"I have to go home."

"It's after two. And, I don't think it's a good idea for you to be alone tonight."

"I wouldn't feel right staying here," I said. The look on his face told me I'd hurt his feelings. "That's not it. But after what happened out there, I want to be in my own house. And I won't be alone. I'll have Rocky."

"Then I'll take you."

"No, I have the truck."

"Leave it here. We can figure that out tomorrow."

"I keep odd hours," I said, now more alert from the heat of the kiss and not knowing what it meant. "And there's stuff from an estate in it. I have to finish unpacking it early tomorrow morning."

"Then I'm going to make sure you get home safely. If you won't let me drive you, I'm going to follow you."

"You don't have to—" I started to say, but realized I was grateful for his offer. "Fine."

He followed me the short distance to my building and circled the lot while I backed the Explorer into my parking space. The partying crowd that occasionally peppered Gaston Avenue had long since turned in or passed out. A large critter, maybe skunk, maybe possum, maybe raccoon, sat by the dumpster and watched me carry Rocky inside. I locked the door behind me. I thought being in my building would make me feel safe, but I felt more vulnerable than at Hudson's. Tomorrow I'd call a locksmith and add another deadbolt to the building, just to be on the safe side.

I looked out the window. Hudson sat in the cab of his truck, staring up at my window. The moon provided enough light for me to see him wave. I waved back. He pulled out of the parking lot. I plugged my dead cell phone into the charger and peeled off the torn shirt and dirty Capri pants and crawled into bed in my underwear, asleep before my head hit the pillow.

I woke to the sound of pounding on my front door. I peered through the peep hole. Tex faced me. I pulled on a robe and opened the door.

His expression changed from anger to surprise. "What happened to you?" he asked instead of good morning or hello or what a normal, polite person would say.

"Good morning to you, too," I said, and turned around. He followed me inside.

"It's not morning anymore."

"What time is it?"

"Eleven-thirty. I thought you were a morning person?"

I went to the kitchen and shook four anti-inflammatories out of an economy-sized plastic jug. I started a pot of coffee, then poured a small glass of juice and swallowed the pills in one gulp.

"Night, what's going on?"

"Why are you here?" I asked.

"I don't like how things ended last night."

"You have been using me, lieutenant, and I don't like being used. There's a murderer out there, in your backyard, and you're spending too much time focusing on me."

"I wanted to make sure you were okay."

"So here I am. I'm okay. Check me off your to-do list and go back to you job."

"Funny, you don't look okay." He collapsed his frame onto a bar stool reupholstered in lime green vinyl. "What happened to your hair?"

"I cut it," I said simply.

"It's kind of an interesting look."

"It had nothing to do with vanity."

"How's that?"

I crossed the room to the pouch that I'd been wearing last night and pulled out the scissors. When I laid them on the table in front of the lieutenant, his expression changed.

"That's more dangerous than a gun."

"Then I should probably keep them with me. I was attacked last night."

He jumped from the bar stool and slammed his palm on the counter. "Where? Did you report it?"

"Yes, I reported it. I'm surprised you don't know."

"Where was this?"

I stopped speaking. Tex wouldn't understand why I'd gone to Hudson's house, or why I now believed in his innocence, one hundred percent. And I was wary of sharing anything with Tex, anything related to Hudson.

"I talked to Hudson. I know his side of the story and I believe it. He's not your killer."

His face grew taut, dark. There was no emotion to read. "You don't know the details that I know, Madison."

"I know that Hudson was the one who called the cops after I was attacked. You can ask your friend Officer Nast. He wouldn't do that if he was guilty."

"Guilty people call the cops all the time."

"Don't try to change my mind. I know everything I have to know."

"Do you know that Sheila Murphy was suffocated twenty years ago, just like Pamela Ritter? And that we never found the murder weapon?"

"No," I said.

"Or that she was at a costume party the night she died, dressed up as your favorite actress?"

"No, I didn't know that either. But it still doesn't prove anything."

"How about this one. Did you know Sheila Murphy was Thelma Johnson's daughter?"

Thirteen

The room started to spin, and I put my hands down on the ivory-tiled counter to get my bearings. An unexpected breeze blew the aqua curtains away from the kitchen window and stopped as suddenly as it had started, turning the curtains back into a motionless wall of fabric.

"How is that possible?" I asked.

"Different marriage, different last name. Happens all the time."

"No, I meant the coincidence of it. And why wasn't anything about it in the paper?"

"We suppressed a few details from the public because of the investigation."

"But—"

"No buts, Night. Face it. You don't know what you're doing."

"You told me I wasn't a suspect."

"You aren't a suspect. You have no motive, and to the best of our knowledge, you never even met Thelma Johnson. You lived in Pennsylvania when Sheila Murphy's murder took place. You were nowhere near this."

"So stop treating me like I'm involved," I said, fists balled up on the countertop.

"Being a suspect and being involved are two very different things and you're definitely involved, that much I know for sure. First, someone wearing your robe, who looks a lot like you, is killed with a pillow stolen from your trunk and left behind your car. Then you get a threatening message at the theater. Then you make arrangements to go to Thelma Johnson's house and another person dressed up like you is murdered with one of your pillows. And now you tell me you were attacked." Tex said, readjusting his weight on the barstool. He looked more comfortable on it than most people would. "We got four dead bodies. And you're in the middle of it all."

"Wait, four bodies? I thought there were three." My stomach turned. "Sheila, Pamela, and Ruth Coburn's daughter." Embarrassed, I realized that I didn't know the young girl's name.

"Carrie. Carrie Coburn."

"Okay, that's three. Who's the fourth?"

"Thelma Johnson."

"That's insane! She was seventy-eight and died in her sleep. I have the article here somewhere." I crossed the room to the makeshift sideboard-desk and pushed small pieces of scrap paper and newspaper articles around the surface, looking for the one with the obituary. "It's here, I just can't remember where I left it."

"Madison, stop looking. You won't find anything in the article."

I stopped what I was doing but didn't look at him. I stared at the clock in front of me, a radial with colorful balls on the end of each of the twelve arms. The second hand snapped forward, ticking off seconds of silence while I kept my back to Tex.

"Night, I told you, we're working with the press. We withheld information from the public. Thelma Johnson didn't die in her sleep. She was suffocated. Just like the others."

The news knocked the wind out of me and I swayed forward. I steadied myself with a hand palm-side down on the top of the desk. Without looking at Tex, I walked down the hall to the bathroom and locked the door behind me.

I took a long shower. Long. When I finished, I dug around inside a bin of rarely needed bathroom-stuff in the closet and found a small pair of scissors, then did what I could to even out my hair. In light of everything, it didn't feel right to schedule a trip to the stylist.

Next I rubbed my knee with steroid cream and wrapped it with an ACE bandage. I could barely bend it, but the restriction subdued the throbbing enough to allow me to move. Temptation wanted me to stay at home with Rocky, take a painkiller, and hide out in bed, but obligation would force me to deal with business first.

Tex suspected Hudson. I didn't. But if I was wrong, then I had put myself in a very vulnerable position last night. If I was right, then the killer was out there. And he wanted something. I didn't have a clue how each of these women were connected. Sheila and Thelma were connected, related, by blood. But Pamela Ritter and Carrie Coburn? How did they factor into this? And was I just an innocent bystander who was getting caught in the middle of the tornado of murder?

I belted the robe around me. My clothes were in the bedroom and I was going to have to leave the safety of the bathroom behind. My cell phone sat on the back of the toilet where I'd left it charging last night. The screen said the battery was full. I unplugged it and the screen changed, alerting me to several voice mails and text messages. Two days without a cell phone left me feeling popular in a way that didn't matter.

I leaned against the pink ceramic sink with my back to the mirror, and listened to the voice mail. Tex. Demanding that I called him. They ranged from *Madison, call me back* to *Damn it, Night, where are you?* His voice had changed from anger to frustration to something I didn't yet recognize. I'd heard the anger and frustration first hand but the later messages held a different edge. Whatever it was, he hadn't used that tone of voice with me before.

After listening to the voice mail messages I cued up the texts. Again, Tex. Same degrees of concern, six in all. I deleted each one as they appeared on the screen.

Call me back
Where r u?
meet me at the mummy tonight
call
call
CALL

I wanted out. Out of the murder investigation, out of range of being used. I tightened the knot on my robe and opened the bathroom door. Tex stood in the hallway, in front of the door, his hand raised to knock.

"You've been in there a really long time," he said.

I held up the cell phone. "That was almost an obsessive amount of messages and texts," I said, and walked past him to the bedroom. He followed.

"I'm in the middle of a murder investigation, Night, and part of my job is to find the killer, and the other part of my job is to protect the people who might become victims."

"Tex," I started.

"You seem to show up at all the right times."

"Because you're telling me to! It's like I'm your puppet!" I waved the phone in front of his face. "First you tell me to go to the Mummy, then you make me leave as soon as I get there. Stop trying to use me!"

"What are you talking about?"

"Make up your mind. Did you want me to go to the Mummy, or did you want me to stay home? If I wasn't supposed to be there, why did you tell me to go?" I stepped backward and tripped over a pair of shoes lying on the floor.

Tex's hands flew out and grabbed my forearms, preventing a fall. "Night," he started.

I balled up my fists and tried to shake him off.

"Listen to me. I didn't tell you to go to the Mummy." The intensity of his voice made me go ice cold.

"If it wasn't you, then who was it? Who texted me six times? 'Call me? Where r u? Meet me at the mummy?'" I punched the cell phone in the air as I repeated each message, but before he had a chance to answer I knew I had been wrong. At least one of those messages hadn't come from Tex. Someone else had texted me to go to the theater last night.

Someone had been waiting there to kill me.

Fourteen

As quickly as I realized what had transpired, Tex figured it out in half the time and had been waiting for me to catch up. Rocky jumped around our feet. His joy in light of my crisis was jarring.

"Madison, I'm going to need to ask you a lot of questions about what you know and you're going to have to answer me. Honestly."

"I need a minute here."

"Okay. Get dressed and meet me in your living room." He walked out of the room and pulled the door shut behind him.

I sat, shoulders hunched, on the bed, and stared at the small TV cart in front of me. The plastic case to *The Glass Bottom Boat* sat on top of the television, where I'd left it after I'd first gotten the idea for the film festival. I felt further from Doris Day and her kind of idyllic life than I could have imagined possible, yet, somehow, it all matched. Rock Hudson's character had tricked her, had made her think he was someone he wasn't. He gained her trust with his lie, and, because she'd wanted to believe so badly that this smart, handsome man who she was falling in love with was the real deal, she left her blinders on and didn't see the truth. As much as I wanted to be like Doris, I couldn't afford to wear blinders. The lieutenant had been hitting me with his one-liners and pretend attraction since we met, to throw me off guard. He wasn't looking for a date for Saturday night, he wanted to know my connection to four murder victims. I had to look at the situation clearly, to see past his come-ons, past Hudson's friendship, to what was really there. I didn't want to believe my life had been spared because of a lost cell phone and a missed text message.

I pulled on a pair of lime green polyester knit pants and a white V-neck pullover trimmed in the same shade. The pants had always been loose and I needed the room for my knee now wrapped in the bandage. I slid my feet into yellow Keds and tied them, while my brain raced with thoughts that wouldn't leave me alone. I grabbed a straw hat from my closet, a tall wicker cone with yellow straw tassels hanging from it, and pulled it over my chopped up hair.

Rocky sat by Tex's feet when I returned to the living room. Tex punched buttons on my cell phone.

"That's an invasion of privacy," I said, trying to make a joke. It fell flat.

"Who else has this number?" Tex asked, holding up my phone.

"Lots of people. It's on my business card," I said.

"Let me see it."

I pulled a card out of my wallet and handed it to him. He studied it.

"This address, is that your studio?"

"Yes."

"When's the last time you were there?"

"Yesterday, I think. No, the day before. The Thelma Johnson project kept me away yesterday."

"The Thelma Johnson project is over. Your new project is working with me."

"You can't do that!"

"You're right. I can't shut down your business or put you under house arrest for your own safety." He stood up and shook his left leg until the wrinkles in his jeans gave out. "But, if you're going to insist on putting yourself in danger, I can make sure I'm there."

"What do you mean by that? You can't be everywhere I am all the time."

"Trust me, I can." He tucked his thumbs into his back pockets, his elbows pointed behind him, his chest swelled out.

"What do you mean by that?"'

"It's pretty simple. You're looking at your new partner."

I pulled the blue Explorer out of the lot and drove down Greenville Avenue to my studio. I needed to finish emptying out the back of the truck. Last night, under a cloud of fear and wine, I thought I'd ask Hudson to help me like I had in the past, but today, with my new side kick, I wasn't looking to complicate matters. I knew Tex still considered Hudson a viable suspect, a threat. I didn't. But if Tex was right and I was wrong....

I shook my head involuntarily and the yellow tassels on my hat bounced. I was not going to think about that, I was not going to let my mind go down that path. It couldn't be. Hudson's story held so much truth, so much honesty, so much pain, that it would be difficult for me to discount it completely. I had to believe in the good of the people around me. It was the only way I knew how to function.

We arrived at the studio and I set Rocky up in my office. He raced to his makeshift bed, and bit into his rope bone. With a fresh bowl of water and a hollow rubber toy filled with peanut butter, he'd be self sufficient for hours. I locked the door and Tex followed me out the back exit.

"So you're a decorator, huh? How'd you get into that?"

"It's a job, just like any other job," I said.

"It's creative without creating anything."

"Who says I don't create anything?"

"Whoa. Calm down." He put his hands up in the air, like he surrendered. "I'm just saying, you know, painters have paintings when they're done. Writers have books. Musicians have—"

"Music. I get it. You don't respect the talent needed to design a room."

He leaned back against the side of the Explorer while I pulled two brass clocks from behind the seats. "I just don't get it. How does someone choose to be creative like this instead of painting or singing, or writing?"

"You know somebody who teaches you. You develop an eye, a way to look at things. You not only see what should be in a room but what shouldn't. You have a decent memory bank, so you remember lots of different things that came from lots of different places, and you figure out how to put them together into something fresh."

"So you're a problem solver," he said.

"At times. You know, our jobs aren't all that different."

He crossed his arms over his chest and leaned a shoulder against the door. "How's that?"

"You look at the big picture, too. You see a bunch of pieces of a crime and try to figure out what belongs and what doesn't. You inundate your brain with information until things fall together into a solution that works."

"You're likening police work to decorating?"

"I am."

"That's a bold statement I'm not sure the boys in blue would appreciate."

"See? Maybe that's a problem. Pride gets in the way of you seeing things from a new perspective." I shoved the two brass clocks at him and picked up a box of china printed with a light blue and light green pattern of starbursts. "Now, if I haven't hurt your feelings, lieutenant, follow me. We have a lot of work to do today *partner*."

105

I shut the door to the van and walked around the corner to the storage locker. He followed a few steps behind.

I set the box by my feet and unlocked the door. Unlike the organized minimalism I maintained in the studio, this nine-foot by nine foot cubicle was stuffed to the gills. At one time I'd lined the perimeter with cheap second-hand bookcases that now held all of the smaller knickknacks I found. The middle was a carefully arranged chaos of sofas, chairs, tables, and wardrobes stacked as tightly as possible. Throw blankets and pillows were wedged between wood surfaces to protect them. Framed pictures sat in upright stacks along the far wall next to canisters of film and colorful sets of glassware.

When I needed something unique, this was the first place I came. I could do a room with what was offered at most retailers today, and I could keep it in budget, too. But these effects were the ones that made the difference. They were original, had probably sat in the same house since they were bought, and were easily repaired. They came cheap because of their condition, but Hudson helped me deal with that small detail.

I stole a look at Tex's face. He took in the room with a sweeping glance and I could tell he was looking with his cop's eyes. He might like to play the flirtatious bachelor, but he was on a case, and I was part of his investigation. Watching him take it all in, what I'd amassed, where it had come from, and how I'd kept it organized, made me feel like he was seeing an aspect of me that I normally kept from the world, that he was looking through a window into my mind. I flashed on the moment days earlier when he'd seen through my pajamas and realized this was yet another way Lieutenant Tex Allen made me feel exposed.

"Where did you get all this stuff?"

"Around. I shop estate sales, auctions, flea markets, dumpsters...." my voice trailed off. I wasn't sure how much he already knew.

"How can you tell when something's going to be valuable?"

"I have to be decisive. That's why it's good to know what I'm looking at."

"So tell me what you see," he said.

"Here?"

"The murders. If our jobs are so much alike, then tell me what you see when you look at the details. Because everywhere I look, I see Hudson James."

"What's his motive?"

"Maybe none. Maybe serial."

"You don't believe that," I said defensively.

"It fits, though, doesn't it?"

"No, it doesn't. Explain the twenty-year lapse between Sheila Murphy and Pamela Ritter's murders. Explain the fact that he stayed in Dallas instead of moving somewhere else. Explain his ability to get people to trust him again."

Tex looked at my face, then the top of my head, then back to my face. "You know, I could take you a lot more seriously if you took off that hat."

"I'm serious, Tex. Hudson isn't your guy."

"There's something's not right with his story. I just can't figure out what."

"Ah-ha! So you are doing it. You're seeing all of the components separately. Seeing what matches. You're trying to force a connection between Hudson and Thelma Johnson, and Hudson and Sheila Murphy, and Hudson and Pamela Ritter." I headed back to the truck with Tex on my heels.

"Carry these," I said, thrusting a pair of squat oval lamp bases at him.

He stared at them for a couple of seconds, then looked up at me. "Where did these come from?"

"Thelma Johnson's house. I took them after you left me the day we met with her son."

"You did what?" Tex demanded. He pushed the lamps back at me, then pushed his fingers through his hair. "Did anybody help you?"

I was angry at Tex, so angry that at first I couldn't speak. I clamped my teeth shut and glared at him. "By 'anybody' you mean Hudson, right? No, he didn't. And he knew I was going there, too. That should prove his innocence."

"Or his guilt. That house is a crime scene, Madison, and he knew you were going to violate it."

I barely heard him. My mind raced to a specific moment two days ago. I had to keep talking to retrieve the memory. "We violated the crime scene, together, Tex. You and me, two days ago, when we went to meet up with her son."

Her son. How had I missed that? How had *Tex* missed that?

"That has to be it! He was here. He made it seem like he should have been there so nobody would question his presence at the scene of the crime, Long enough to make sure he covered his tracks."

"So you went from being a decorator to a profiler?"

"The charitable donation. The rush to get out of town. The attitude when I first called and the change of heart. It all makes sense."

Tex's smile froze on his face. He leaned forward and touched my shoulder. "What is it? Did you think of something else?"

"Have you checked out Steve Johnson? Thelma Johnson's son?"

"Keep it down," Tex said sharply.

I dropped my voice. "We met him. At the house. That's why he was so angry when I first called, he wanted to get out of Dallas before anybody put it all together. That's probably why he changed his mind and sold me this stuff. He wanted me to get rid of any evidence!" It was my turn to gesture toward the van. "He lives in Cincinnati. He probably already skipped town." I ticked facts off on my fingers, waiting for Tex to catch up.

"Listen to me. That guy has nothing to do with the murder," Tex said, now with a hand on either of my shoulders, squaring me off, forcing me to face him.

But I was unstoppable, barely hearing him. "If he was Thelma Johnson's son, then he was related to Sheila Murphy, somehow. He said he and his mom used to be close but they aren't now. He was even listed in the paper as her only surviving relative. Don't tell me you didn't check him out like you did me," I said.

"Night, try not to react to what I'm about to say." He stared at me, his crystal blue eyes piercing my thoughts. "There is no Steve Johnson. The man you met was one of us."

Fifteen

"One of who?"

"A cop."

If the reality of his words had hit me right then and there I might have slapped him, but it took longer than that to process the information. Long enough for him to guide me back inside the studio and into a chair in the office. By that point I had moved from a slapping mood into one of numbness.

"Do you want a cup of water?"

"I want you to tell me what's going on."

"There is a homicide investigation at stake, and there are things I'm not at liberty to tell you."

"You were with me the day I went to Thelma Johnson's house. You met the man I thought to be Steve Johnson. There is a reason you allowed me to be in that position and I want to know what it was. As far as you can see, I've been completely cooperative even when I didn't think I was being cooperative. So spill."

Tex filled a small Dixie cup with water from the cooler and sat in the chair opposite my desk. His head tipped to one side and I imagined him weighing his words, deciding what to share, what not.

"When Thelma Johnson died, it reopened the case of Sheila Murphy. Both women were suffocated. It was eerie; twenty years had passed. A lot of people who were involved with this investigation had come and gone. Most of the guys only heard about it through other sources, or remembered it from the news." He didn't say anything about not knowing who the killer was and I knew, for him, that question already had an answer.

"Thelma Johnson does have a son. He does live in Cincinnati. And you did talk to him. Once. His name isn't Steve, it's Terry. He agreed to cooperate with the investigation. Homicide planted bait in Thelma Johnson's obituary, thinking they might draw out a lead. The phone number rings at the house, and also at the station. It was a long shot but we were desperate. Most people who read the obituary wouldn't think twice about a son who outlived her but someone who wanted something from her, someone who had something to gain from her, would try to make contact and maybe even set up a meet. You called the number. Our guy called you back. He was a rookie cop with a phone number and an address that anyone who did a half-assed search on the web would find." He leaned back in his chair and met my stare. "No disrespect."

"None taken." I'd fallen into a trap they'd set for a killer. I shuddered.

"A background check said you were on the level, so he arranged a meet."

"You checked my background?"

"Standard procedure. I already told you we checked you out."

That day, when he'd driven me to Thelma Johnson's house, was the day he'd asked me about my business. It was the day he first asked about Hudson. Hudson and I had worked together often; there would have been a record of phone calls to him and checks written for work I'd hired him to do. A background check would have turned up our interaction. Tex had known from the get-go that I had a relationship with Hudson James.

"Fine. So you had to do something."

"Our guy told you he'd arranged to donate the estate to a local charity. That was supposed to make you lose interest. But after you made that offer we figured you might be looking for something—or working for someone. We had to follow up on any lead we got."

"You were at the Mummy when he returned my call. You knew all along." I felt like an idiot for playing directly into their plan.

"C'mon, Night, I'm a cop. I've done this before, and with good reason. Four women are dead. I want to stop that from happening again."

If it had been happening to someone else, I would have probably seen things from Tex's side, but I couldn't help feeling violated and used.

"How do you expect me to feel right now? You played me."

"A lot of people fall for something like this. Don't underestimate how smart these criminals are."

"You're actually telling me these criminals are smarter than I am?"

"That's not what I said."

"Sure sounded like it to me."

"Night, let me ask you a question. Who else had access to your trunk?"

It was the one question I didn't want to think about. I averted my eyes and looked at the floor. Something wasn't right. I stood up and scanned the corners of the carpet.

"Where's Rocky?" I asked suddenly, my voice laced with panic.

His eyes followed mine around the room.

"He was here a second ago."

"Did you shut the door?"

We both looked at the office door, open the width of one Shih Tzu.

"Damn it, Tex," I said, and rushed into the studio, just in time to see an eight-foot silver arc lamp crash to the ground.

Rocky's head and tail were lower than usual when I found him next to the marble base. Both the perfect round shade and globe-shaped bulb had shattered upon impact. The metal arc was bent from landing on a glass top table that now had a large crack across the middle. A small wet spot stained the rug next to the crash.

I scooped Rocky up and stepped around the furniture. I doubted any of it was fixable. The scared puppy pushed his head next to mine and wrapped a paw around each side of my neck like a hug. He was asking for forgiveness. It was easy to forgive a puppy. It was the only emotion I could handle.

I clipped Rocky's leash onto his collar. "I'm taking him outside."

"I'll take him," offered Tex.

"No, you won't."

"Then I'll clean up the broken glass."

"Leave it."

"Night," he started.

"It's my problem. You work on yours, I'll work on mine."

I stormed out the back door and set Rocky on the sidewalk. He pulled me toward the back of the alley. After the near miss of an eight-foot tall metal arc lamp anchored in a 20-pound marble block, I was betting on a record-sized poo.

While Rocky arched his back and stared up at me with guilty eyes, my mind raced. Something still wasn't right. If the cops had invented a son and planted him at Thelma Johnson's estate, then my being there had put a wrench in their whole plan. Tex knew I wasn't involved, so why allow me to show up at all? Did they really use me because of my affiliation with Hudson?

Tex was looking at the big picture but he wasn't seeing the right one. It was like watching the director's cut of a movie. It was something I'd learned after I first started volunteering at the Mummy. Occasionally we landed a print that included footage cut from other versions. At times, when I watched movies I knew well, I was surprised to find more to the story than what I remembered. So much was lost on the editing room floor the end result often lacked the scenes of continuity that tie the whole vision together. Tex wasn't seeing the whole movie. He was seeing the edited version he'd been replaying for twenty years.

That's what I needed to see. The whole picture, cutting room floor scraps and all.

I had half-expected Tex to come looking for me out back. He didn't. When Rocky finished up his business and I finished cleaning up after his business, we walked back down the length of the alley. No Tex. I poked my head into the studio and called out for him but he wasn't there. I went out onto the street, expecting to find him unloading the rest of the truck. I couldn't have been more mistaken.

Not only was there no Tex, there was no truck.

The lieutenant had stolen my car.

Fear, doubt, and anger converted into a shot of adrenaline with a don't-mess-with-me chaser. I went inside and called the cops.

"Police Dispatch," said a monotonous voice on the other end of the phone. He sounded like he was chewing something. My bet was on sandwich.

"This is Madison Night. I want to report a stolen car."

"Where you at?" asked the voice.

"Don't you have that information on your caller ID?"

"Ma'am, it's a routine question. I'll need your address."

I gave him my contact info and answered a series of questions. He said he'd send a patrol car out to take my report. The proper channels were doing little to diffuse my attitude.

If Tex had known about my knee injury, I didn't think he'd be so willing to hijack my car. Not one to play the victim, that was fine by me. The him-not-knowing, not the carjacking. That was definitely *not* acceptable.

I unlocked the front door and flipped the Closed sign to Open. As long as I was spending more time at the studio, it didn't hurt to be available should opportunity come knocking. I shut Rocky inside the office and spent the next half hour cleaning up the lamp mess. After hauling the broken pieces to the dumpster, I selected a replacement floor lamp from the storage unit. I hoisted it onto a dolly and pushed it inside close to the now-empty spot. A rectangular impression on the carpet marked where the marble base of the arc lamp had sat. The round metal base of the new lamp covered most of the impression but left exposed corners. I could fix that with a vacuum but it would have to wait until later. A royal blue squad car with *Dallas Police* emblazoned on the side in aggressive italics pulled up to the curb in a red zone.

"Madison Night?" asked the chubby officer who stepped out from behind the wheel. I quickly recognized him as Officer Clark, the same officer who had been with Officer Nast when I was attacked outside Hudson's house.

"Yes. My car was stolen."

"Where was your car when this happened?"

"Right where yours is now."

He took notes on a form clipped to a board and asked questions about the make, model, and year without looking up.

"License plate number?"

"I don't know. It was a rental."

"Where were the keys?"

"Probably in the door."

"You left your keys in the door of the car?" His head snapped up.

"I was unloading the truck with the help of a—a volunteer. I believe he's the person who stole it." The officer took notes. "You probably know him. Tex Allen?"

"Lieutenant Tex Allen?" His head snapped up again.

"Yes. Lieutenant Allen stole my car."

Officer Clark turned his back on me and went inside the squad car. The windows were tinted to protect against the hot Dallas sun but through the crack in the door's opening I saw him pick up his radio. He glanced at me, pulled the door shut behind him, and turned the other way. Finally he got out of the car.

"Looks like a mix-up. Lieutenant Allen says you knew he was borrowing your car to help out with your work here. He's at a..." He flipped through a small notepad. "He didn't say. A local residence? Says you borrowed some stuff from somebody and he's helping you put it back?"

"He and I did not arrange that."

"Listen, ma'am, if you want to file this as a stolen vehicle to make up for some one-night stand with Lieutenant Allen, that's your decision." He tipped his head and made a note on his pad. "One of the more creative ways to get back at him, I'd say. I'll write up the report and we'll start the investigation but you will have wasted a lot of people's time and tax money, and chances are you'll have your car back in a couple of hours. I'd say you need to forget about Loverboy Cop and move on."

Oooooh!

"Despite what you think, this isn't about a one night stand. He stole my car and I want it back."

"Tell you what. I'll take this back to the station and fill out the paperwork. But I just spoke to the guy and sounds like this was a big misunderstanding. You have Lieutenant Allen's number?"

"Yes."

"You might want to give him a call and straighten the whole thing out."

"I want you to fill out the paperwork and treat this like Grand Theft Auto."

His eyes went wide. "That was either one hell of a night, or you're one hell of a woman."

I stormed back to my office as best as I could with a bum knee. I fished a bag of ice out of the freezer in the office and held it against the lime green fabric over my knee. I needed to cool down.

With my free right hand I checked the messages. Two hang-ups. One from a couple who had recently bought a mid-century modern ranch that had been renovated in the eighties. They needed a contractor to undo the damage. I could recommend Hudson, like I had done so many times in the past when these types of calls came to me. I went as far as dialing the first four numbers before I hung up.

I thought about last night, the attack, and the kiss. His explanation for what had happened years ago. I hadn't been lying when I said I believed Hudson's explanation, but Tex had raised questions in my mind. I dialed their number and, after a brief welcome to the neighborhood, gave them his contact information.

While I should have spent my afternoon trying to find my next clients, I couldn't. My mind wasn't on square backed sofas and floor to ceiling curtains and bullet planters and tulip chairs. It was on four murders that had taken place around Lakewood. I pulled a new lined notepad from the drawer of my desk and jotted a few notes.

Sheila Murphy
Thelma Johnson
Pamela Ritter
Carrie Coburn

What did I know about these women? I put pen to page next to Pamela's name. *Real Estate Agent. Swimmer. Twenty-something.* Outside of those few items, I didn't know much about her. I knew even less about the others.

I turned to the Internet and typed "Sheila Murphy murder" into Google. The top hit was the article from the recent Dallas Morning News. I didn't click the link. Instead I scrolled down the page for older information. On page two I found what I was looking for. A copy of the newspaper articles from when she was killed.

I clicked the link and stared once again at the smiling face of young, blonde, Sheila Murphy. It was the same picture the paper had used in the more recent article.

I learned nothing new from the article. Sheila had been at a costume party near White Rock Lake. She'd gotten into a fight with her boyfriend and left. Witnesses at her apartment building saw her return home in an unfamiliar truck. The next morning, her body was found by White Rock Lake, wearing a shirt that could be traced back to Hudson James, identified as the driver of the truck. Other evidence placed her in his truck, and his truck at the lake, but ultimately a jury did not find him guilty.

The details matched what he'd told me. Almost eerily so. It was as though he'd been plagued by the account of that night since it had happened, like he relived it so many times that the memory was untainted by age. I wondered if that was true, if he was locked up to this murder like Prometheus bound, waking every day to have his liver pecked at by vultures who continued to believe in his guilt.

One little fact of Sheila Murphy's murder nagged at me. There had been no evidence of rape or sexual assault, yet Hudson told me she was in her underwear. He'd been a gentleman and given her his shirt, and that one piece of evidence had been more damning than the rest combined. I clicked around other articles but found no mention of this fact. Yet, the question remained. Who had taken her clothes? Maybe it had happened at the party she'd fled. A costume party, the article said. A fight with her boyfriend.

Of everything I read, this was the only article that even mentioned that a boyfriend existed. There had to be a way to find out who he was, and not just by asking Tex. If the lieutenant could operate his investigation on his own terms, telling me bits and pieces of information while using me as bait, then I would compartmentalize what I found out, too. If I was indeed connected, then I was at risk and I had to take care of myself. Last night's attack was proof of that.

I did a Google image search for Sheila Murphy, hoping to find a virtual memorial that showcased a series of pictures dedicated to keeping her memory alive. I hit pay dirt.

www.Findmykiller.com/SheilaMurphy featured the same smiling image of the young victim I'd come to know from the papers, but below a brief paragraph that summarized the unsolved crime was a gallery of images. I clicked on the first few and found photos of her childhood. I scrolled through three pages and clicked on the last picture. My breath caught in my throat.

Sheila Murphy was smiling into the camera, dressed in a light blue double-breasted skirt suit with a white collar and buttons. I had a similar one in my closet at home. Her likeness to me was less powerful than her likeness to Doris Day. It was obvious that she was at the costume party, based on a background of vampires, werewolves, and witches. But the most unnerving aspect of the picture didn't have anything to do with Sheila Murphy or Doris Day or monsters. It was the man who had his arm slung around her shoulders. He was dressed in a vintage suit, skinny tie, close cropped dark hair that was parted on the side. The sideburns were darker than they were now, but the eyes were cool blue and pierced my soul.

Her boyfriend was Tex.

Sixteen

wanted to think that this changed everything, but it didn't. It was one more piece of the puzzle that eventually would make sense. Twenty years ago, Tex might not have been a cop, and if he had been, he would have been pretty new to the department. He wouldn't have been a lieutenant, because achieving that title takes time. If the police had determined a connection between Thelma Johnson, Pamela Ritter, Sheila Murphy, and Carrie Coburn, then there was no way Tex was assigned to work the case. His personal history tainted his objectivity. So his actions, his trickery, and the way he'd attached himself to me like glue were for one reason and one reason only: the homicide division had shut him out of the investigation and he couldn't let go. I was his only lead.

I couldn't help thinking about Tex's role in Sheila Murphy's life. He'd been with her the night she was killed. No one had ever been found guilty of the crime. His job put him in the line of duty, sworn to serve and protect, and it must eat away at him like a cancer that the person who killed his girlfriend twenty years ago was still free. I started to understand his unwillingness to accept that Hudson might be the wrong man and that the real killer was still out there.

Tex needed closure. And while the trail had gone cold in the past two decades, he would have held that anger and need for closure close to his heart. Close enough to keep him from feeling anything real, to keep his relationships short, easy, and unencumbered. To shut out the world, and to not let people in.

No wonder he was the love-them-and-leave-them type. I began to understand his flirtatious nature and reputation. I hated to admit it, but he wasn't all that different from me. It was easier to push people away, to not let them in, than to chance losing someone I cared about. I hadn't been looking for love when I met Brad, but knowing him had changed my life. Tex had been pushing for me to expose something of myself since I'd met him, for the purposes of his investigation, and I'd responded with undeserved animosity.

I guessed that Officer Nast was one of a number of women he'd dallied with along the way. He hadn't even been bothered by her cold shoulder. Here was a man with enough emotion bottled up thanks to his own connection to a murder twenty years ago that it had affected his life as much as it had affected Hudson. The only difference between them and me was that both of them were trying to move on and I wasn't.

Both men were prisoners of their pasts and I was becoming a prisoner in my present.

I fleshed out my notes, with Tex's name next to Sheila Murphy, then printed out their picture and taped it to the page. Seeing it, with the two of them dressed up like Rock and Doris, it was hard to imagine what the following twenty-four hours of Sheila Murphy's life must have been like. It was hard to imagine that twenty-four hours from that state of innocence she would be dead and at least two other lives would be changed forever. And that twenty years later, no one would know why.

The other three names stared back at me from the piece of paper. Chances were, I wasn't going to find out a lot about Thelma Johnson. And Pamela Ritter's death was confusing, too. That left Carrie Coburn, and after seeing the text message left on my phone, I was pretty certain her death was an accident. Someone had tried to lure *me* to the Mummy last night. Carrie Coburn was a senior in high school. I looked young for my age, but not *that* young. There had to be something more to confuse us.

I spun the Rolodex to the letter M. Behind the theater's contact information were several cards with the phone numbers of Richard and the rest of the volunteers. Occasionally we invoked the phone tree and I'd found it best to file all Mummy contacts under M instead of their respective last names. I was organized in a way that only my brain would understand. It works when you're in business for yourself.

I dialed Ruth's number and she picked up after three rings. Her hello was shaky.

"Ruth? This is Madison Night."

"You've got a lot of nerve, calling me. What could possibly be so important, in the wake of my daughter's death?"

"I'm sorry for your loss," I started, trying to keep calm. I ached for her; the loss of her daughter was one I'd never know.

"To think she went down there to impress you! It was her idea to dress up and everything! That stupid film festival of yours," she spat the words like she were dropping the F-bomb, "That's what killed my Carrie. You, I never want to speak to you again."

The phone went silent. I didn't waste time calling her back. I flipped a few cards forward in the Rolodex and called Richard. He answered almost immediately.

"Richard, this is Madison." I paused, not sure what to say next.

"Madison, man, what are we gonna do?"

"Richard?" I asked tentatively, now not sure if he thought I was someone else.

"Ruth's daughter, that's crazy, right? I can't even figure out how it happened."

Okay, so maybe he knew who I was and was dealing with his stress with a bag of marijuana. He'd been known to smoke it in the past before screenings and I sensed a coping mechanism in place.

"Richard, were you there when it happened?"

"No, man, no. I got called down by the cops. My number's the one that rings off-hours when the theater's closed."

I wanted him to stop calling me man but I wanted information more. "What did you find out when you got there? Anything?"

"Have you talked to Ruth?" he asked.

"I tried to, but she won't talk to me."

"It's no wonder, really."

"Why? Why is she so specifically mad at me?"

"Her daughter was dressed up like Doris Day. When Ruth told her about the film festival she got all excited and wanted to get the part."

"There wasn't a part."

"The Doris Day look-alike part."

"Ruth came up with that on her own. Nobody agreed to it."

"That's not how she remembers it. Anyway, her daughter went down to the Mummy after hearing you were going to be there. She must have been taken by surprise. Hit on the head, I heard. Poor girl never saw it coming. Somebody suffocated her while she was out cold."

My stomach turned. "Is that all you know?" I asked him softly.

"Not sure but I think I figured out what they used to kill her." There was a long pause. Richard might have moved on to another plane.

"Richard? Are you still there?"

"Yeah, man, I'm here. What were you saying?"

"What killed her?" I prompted.

"Oh, yeah, there were all of these numbered markers around the front of the Mummy in the dirt and on the street.

Everything the cops thought looked suspicious. And laying a few feet from her hand was one of those pink velvet pillows, you know, like the ones you have in the trunk of your car?"

My mouth went dry and I couldn't swallow the lump in my throat. "How do you know about the pillows in the trunk of my car?"

"Last week, after the meeting, you were talking to the group. Leonard had a dead battery and we needed jumper cables. I borrowed your keys, thought you might have one."

"Did you have any trouble with the lock?"

"No. Why?"

I stared at Rocky, sleeping on his dog bed in the corner. Those pillows in my trunk connected me more than my appearance. They were as unlikely a murder weapon as I could imagine. But someone who had used them twenty years ago was using them today. Like a calling card. It meant something, but I didn't know what, and I wanted to keep it to myself, until I figured it out.

"Just curious," I said.

"So you understand, we can't run the film festival now."

It was a fact that I had to accept. As much as I wanted to lose myself in the light tone of Doris Day movies, I knew he was right. What had started as a tribute to Pamela Ritter had ended as an insult to the memory of Carrie Coburn.

"Richard, do you know when we can get back into the theater?"

"Why?"

"I started working on the project a couple of days ago. Sent a few emails and made a few calls and I'd rather get in touch with everyone and tell them the project is off. All of my work is saved on the Mummy's computer and that's the only place where I can check the theater email."

"I never gave you the go-ahead on that project, Madison," he said, the deadhead persona gone, replaced with a strict, business-like tone.

"I know. I just put out a few feelers because we had a limited window of time and I thought it would be best to have answers ready at the next meeting."

"When did you do this work?"

"A couple of days ago. Why?" I asked.

There was a long pause in our conversation, long enough that I wondered if he'd hung up.

"Richard? Are you still there?"

"Don't sweat it, man, the crime happened outside the theater so the whole area is closed down. The fuzz said I can get back in tomorrow. I'd say the same goes for you. Don't try to get in ahead of them. I don't want to them breathing down my neck because of something you did."

"Fine," I said, getting whiplash from the Pineapple Express.

After I hung up, I stared at the list of names on the paper in front of me, only this time I knew a little bit more. Carrie Coburn had been suffocated just like the others, with one of the pillows stolen from my trunk. That made four victims of suffocation. Sheila Murphy's murder had taken place long before I had come to be in possession of those pillows. But still, it was clear. Someone who had access to the trunk of my car was out there stalking the women in Dallas with my vintage velvet pillows.

If Tex was planning to return my truck he would have done it by now. I called police dispatch back and asked for Officer Clark. After a ten-minute hold, while Rocky chewed his way through the yellow velvet piping on his deluxe faux fur dog bed, the officer came on the line.

"Ms. Night?

"Yes, this is Madison Night. Have you finished filling out the paperwork on my stolen car?"

"You're not serious, are you?"

"Of course I'm serious! My. Car. Was. Stolen. What part of that don't you understand? I don't care what kind of code you cops have between you but this is a crime and I expect you to treat it as such!"

"Lady, lady! Calm down." His voice had an edge to it that he hadn't used when he filled out my report. "First of all, I don't appreciate your inference that I'm not treating this like a crime. If there were a missing car in question, I would have filed a report. If we had confirmed that Lieutenant Allen stole your car, we would have gone after him just like we would go after any known felon. And may I point out that what you accused him of is Grand Theft Auto. A felony. That's a big deal. Especially for a cop."

"Officer Clark, what exactly have you done to help recover my vehicle?"

"Ms. Night, your car is sitting here in our lot waiting for you to pick it up. Lieutenant Allen dropped it off because he got a call and needed a police cruiser. I have the keys in my hand."

"Of all the nerve," I started.

"You going to come get your car or not, ma'am?"

Another call beeped on the line. I had yet to program the number into my phone but I recognized it nonetheless. Tex Allen.

"Officer, I have another call I have to take."

"Fine by me. Just pick up your car by five." I heard his click before I punched the call-waiting button.

"Hello?" I answered in a voice more calm than the one inside my head.

"Night? Did you report your car as stolen?"

"Did you steal my car?" I asked back. Silence. "You did!" More silence. I met it with silence of my own. If one of us had hung up the other would have been none the wiser.

"Did you stop to think about what you were doing?" he finally asked.

"Did you, Tex? You need to start taking me seriously. I'm not one of your one night stands," I said, with Officer Clark's earlier words still ringing in my ear.

"No, you're more like a one night stand-off that never ends."

"I need my car back."

"It's at the station."

"I know."

"So go to the station and pick it up. No harm, no foul."

Oh, there was harm. There was the hundred and twenty-four dollars a day I was paying for the rental car, and Lieutenant Allen was going to be getting the bill.

"Night—"

"Must you refer to me by my last name?"

"Madison, it was for your own good. You interfered with a crime scene when you went to Thelma Johnson's house. You're lucky I was willing to put my ass on the line to take that stuff back. Just call a girlfriend and get a ride to the station. You could probably walk it if you wanted. It's only a couple of miles from your studio."

"You're going to pay for this, Lieutenant Allen," I said with abstract grim determination, and jabbed at the disconnect button.

For my own good, he said. Call a girlfriend, he said. You could probably walk, he said. He might have done a background check but there was so much he didn't know about me, not the least of which was that I had no one to call in the event of an emergency.

Seventeen

A s a small business owner, I had clients. I had contacts. And because I believed in customer service and referrals, I maintained good relations with all of them. When I moved to Texas with the plan to start over, I had startup cash, a loan from the bank, and my business strategy for Mad for Mod. The income from the apartment building kept me afloat during the months where appointments were slim. By now, I had quite a network.

What I didn't have were people to call spontaneously and ask if they would give me a ride to the police station.

I had friends, but they remained in Philadelphia. We all still rooted for the Phillies but they did it from the home section and I did it from the away, and in Dallas, when you root against the Rangers, you're not doing yourself any favors in the Making Friends category. I stopped going to games because I tired of the heckling. So I was in need of two things: a person who would give me a ride to the station and a good ballpark frank.

Reluctantly I looked up the number for the closest cab company and requested a pickup. Tex's "not that far" translated to three and a half miles on foot and while the feet

128

might be up for it, the knee was definitely not. I hated to admit it, but more likely than not there was a cortisone shot in the very near future.

It was afternoon and it was hot. If the temperature was this unbearable in May it would be insufferable by summer. Quite a city I had chosen to live in. I refilled Rocky's water bowl from the sink in the small bathroom and let the cool stream of water run over my wrists and hands. It was refreshing. I pressed cold wet hands against the back of my neck and against my forehead. The straw hat tilted backwards then fell to the floor behind me. I turned around to pick it up. It had fallen with the tassel side down, the inside exposed. On a small white label that marked which side was the back it said, *Property of Jan Randall.*

I picked up the hat and faced the mirror, first smoothing my choppy blond hair off my face then setting the hat back on my head. I still remembered the day I'd found it, at one of my first estate sales. I had a less practiced eye back then and had tagged way more merchandise than I could ever use. The surviving family had made it easy on me, or so I'd thought. "At this point it would be easier for you to take everything."

I'd been about to flip through my agenda for the number to the nearest women's shelter, who would not only be happy with the donation but also would make the pickup, when I got a glimpse into the deceased woman's closet. The first shelf was lined with pristine hatboxes. The second shelf held a row of Styrofoam heads that showcased an assortment of the wildest wig collection I'd ever seen. Her clothes, hung on kaleidoscope-patterned padded hangers, were treasures: Pierre Cardin, Biba, Mary Quant. The woman had even owned a pair of white Corregés boots.

I accepted the family's offer to let me have it all and wrote a nice fat check to the women's shelter to assuage any feelings of guilt. The clothes now hung among the other items I'd accumulated on buying trips but were saved for special occasions. You could learn a lot about a person by the contents of their closet and it almost saddened me to know that Jan Randall had passed away. I would have loved spending time with her. Based on what she wore, I'd bet she was a heck of a woman.

I heard a repeated car horn out front and looked through the front windows. A taxi sat at the curb. "Come on, Rocky, time to undo Lieutenant Tex's mess." I met the taxi driver by the curb and told him it would take me another minute or two to lock up.

"Whatever you want, lady. Meter's running."

One more thing to add to Tex's bill. I didn't expect him to actually pay for this, but the idea of sending him an invoice was mildly satisfying.

"Since you're already running the meter, my dog can sit in the back. I'll be out in a second." I set Rocky inside the back seat and he poked his little black nose through the open window. "Wait here," I instructed.

I flipped the Open sign to Closed and locked the front door, then pulled the office door shut and locked that, too. Unnecessary precaution but I did it all the same. I flipped off the lights from the back of the store and left, locking the back door behind me. When I returned to the front, the cabbie was bent over, nose to nose with Rocky. It was hard to say which was having more fun.

"Cute pup you got here."

"Yes, he is, though he's also a troublemaker."

"It's easy to forgive when they're this cute," he said and ruffed Rocky's fur. I got into the cab and Rocky jumped onto my lap. The driver got in also and made a show of resetting the meter.

I glanced at his license mounted on the glass partition behind his headrest. Maxim Smith. But by the sound of his accent, Smith was short for something Russian.

"Take me to the police station off of Loop 12," I said.

"You're taking cab to the cops? You're not bad lady, are you? Turn yourself in?" he joked.

"No, but it's a long story." I leaned back against the torn seat. "Loop 12 is going to be murder right now. Can you take the shortcut by White Rock Lake?"

"Fine by me," he answered.

Rocky hung his head out the window while the passing air created by our speed whipped his fur away from his face.

I'd left the notes on the murder victims on my desk at the studio, buried under swatches of five different shades of yellow, but the questions that I'd been thinking about were still weighing heavily on my mind. Pamela. Sheila. Thelma. What did these women have in common? I stared out the window as we drove around the lake. Sheila Murphy's body was found somewhere around here. This was where Hudson had picked her up. But still, aside from knowing that she had dated Tex, I knew little else. If only there was a way to learn more about them. But deceased, with no surviving relatives, left me with no direction to turn. Unless . . .

Like I'd learned with Jan Randall, you can learn a lot about a person by looking in their closets: how they lived, what they spent money on, what was worth keeping out on display and what they kept hidden out of site.

And then my brain exploded and I knew why Tex had taken my truck. He wasn't covering for me, he had found a way to gain entry into an investigation he wasn't supposed to be working. He'd had the same thought as me, and by taking my truck back to Thelma Johnson's house, he had access to what I already had taken from her estate and access back into her house.

By leaving me behind, he was one step ahead. Tex's motivation may have been rooted in solving a homicide but mine was rooted in a little something I liked to call Not Becoming the Next Victim.

"Here you are," the cabbie announced. I'd been so lost in my thoughts I hadn't realized that we'd covered the three and a half miles already. I fished into my wallet for a couple of bills and paid him.

"Can I get a receipt?"

His brow pulled together. "What are you paying me for? It's already taken care of."

"By whom? I called the cab company myself."

"Lady, I was sent out to studio by some guy Allen. He gave me credit card number for to pay." I was more confused by the content of his message than his improper English.

"But I called for a taxi. Isn't that you?"

"Another cab showed up when you were inside. I told him to hike. I thought I was supposed to take you home, but you want for to be here, that's fine by me."

Tex's arrangements completely took me by surprise, they didn't seem his style. I handed the driver a five, a generous tip if I did say so myself, and opened the car door.

"May I have your card?" I asked.

"What for?"

"In case I want to hire you again."

"I'm out. Sorry," he said, feeling around the dusty dash and center console.

I pulled Rocky out of the back seat. Together we walked to the front doors of the police precinct and, after more sarcasm than I wanted to acknowledge, I drove away in the dark blue Explorer. To get back at them I let Rocky leave a small present next to a row of squad cars.

I stopped off at CVS for a bottle of water and swallowed the maximum dosage of anti-inflamatories. My knee was swollen and straining against the elastic bandage. Instead of driving home like I really, really, really wanted to, I drove to Thelma Johnson's house. I didn't know if what Tex had said was true or not. I didn't know if I had a right to be there or not. But I wouldn't sleep until I had a chance to walk through her house and look at it with a different perspective.

The neighborhood was quiet, though people would soon be arriving home from work. Rush hour was full-on. Soon, the street would be lined with luxury cars. Most of the houses in this neighborhood were owned by secondary owners. Thelma Johnson must have been one of the last of the original residents.

The house looked vacant. I parked in the driveway and walked Rocky around back, where I found the spare key under the Dracaena tree by the back door. We went inside and I flipped the deadbolt behind me. Locking doors behind me seemed like a good habit to keep up these days.

There wasn't much left in the kitchen, and I hadn't touched the living room on my last trip. But that wasn't where I wanted to go. I walked further down the hallway. The pull-down steps to the attic confirmed my suspicion that Tex had been here earlier. I eased past them to the master bedroom and crossed the room to the closet. What could I learn from Thelma Johnson's belongings?

A call from Tex interrupted my project.

"Night, I hear you got your car from the lot."

"Yes, I did, and as much as it pains me to admit it, I suppose I owe you a thank you."

"I told you I did it for your own good."

"I don't really know what you mean by that, but I do appreciate the cab."

"What cab?"

"The cab, the cab. The taxi," I said.

"You called a taxi?" he asked.

"You sent a taxi to pick me up from the studio."

"No I didn't."

"You can stop playing dumb. The driver told me. He said you'd made the arrangements to pay the bill."

"Night, are you at home?"

"No, I'm at Thelma Johnson's house," I said.

"What the hell are you doing there?" his voice snapped. "Get out of that house!"

"What? Why? I know you were here today. Are you afraid I'm going to discover something you didn't?"

"Night, that house is a crime scene. You should not be there, you have no authority to be there. I took your car because it was filled with stuff you took out of that house, and I don't care how much you like that stuff, it's evidence in a homicide investigation."

"I wrote a check for this estate," I said, but my sentence fizzled as I remembered that the Steve Johnson who took my check wasn't who he said he was. "My check hasn't been cashed, has it?"

"No, and it's not going to be. Now get out of that house before the cop that's watching the residence calls you in for B&E. Drive to the nearest police station—Highland Park. I'll meet you there."

"No, Tex, I'm tired of playing games. I want to go home."

And then I heard footsteps in the attic above me and realized I wasn't alone.

Eighteen

I scooped Rocky up in my arms and moved to the hallway. The fold-down attic steps bisected my path to the front door. Silence surrounded me, and I wondered briefly if I'd imagined the sound. *Tex is playing with me*, I told myself in an attempt to calm down. I eased sideways past the collapsible staircase. As I passed it, I looked up at the black hole of the attic. The tip of a man's rubber sole hung over the top step, the rest of him lost in the darkness.

Adrenaline propelled me to the front door, despite the pain in my knee. Clumsy footsteps thudded down the wood stairs behind me. I didn't look back. Rocky whimpered as his tail knocked against the small counter in the kitchen. I pushed against the door and hobbled through the small, enclosed porch. My fingers threw the deadbolt and I yanked the front door open. I stumbled down the three front stairs and ran to the Explorer, fumbling with the keys for the remote.

I slammed my palm on the lock switch once we were inside. Rocky's leash was caught on the other side but I didn't risk opening the door. I unclipped it from his collar. My eyes flicked up to the house, back to the ignition, checking to see if anyone was there, if anyone was coming to get me. I jabbed the key at the ignition. On the third try it slipped in. I tore away from the sidewalk, tires squealing. I drove fast—too fast for a truck this size—out of the small neighborhood. Twice the truck swayed dangerously to the side. I had to slow down but I had to get away from that house.

My cell phone flew from the passenger seat to the floor, the screen still a blue glow. I hadn't hung up when I ran. Tex was probably still on the line, but I couldn't take my hands off the steering wheel.

"I'm out of the house!" I shouted at the floor. "I'm out of the house!"

His reply was lost in the sound of the vibrating floorboards and the pulsating rush of blood in my ears.

I didn't drive directly home for fear I was being followed. There was no mistaking the fact that someone had been in Thelma Johnson's attic and they'd started to come after me. That much I knew. I checked and rechecked the rearview mirror. Something, a blur of a memory I couldn't focus on, told me he'd stopped his pursuit at the threshold of Thelma's front door, but I was still scared. He'd had a clear view of my car; if he wanted to follow me, he could. If he didn't want to follow me tonight, he'd know what to look for tomorrow. And if he knew who I was, he probably knew where to find that car, and therefore, me.

I turned up and down side streets, constantly checking the rear view mirror. Occasionally a car appeared behind me, and I took a series of right and left turns to ensure their presence was coincidental. I turned onto Mockingbird and drove the length of it until I arrived at the Highland Park Police Station.

I pulled into the lot and stared at the army of patrol cars. Shiny, clean. Newer than the cars that were parked in the station north of White Rock Lake, but Highland Park was the richest area in Dallas. The women and men they protected and served were of a different social background than the ones Tex's team watched over.

I didn't get out of the car. Just being there, in the well-lit lot, surrounded by cop cars, allowed me to stop and slow down for a moment. Rocky thwomped his furry paws onto my lap and he looked up at me, fear visible in his giant brown eyes. I kissed the top of his head and ran my hand over his fur. He was trembling as much as I was.

I fished the cell phone off the floor. The call had dropped. I called information and asked for the number to the Budget Rent-a-Car. They were closed for the night. Tomorrow morning I would trade the SUV in for something else.

I called Tex back.

"Madison, where are you?" he asked.

"I'm at the police department in Highland Park, like you said. I don't think I was followed."

"Good. Stay there. Tell them I'm coming to get you."

"I'm okay now. I just need a second to calm down. I want to go home."

"Not in that car, you're not. I'll take you home. You can leave that car there."

"*No!* You are not placing me under house arrest!" I flipped the phone shut and threw it back to the floor. Immediately it rang, but I ignored it. I reached across the passenger seat and opened the door, freeing Rocky's leash. The handle had become frayed from dragging outside of the car, but it was still in one piece. I wound the leash into concentric circles and set it on the floor, then kissed Rocky's head again and positioned him on the passenger seat. "Time to go home, Rocky."

I rebuckled my seat belt and started the ignition. As I released the parking break, knuckles wrapped against my window. I jumped, despite the cross-chest seatbelt strap holding me in place. An officer dressed in an immaculately cleaned and pressed navy blue uniform stood next to the car. His mirrored aviators were both clichéd and unnecessary with the waning sun.

"Ma'am?" he said, to the shut window.

"I'm just leaving, Officer," I yelled at the glass.

"Turn the car off and come with me," he said.

"No, thanks, I'm fine."

"No you're not. I booted your car."

There was no way I'd heard that correctly. I cracked the window. "What did you say?"

"We got a call on the radio from a Lieutenant Allen saying you were in our lot. Said for us to keep you here."

"You can't do that. I've done nothing wrong."

The officer adjusted his aviators and gave me a half-smile. "Said you racked up a whole lot of unpaid parking tickets, and he's been after you for awhile."

I had no unpaid parking tickets, but Tex couldn't tell them I was involved in a homicide investigation that he wasn't supposed to be investigating. Seems we both had cards we weren't playing. I wasn't pleased by this turn of events.

"Officer, can I see some identification so I know who I'm talking to?"

He held an identification card and badge up against the window. I grabbed a pen from the center console and wrote his name and badge number on the back of the rental car papers that had scattered on the floor.

"Ma'am, it's for your own good. Come with me and I'll get you a cup of coffee while we wait for the Lieutenant."

"No. The Lieutenant has me confused with someone else, and I want to go home now." I unlocked the parking brake and put the car in drive. The car jerked but didn't move. I checked the brake and the gears and tried again. The same thing happened.

The officer again rapped his knuckles on my window. "Ma'am, I wouldn't do that if I were you. You're goin' to ruin a nice set of tires and these ones here are expensive."

I rolled the window down completely and hung my head out the window. Sure enough, an orange boot was locked on my rear tire. "You already know I don't have any outstanding parking tickets."

The officer tried, unsuccessfully, to hide a smile.

"There has to be against some kind of law against that," I added.

"Yep, there probably is."

"Then unlock it and let me go."

A black Jeep swung into the lot, Tex behind the wheel. He parked in front of the Explorer and hopped out. He flashed a badge.

"What's going on here, Officer?"

"Lieutenant Allen? This here's the car you wanted us to hold up, right?"

"This one? Nah, it's a different one. You can go ahead and take the boot off now."

The young officer unlocked the orange contraption with an ear to ear smile on his face. Now that Tex's Jeep blocked my exit, I was as trapped as before.

Tex leaned his elbows on the now-open door window and rested his chin on his crossed wrists. His light blue eyes drilled into me. I matched his stare with my own but it didn't matter. We were on his turf.

"Night, this is for your own good. Get out of your car, get whatever you need, and I'll take you home."

"And then what happens? I can't leave my apartment? I'm trapped and out of your way? I don't think so."

He opened his fist and dangled a set of keys in front of me. "There's another rental waiting for you at your building. I'll return this one tomorrow. I don't think it's wise for you to drive around in this car if—" he stopped talking.

"If the killer saw me get into it and knows how to find me," I finished for him.

"Did he?"

"I think so."

"We need to talk, Night. I need to know what you know because you know something."

"I want to go home."

"Get into my Jeep."

I clipped the frayed leash onto Rocky's collar and reluctantly got out of the truck. We walked toward Tex's Jeep, me favoring my knee. I got into the black vehicle and rubbed my hands over the swollen joint. It was the second time I'd been chauffeured by Tex in a week and the circumstances hadn't improved.

He spoke to the young officer briefly and joined me in the car. I would have been very happy with silence but it was not to be so.

"Why did you go back to Thelma Johnson's house, Night?" he asked as we pulled onto Turtle Creek Boulevard.

"Why did you?" I asked.

He kept his eyes on the road.

I was silent. It wasn't a long drive from the Highland Park police station to my apartment. He didn't ask any more questions but I sensed the conversation was not over.

He pulled the Jeep into the driveway on the south side of my building and drove it to the parking lot in the back. He left the engine running. Something stopped me from getting out.

"I don't know why I went to Thelma Johnson's house. I was looking for something, only I don't know what. A connection." I looked down at my hands. "I'm trying to figure out what this all means, these four murders, and what they have to do with me."

"That's not your job, Night."

"It's not your job either, Lieutenant."

"My job is to look out for the citizens of Dallas. You're a citizen of Dallas."

"So I'm supposed to sit back and trust you'll figure it all out before I get killed? I've been in more dangerous situations since I've met you than I have in my whole life."

140

"I admit, these aren't the best circumstances for us to have met."

I wanted to smack him. "There is something very wrong about the way your brain works, Tex Allen. I'm afraid for my life and all you can do is joke around. My life is in danger and *I don't know why*. And everybody acts like I'm one of your disgruntled conquests, like I'm only around because I'm trying to get your attention."

He leaned back and put his hands behind his head. "It's been known to happen."

"But I can't begin to imagine under what circumstances I would be happy to see you."

He smiled but stared straight ahead. "You'll come around."

"OOOooohhh!" My fists instinctively balled up and pounded the dashboard. I tried to unlock the door but Tex had the driver's side locks engaged and I couldn't get out. Heat lit up inside of me, at playing the mouse to his role of cat.

"I'm right about the case, aren't I? You're not supposed to be working it," I asked, still half-fighting a losing battle with the door.

"How did you find out?"

I gave up on the door. "I found an article online." I watched his expression.

His jaw flexed a couple of times. He was fighting his own reaction and it hit me, why he worked so hard to keep up the joking, two-dimensional personality. How hard this must be for him, how I hadn't stopped to think about any of it from his perspective. Involuntarily I put my hand on top of his. I was as surprised by the gesture as he was.

"I'm sorry you've had to live with this."

He turned his hand over, so our palms touched, then he placed mine back in my lap. "Don't go soft on me now, Night," he said, his voice catching as he said my name. He hit the unlock button and put the car into drive. Rocky bounded out of the Jeep and pulled me toward the back door.

Tex backed the truck up and pulled next to the door. "And Night? Those other cops are wrong. You're nothing like any of my conquests. You're in a class all your own."

He drove through the narrow driveway to the north side of my building and I unlocked the back door, to the building, then locked it behind me and started up the stairs to my unit.

"We're home, Rocky. Finally." Rocky bounded ahead of me, yipping in my direction when he reached the door. I gripped the banister and stepped slowly up the carpeted treads. "How does spaghetti and meatballs sound? I think we deserve comfort food, don't you?"

I turned the key in the lock and pushed the door open. Rocky ran ahead of me, into the darkness, yipping with excitement. "I didn't know you'd be so happy to get home," I said. My hand clumsily sought the switch to the lamp, and a hand clamped down over my mouth from behind and pulled me tightly against a rigid chest.

Nineteen

I tried to fight against the strong cage of arms but couldn't. And then I heard the voice.

"Madison, Madison, ssshhhhh, it's Hudson. It's Hudson, it's Hudson. Don't fight me. It's Hudson."

Like yesterday, when he'd found me in front of his house after being attacked, the repetition of his soothing voice calmed me. I relaxed slightly, but not entirely. He removed his hand from my mouth. Moments later he turned me around to face him. My own fear reflected in his eyes.

"Madison, I'm not going to hurt you."

My chest heaved and fell with deep penetrating lungs filled with air. "Get your hands off me," I said in a low, gravelly voice, my heart pounding in my chest from the surprise.

He let go and held up his palms facing me like he was proving he wasn't a threat. I took two steps backward to put distance between us. Rocky yipped around our ankles like we were playing. He put his front paws on Hudson's jeans and stared up at his friend's face, not understanding that sometimes friends were not to be trusted.

I reached in the bag slung across my chest and pulled out my cell phone. "I'm calling the cops."

"Madison—"

I put a hand out palm first in front of me to stop him from closing the space between us.

"How did you get in here?" I asked.

"You gave me a set of keys when you asked me to do maintenance on the building." He reached into the pocket of his black jeans; I took another half step back. He extracted three metal keys that still hung on the cheap key ring the locksmith had used when he'd cut the set. Gently, Hudson set the keys on the low wooden hutch.

"Please let me explain."

"Damn it, Hudson!" I yelled. I dropped the phone. My fingers splayed like I was holding an invisible basketball and my hands jabbed forward like I was looking for a teammate to pass the ball to. "I can't live like this," My breath caught. "This is not a normal life!" I pushed fingers into my temples and the tasseled hat fell off my head. I felt my face contort with emotion. "People are chasing me and jumping out at me. Everybody knows more than I do and nobody is telling me anything. I can't live like this!" I repeated.

Before he could speak there was a knock on the door. Instantly we both went quiet.

"Ms. Night? It's Kirsten from Apartment B. Are you okay?"

I remained silent.

"Ms. Night? I heard you yelling. Do you want me to call that police officer who drove you home? He gave me his card when he was here on Wednesday."

Hudson had a finger up to his mouth but her last words made his hand drop. It was do or die time. I took a deep breath to steady my voice.

"Kirsten, it's okay. I'm on the phone."

I watched the shadow below my door stay steady then retreat. "Okay, sorry to bother you. Give Rocky a kiss for me!"

I suddenly pushed Hudson against the wall behind the door and opened it. "Kirsten, can you do me a favor? Can you take Rocky out one last time tonight?"

"Sure!" she replied. "I have a Milk Bone for him, too." Rocky was all too happy to follow her down the hall to the front door. I shut the door behind her, but didn't turn the lock.

"Thank you," Hudson said.

"You've got about two minutes, maybe three, before she gets back. Start talking," I said.

"Remember I told you I saw someone hanging around my house?" he asked.

I nodded.

"I don't know if it's the person who attacked you or not. I'm starting to think it might be a reporter from the Dallas Morning News. He's watching me. Taking pictures. I work in the garage but it's getting to me, being watched. I can tell he's there, I can hear the shutter of his camera. I tried to confront him once but he took off and now he stays further away. I can't concentrate. I'm really sorry, Madison."

"Why are you apologizing to me?"

"It's about the job you hired me to do."

"You're under surveillance by a reporter who wants to write some kind of expose on you and you came here to tell me you can't finish a job?" I asked.

He didn't answer my question. "I was in the garage, working on the table legs. Mortiboy was sitting on the driveway one second but the next second he was gone. I found him halfway across the street. The last thing I need is for him to get into a fight with another cat or start tracking a squirrel so I went after him. When I got back to the garage, the stuff was gone."

"What stuff?"

"I had a couple sheets of paper on the workbench. Your name was written on them, along with the address of your studio. Dimensions of the table and what I needed to do to the legs. When I got back the papers were gone and the table leg was on the floor. The wood was chipped like it had hit something hard. I don't know if it can be fixed. If it can't I'll reimburse—"

"Hudson! Forget about the table leg."

"When I realized the invoice was gone I drove to your studio. You weren't there. I got worried and came here looking for you."

"How long have you been here?"

"I'm not sure. I left the lights off."

"Where's your truck?"

"I parked it on a side street and walked. I thought it was best not to be seen."

My mind raced in a thousand directions. If Tex had taken two minutes to cruise the side streets around my apartment building looking for something suspicious, he would have seen Hudson's truck. Whether I was high up on Tex's radar or not, he was a cop first, and I doubted a detail like that had escaped his vision.

Before I could talk, there was a knock on the door. "Madison? It's Kirsten."

Hudson stepped back into the shadows. I hobbled to the door and opened it. The teenager handed Rocky to me.

"Why are you carrying him?"

"I don't know. He seems awfully tired. We got outside and he just wanted to sit by my feet. Are you sure he needed to go?"

"No, just thought it would be a good idea. Thanks, Kirsten."

"Anytime. Good night!" She bounded back down the stairs to her apartment below mine. If she'd heard Hudson and me earlier, no doubt she'd hear two sets of footsteps all night if he stayed and that would raise more questions than I was ready to answer. Including whether or not I was capable of allowing Hudson to spend the night.

When I locked the door behind me I heard Hudson opening and shutting the freezer. He returned with a Ziploc bag filled with ice. "Your knee. You're hurt. Sit down."

"Not now."

"Madison, you can't keep going like this. Ice it."

I sat down and held the ice bag against my joint. The shock of cold against my skin shot through my whole body but I fought the instinct to pull it away. He was right. Icing it for fifteen minutes was the best thing I could do for the painful, inflamed joint right now.

"I shouldn't have come here but I had to warn you that someone out there might be coming after you. I don't think he took anything else."

"Could it have been the person who attacked me outside of your house?"

He nodded. "I thought of that, too."

"You can't stay here tonight."

"Madison, I'm not looking for that."

"No, that's not what I mean. I don't think you should go home yet, but too many people could become suspicious if you stay here with me. I have an idea."

"I don't want you getting any more involved with me than you are right now. Someone's trying to bring up a lot of dirt from a long time ago and you don't need to get muddy, too."

"Hudson, I am involved. I don't know how or why, but I'm fairly sure one of the victims was supposed to be me. I was attacked outside of your house. I was chased away from Thelma Johnson's house today. As much as I like you, I'm not getting involved purely for your benefit. Whatever this is about, I want it to be over, too."

"What's your idea?"

The man who rented the last apartment on the first floor, opposite Kirsten's, was away on business. Luckily, the apartment above his was vacant. Hudson could stay there, undiscovered. I instructed him to wait for me inside while I got a few things together to help him get through the night.

Rocky was exhausted, more so than I'd ever seen. He padded his little furry feet to a spot under the low coffee table and lay down. I moved through the apartment, opening closets and stuffing items into a suitcase: pillow, blanket, overnight kit. When I finished I pulled it across the hall and opened the door. Hudson stood by the back window staring out over the parking lot.

"Still no car?"

"Still no car."

"New rental?"

"New rental."

"Madison, I wish you weren't involved," he said, turning to face me. I was embarrassed that my personal boundaries kept me from inviting him to sleep on my sofa, but I wasn't there yet. I needed space and control, two things I was used to having. The past few days had shaken me up more than I wanted to admit to myself and I was clinging to whatever I could.

"Here's a pillow, comforter, and blankets. There's some other stuff in the suitcase. I know it's not much. The water's on so you can shower or. . ." my voice trailed off. "I should just—"

"Don't. I'm fine here. This is more than I expected. Thank you."

There were several feet separating us, unlike last night when his arms were around me, yet our eyes connected in a way that made me feel like we were inches apart. I wanted to cross the room and have him fold me into his embrace to comfort me but knew that was little more than a selfish thought. He needed comforting, too.

"Hudson, I need to ask you something."

"Shoot."

"What were you doing at White Rock Lake the night Sheila Murphy was killed?"

148

His head dropped and he stared at the bleached wood floor. I was afraid of the question I asked him and afraid of his answer, but it was something I had to know. I waited. He pushed one leg out further than the other and rested the heel of his black sneaker on the floor, his toe pointing up, then nervously bounced it a couple of times.

"I was going through a rough time. Getting desperate and thinking about doing some stuff that would have been a really bad idea. I was out of work and needed someone to talk to. She was right there, and it had been a long time since I talked to anyone the way I talked to her. I didn't want to wait until morning so I broke in."

I didn't like what I heard but if he'd been with someone, a woman, than he'd have an alibi. All he had to do was say who she was.

"So you had an alibi. Whoever she is, whoever you're trying to protect, wouldn't she confirm that you were with her?"

Unless he was with a married woman who had more to lose than to gain. It was the only scenario I could imagine, the only reason someone wouldn't defend him or give him something to cling to during the murder investigation.

"Hudson, why can't you ask this woman to tell the cops you were with her?"

"Because she's dead, too."

My head started to spin.

Twenty

"I was visiting my grandmother's grave," Hudson said. "I was low, lower than I ever remember being, that night. You know, you try to do the right thing, you work hard and think being honest and having integrity is going to get you somewhere, but it doesn't. My friends were getting into some bad stuff, stealing and holding up convenience stores. I broke away from them before I got pulled into their shit, but it was tough. They thought I was going to turn on them. I thought about it, you know. I was at rock bottom, I thought I was going to lose the house, lose everything I had. So I went to her grave in Cox cemetery."

He laid back and reached a hand into the front pocket of his jeans, and pulled out a pristine white linen handkerchief that he unfolded. Nestled inside was a decorative silver hat pin.

"This was hers. I carry it around with me as a reminder of what it was like before—before. She was the only person I had." He stared at the hat pin for several seconds and I didn't interrupt him. He rolled it between his thumb and index finger, as though it had special powers, and for a moment I started to wish that it did.

"It was the first time I'd been there since she died. I didn't like looking at that headstone and thinking about her under the ground. But that night I went to the cemetery and sat next to her plot and talked about everything. I told her what my friends were up to, and how I thought about doing it, too. It felt like I was talking to her. I could hear her voice. I could feel her presence. It was like I wasn't alone any more, like someone was there to make sure I made the right decisions.

"When I left I felt better than I had in a long time. I drove home and saw a woman running down the side of the road and stopped to help her out. You know the rest."

"Hudson, why didn't you tell me that the lieutenant was her boyfriend? It was in the papers. You must have known."

He stared at the ground. "I've got my own demons. If I want people to move on, it's not my place to dredge up somebody else's."

I couldn't leave him alone, not now, not after he'd opened up to me about that. "Wait here," I said. "I'll be right back."

When I returned to the apartment it was with another pillow and blanket under my left arm and a tired dog draped over my right shoulder. I set everything down on the floor and set up camp next to him. Rocky's eyes were only half-open. He walked toward Hudson and sprawled on top of his blanket and promptly fell asleep.

"Madison, go back to your apartment."

"Not yet. I want to talk to you."

He reached a hand out and pushed a piece of blond hair away from my forehead. I didn't want to think about how I looked after the day I had. His finger was rough, calloused from working with his hands, but gentle as it traced down my cheekbone and under my chin. He pulled his hand away as if he realized what he had been doing and thought I'd find it inappropriate. The fact that I hadn't stopped him should have clued him in that I didn't mind.

"Hudson, what did you and Sheila talk about during that ride?" I asked.

He lowered himself to the floor and untied each of his sneakers, then set them along the baseboard before answering.

"Not a lot. She was scared, but she didn't want to talk about it. I asked her if she wanted to go to the cops and she said no. I got the feeling she knew who was chasing her and wanted to handle it on her own. I know he didn't hurt her, not before I found her, only shook her up and took her clothes. She tried to act brave but when she flagged me down, she looked terrified. I'll never forget the look on her face. Think about it, she was alone by the lake. Some weirdo in a mask shows up and chases her through the woods."

"And takes her clothes. She wasn't hurt?"

"Not that she said. And she didn't look like she'd been touched. Just panicked. Like she didn't know if she should run or not, if it was some kind of a joke. I think that's why she didn't go to the cops. She'd been drinking at the party, and someone in a mask shows up and demands her clothes? Almost doesn't sound real." He sank down under the light sheet and rested his head on the pillow.

He was right, it didn't sound real. Something was missing from the puzzle, but I couldn't focus. The ice had helped my knee significantly but my body and my brain were slowing down with the lack of sleep. I wanted to keep talking. There might be something he knew that I didn't, but all I wanted to do was close my eyes. I folded the light comforter around me like a soft taco shell and rolled onto my side to face him. His eyes were shut and his even breathing blended with Rocky's own puppy breaths. Whether or not I could keep myself awake enough to keep talking, Hudson was out cold.

My internal alarm clock woke me first and it took several seconds to figure out where I was. My joints were stiff. I looked at Hudson, still asleep, with his arm draped over Rocky's fur. It was the most peaceful sight I'd seen in days. I cocked my head to the right and looked at the watch still strapped on Hudson's wrist. Five-ten.

I stood up slowly and crept toward the door. Rocky's head lifted from the blanket, but his eyes remained drowsy. I held a finger to my lips even though I knew he didn't know what I meant. I tiptoed to my own apartment and changed into a bathing suit and pink sleeveless dress that zipped up the back. It had an oversized collar and matching necktie. It made me feel like a flight attendant. I slid my feet into my daisy flip flops and packed flat gold sandals in my bag, collected Rocky's leash, and left, returning to the vacant apartment to leave a brief note to Hudson about where I'd gone. Seemed polite.

Rocky had anticipated my return and sat right inside the door. I clipped his leash on and set the folded note on my pillow. Hudson rolled over as I left. Soon enough he'd wake up alone.

I drove to the Swim Club. A few familiar cars were parked in the lot. My posse. I walked Rocky to the front desk and paid my dues.

"He can't go with you," said the man behind the desk. He held a powdered donut in one hand. A dusting of powder down the front of his shirt indicated that it was not his first one of the morning.

"I'll tie him up to the benches. He'll be fine."

"No pets allowed in the pool area."

"Give me a break. It's six in the morning. Nobody's going to know."

"He can sit in the pet room third door down on the left."

"I don't want to leave him alone."

"You could leave him in your car," he said.

"Listen." I channeled my most polite lady-of-the-pool manner. "He is a well-behaved dog, smaller than most cats. He is tired. He will sit in a corner and chew on a bone for the next hour while I swim. Is there nowhere else he can stay?"

The man stared at me and I stared at him, until finally I pulled my wallet out and flipped through a couple of bills.

"The manager's office is right back here and he doesn't get in until seven-thirty. I could maybe let him stay there, if, you know . . . ." His voice trailed off.

This was absurd. I pulled a twenty out of my wallet and handed it to him. "I will be back out here before seven-thirty."

"If he comes in early, your dog's going into the pet room," he called behind me as I walked down the faded hallway.

I went directly to the pool deck and dragged the toe of my foot through the water. It was cooler than before. Someone had the sense to adjust the temperature. A few more people from the Crestwood crowd had migrated, sitting on the bleachers, mingling before they started their swim. These people were regular morning swimmers, more reliable than the post office. I waved to Alice. She waved me toward the bench where she sat next to Jessica, Andy, and a new younger man closer to my own age. Reluctantly I approached them.

"Madison! Did you hear? We can go back to Crestwood on Monday. Isn't that good news?" Alice said.

"That's a relief. They wouldn't let me bring Rocky in to the deck today."

"Poor guy got stuck in the pet room," said Andy. "It's stinky in there, kiddo."

I smiled.

He scooted a few feet away from Alice and left a vacant space on the bleacher. "Have a seat."

No way, I thought to myself. *Those are pinching parameters.* "No, thank you, I'm going to put a few things in my locker and I'll be out. Mind if I take the left lane this morning?"

Amidst a collection of approvals and okays I walked away from the group. Something happened behind me because I distinctly heard Alice say, "Andy! Be nice!" I was happy to have the locker room for privacy.

I returned to the pool deck while the older crowd continued with their stretching. Within minutes I plunged into the deep end. My body instantly tightened up, reacting to the cold. I sank to the bottom of the pool, then slowly rose, expecting my own temperature to adapt to that of the water. My flesh broke out in goosebumps. When I reached the surface I gulped a large breath of air then started swimming. It would take more than a lap and a half for me to adjust to the temperature.

I did a flip turn at the end of the lane and started into lap two. My legs trailed behind me, kicking ever so slightly. I wanted to warm up, to become one with the water, to relax and allow my brain to move into its own direction. The tranquility of the water might help me sort through the details I otherwise couldn't begin to understand.

Five laps into my morning swim and I hadn't adjusted to the temperature. My shoulders were stiff and I had a hard time getting my arms over my head in a basic freestyle. When I curled into a ball to flip at each turn the raised bumps on my thighs and arms brushed against each other. After six laps I stopped and rubbed my hands up and down my arms rapidly. Why couldn't I warm up?

"What's wrong, missy? You don't usually stop so soon!" said Andy.

"What's the temperature in here?" I called out.

"Whatever it is, it's hotter now that you're in it," he called back.

I didn't have time for his one-liners. "Alice? C-c-c-an you ch-ch-check the temp-p-p-erature?" My teeth rattled against each other.

The small older lady walked slowly to the corner of the pool where the thermometer was tied to the silver ladder. She reached into the water and immediately pulled her hand out, like the water had bitten her. "Oooh! It's cold!"

I started to swim to her, but couldn't control the shaking. I hopped down the lane, my arms wrapped around my body. The red and yellow plastic flags that marked the fifteen feet from the end of the pool mark flapped above my head.

"Missy! You're blue!" said Andy.

I could do little more than bounce on one foot, my other foot wrapped around my calf. I had to get out of the ice water. Shaking to my core, I submerged under the lane dividers and tried to swim under the surface, though my limbs were paralyzed with cold. When I reached the side of the deck I shook visibly. I couldn't unwrap my arms long enough to get out of the pool.

"Andy, help her!" I heard Jessica say.

The old man wrapped a tight grip around my wrist. I went limp and he hoisted me out to my waist and laid me face down on the deck. Alice and a few other seniors covered my torso with towels while the old man grabbed at my inner thighs and dragged my legs out. His fingers bit into my flesh, but I didn't care. I was happy to be out of the pool.

"I'm getting the manager," Andy said and left. The women crowded around me and rubbed at my limbs to improve my circulation. When one person's hands left my arm or leg it started shaking all over again.

The man from behind the desk appeared on the deck. "What's going on here?" he asked.

"C-c-c-cold," I said between chattering teeth.

"What do you mean cold? We keep the pool at eighty degrees." He knelt down next to the silver ladder and fished the thermometer out of the water. "What the hell?"

I focused on creating body heat instead of what the man was doing, but it was hard not to notice him shaking the thermometer and running his hand through the water. He stood up and crossed the pool deck in important strides, stopping only to unlock a small door and disappear inside a hallway. Moments later those of us within range heard a string of curse words and he reappeared.

"We had an equipment malfunction. The heater's off. The pool's closer to sixty than eighty! Get her into the showers. Put her under hot water!"

I tried to stand, with two old ladies on either side of me. I didn't think we were going to make it. Slowly we advanced toward the locker room. Andy appeared at the doorway and guided me inside.

"Andy! You can't go in there!" chided one of the ladies.

"She needs a man to help her. At the rate you old coots are going she'll die of hypothermia." He put my hand under his elbow and I shuffled next to him, for once happy that he'd taken an interest in me. "Okay, missy, which one's your locker? I'll bring your stuff closer to the showers."

"Forty-six A," I said. He walked me to the shower stall and turned on the water. I stood under the stream, absorbing the intoxicating warmth like an addict getting washed over by a much needed rush. With my hands on the wall, I lowered myself to the floor and huddled under the spray.

It was over an hour later when the manager offered his profuse apologies and handed Rocky's leash back over to me. "Ms. Night, I can't begin to tell you how sorry I am that this happened."

"Did you call the cops?" I asked.

"The cops? There's no need to involve them in this. It was a system malfunction. We're going to remain closed for today, tomorrow, too, if necessary, to make sure the pool is heated to the correct temperature."

"But what about sabotage?"

He spun a ballpoint pen around in his fingers and clicked the point up and down several times before he spoke. "Ms. Night, no disrespect, but aren't you a decorator?" he asked.

"Yes, I am, but—"

"And getting your name in the papers would bring you publicity, wouldn't it?"

"Are you insinuating that I had something to do with this?" I asked.

"Absolutely not, I doubt you would be able to tamper with the temperature gauges even if you wanted to. It's not an easy system to figure out, unless you're a highly technical person familiar with this kind of equipment. Like I said, it was a malfunction. I've already called the service technician to come out and give it a once over, but since you've been in the shower the temperature of the pool has already risen three degrees. Maybe it was a power outage. Maybe it was an electric surge. I'm not sure. But I see no need for you to take advantage of us for your own benefit. Face it, Ms. Night, accidents do happen."

I wasn't so sure I agreed with him.

Twenty-One

I drove home and took another shower, longer than the first, in the comfort of my own apartment. Maybe he was right. Maybe accidents did happen. Only, too many accidents had been happening to me or around me lately, too many to call it coincidence. Problem was, once he'd mentioned getting my name in the papers for publicity, I realized what a bad idea publicity would be. If someone really *was* after me, and this *was* a simple accident, publicity would expose a lot of details that would make me an even easier target. And if this wasn't an accident then someone was closer than I thought.

After my shower I dressed in an aqua and white three-quarter sleeve tunic, aqua jersey pants, and my yellow Keds. The temperature threatened to go well into the nineties but I couldn't shake the morning's bone chilling cold. I wrapped my knee in the bandage and pocketed a travel-sized container of Advil along with a picnic basket of bread, cheese, and fruit. Rocky led me down the hall to the apartment Hudson and I had shared last night. The door was locked and my knock went unanswered.

I turned the key and stepped inside. The blankets were folded neatly with the pillows nestled on top. My note sat on top of my pillow, a new scrawl below my own. *Madison, thank you for everything. Your generosity means more than you know. Take care, –H.* It was short and sweet and I was let down that there wasn't more to it. I put it into my straw handbag next to the Advil and left.

After dropping Rocky off at the neighbor's apartment, I drove the white SUV, today's rental, to the Mummy. It stood deserted, like a ghost of the theater that had been running only a week before. It was going to be difficult for it to bounce back from the impact of the murder. It had taken a long time, longer than anticipated, to reopen after being closed indefinitely by the original owners, passing through the hands of too many potential buyers who abandoned the project mid-way, and a few additional years of neglect colored with graffiti. And it had taken more money than anticipated, too, to finish the job right. Richard had relied on the generosity of countless people in Dallas to donate money, energy, skills, and enthusiasm to achieve his goal of owning and operating a cinematic treasure. A piece of film industry history. And now, it stood quietly alone, pieces of yellow crime scene tape flapping in the slight breeze out front, as if marking off the death of the business.

I parked in the lot and went in through the back door like Richard had asked. I assumed the cops had left little behind in their investigation but I didn't want to look for myself. I walked down the hallway to the desk where I'd sat days before and booted up the computer. The Rolodex was still open to Susan's card at AFFER and the messy piles of invoices and chicken-scratch notes still covered the desktop. I sank onto the chair held together by duct tape and turned the small space heater on my ankles. I wondered if I'd ever feel warm again.

I dialed Susan's number and she answered on the second ring.

"Susan, this is Madison."

"What kind of a show are you running over there? I've been waiting for a call or an email from you for the past three days. I tell you I have something that nobody-*nobody*!-knows about and you bail on me?"

"I'm sorry. Things have gotten a little intense around here."

"Listen, you're still doing the thing, right?"

"What thing?"

Her voice dropped. "The Doris Day thing. You're not going to flake on it, are you? Because on top of everything else, we actually have a stunning print of *Pillow Talk*. For some reason it was marked as never shown."

"Oh, no, that's not why I'm calling you. The project was put on indefinite hold."

"You are kidding. Somebody found out? You told somebody what I had? No, if you told someone they'd be chomping at the bit for this. What did you say? Do you need me to talk to Richard to let him know you're not making this up?"

"It's not related to that. It's just, there's been a murder."

"Another Doris Day murder?" she said.

"What did you call them?"

"The Doris Day murders. The former director told me about them when we spoke yesterday. Is that what this is about?"

I didn't answer at first, because it sounded too strange, but it hit me, like a flower pot dropped on my head, that Doris Day was the connection. Sheila Murphy and Carrie Coburn had both been dressed as the perky blonde actress when they were killed. And Pamela Ritter's photo on her promotional flyer was a pretty darn close likeness, too.

"Madison, are you still there?"

"The most recent murder was at the Mummy. Richard thinks it would be best if the theater stays closed until. . . ." I stopped talking again. I thought whatever she would supply to fill in the blank would be better than me saying *until the killer is caught.*

"Did you tell the cops about your film festival? Or the dirty Doris Day film?"

"This has nothing to do with that."

"I wouldn't be so sure about that. Remember how I told you about that letter, about destroying all Doris Day movies?"

"You can't be serious."

"Listen to me. When I told John what you were planning and asked him about the letter, he said 'it's happening all over again'. He wouldn't tell me what he meant."

"Do you think he knows something?" When she didn't answer, I continued. "Do you think he still has the letter?"

"He took it with him when he retired."

"How can I get in touch with him?"

"I'll have him call you. Give me your number, all of your numbers. Home, cell, business, pager. I'm not letting you out of this thing again."

We exchanged contact information and disconnected. I leaned back in the chair and thought about her words. I thought again about my realization. Was it really possible that four murders around Lakewood had something to do with Doris Day?

I pushed the piles of paper around the top of the desk searching for something to write on. Under last month's catalog was a lined notepad with frayed pieces of paper along the top where pages had been torn off. The only pen in the chipped King Kong mug that served as a flotsam holder had an hourglass timer in the middle and a miniature Boggle game secured to the end. I pulled it out and wrote each of the victims names on a separate line. The tiny Boggle letters rattled when I crossed Thelma's T and dotted the I's in Sheila, Carrie, and Ritter.

What.

What.

What.

I tapped the ballpoint of the pen next to each of the names until the rattling drove me to lay the pen down. I had to find something else that these women had in common, something other than their wardrobe choices the night they were killed. Slowly I drew a line through Carrie Coburn's name and wrote my name next to it.

A real estate agent. A decorator. A mother, and a daughter.

And then it hit me like a bucket of ice water colder than the pool water at the Swim Club. *I wouldn't be caught dead in that,* Pamela had said when I offered her my robe. Yet she put it on and went outside and was killed. And in the pocket of that robe was her flyer, with the phone number for Thelma Johnson's son—a son who wasn't her son, a son who worked for the cops. It wasn't Doris Day that connected the four women, it was Thelma Johnson.

The phone rang a shrill tone like the Rockford Files opening sequence and I jumped.

"Hello?" I asked.

"Great, you're still there. Okay, you're going to love me. Not only do I have John's number, but I called him and he really wants to talk to you. Like today. Like now. Like, get a pen and write this number down."

"Susan, slow down."

"No, Madison, hurry up. This guy is, like, seventy-eight. He'll be going to dinner in about an hour. You don't want to miss your window of time."

I picked up the Boggle pen and started flipping pages of the notepad to get to a fresh one.

"What is that sound?" Susan asked.

"It's Richard's Boggle pen. It's the only thing here to write with."

"You can pull the end off, you know."

I yanked on the end and the miniature game board popped off. The small hourglass timer flew out and landed on

163

the floor. I picked it up and set it in front of me on the desk, watching the tiny granules of sand filter down into the base.

"Okay, I'm ready now."

She gave me the information and I promised to call right away. We hung up and I flipped back a few pages to check my notes. That's when I saw it, on one of the sheets between the page where I'd started and the page I was on now. *MADISON, YOUR DAYS ARE NUMBERED.*

Twenty-Two

I t was planted in a place where I couldn't have missed it, and that was not a good feeling. I scooped my cell phone out of the picnic basket and did the sensible thing. I called Tex.

"Allen," he answered.

"Tex, it's Madison. I need to see you."

"I knew you couldn't resist my charm," he joked.

"Can you come to the Mummy? Now? I have some information you need to know."

"Are you alone?"

"Yes."

"Don't move, don't talk to anyone, I'll be right there."

Lieutenant Tex Allen was a lot of things, but right now the only one I was concerned with was that he was a cop. And even before this morning, when I'd sunk down to the bottom of a freezing cold pool, he knew I'd been in over my head.

He arrived quickly, as if he'd already been in the area. I didn't ask. He smelled like cut grass and cinnamon. He took the seat in front of me and leaned back and I showed him the notepad. Then I told him about the pool. His fingers grasped the sides of the chair tightly enough to show he was keeping his true thoughts in check.

"What else?"

"What do you mean, what else?"

"Your friend Hudson. What about him?"

"What are you driving at?" I asked instead of answering.

"His truck was parked three blocks from your apartment last night. We put a car on it and it never moved. Do you want to tell me where we can find him?"

"I don't know where you can find him. Did you try his house?"

"He's not there. A couple of officers have been watching his house since you were attacked, and it looks like he skipped town."

"He wouldn't just leave."

"Said he loaded up the back of his truck and put a cat carrier on the passenger side."

That didn't fit. I didn't see him leaving town now, not after everything he'd told me, not after all of the reasons he had chosen to stay in Dallas.

"If he left, he'll be back. He has nothing to run away from."

"What makes you so sure, Night?" Tex asked and for the first time that day I grew uncomfortably warm. I bent down and turned the small space heater off.

"I don't think I'm a bad judge of character."

"Your last boyfriend. The married furniture designer in Philadelphia? Do you think you correctly judged his character?"

I leaned forward, right in Tex's personal space. "That is *not fair!*" I shouted, and slammed the palms of my hands down on top of the desk. "How do you know about that? And how *dare* you bring that up to me. I am trying to help you find a killer, not go after an innocent man." I pushed the chair away from the desk and stood up, needing fresh air and space from the lieutenant. I took two steps and my knee cracked loudly, like a twig underfoot. I winced and buckled slightly, closed my eyes, and hobbled toward the front door.

166

"Night, your knee. Was he the one that caused the injury?"

Like a poison-tipped dart intended to injure me long after it penetrated my flesh, Tex's comment pierced my spirit. I realized the extent of his background check on me, how much he'd known all along, how much he had kept to himself. There was no denying my reality, not to him.

"No, Lieutenant, I'm the only one responsible for my injury. I wasn't watching where I was going." I pushed the doors open and limped through them, leaving him behind in the office.

My exit would have been that much more effective if I'd thought to grab my keys or phone before storming out the front door. I had to give Tex credit. He waited a solid twenty minutes before coming to find me, leaning against the front exterior of The Mummy. He had my picnic basket in one hand and my personal belongings in the other.

"You got enough in here to share?" he asked, rocking the basket slightly toward me.

"Possibly," I said.

He sat down on the sidewalk and set the picnic basket next to him. I didn't move. He opened the basket and pulled out plastic tumblers and a container of tea. After filling two cups, he set them down and tore the end of the loaf of French bread. I crossed my arms over my chest and watched him bite into the loaf and chew, washing it down with a good sized gulp of tea. I was hungry. I was thirsty. Most of all, I wanted to sit back down.

And, it was my food.

I took a seat next to him on the sidewalk and snapped a branch of grapes off the vine. My legs stuck out in front of me. I popped three grapes in my mouth, swallowed some tea, and tore off a piece of bread, all without making eye contact.

"I don't want to talk about that." I said before biting into the bread.

"Fair enough," he replied.

We ate together in silence. When a good amount of the bread and grapes and cheese were gone I leaned back, letting the hot sun sear my face with my eyes closed.

"Night, I want you to steer clear of all of this for the next couple of days."

I took a deep breath and kept my eyes closed. "As in, what?"

"As in, let homicide do their job. Find something else to occupy your time."

For the first time since the murders had started, I heard him. He had sworn to serve and protect, and at the moment, those responsibilities included me.

"Fine. I need to focus on business before I go bankrupt."

"You'll have plenty of time for theater stuff when this is over."

I leaned forward and opened my eyes, then turned to him. "I know."

He stood up and extended a hand toward me. I didn't want to need his help, but maybe, just this one time, it wouldn't hurt to let someone help me. I took his hand and let him pull me up off the ground.

"So what are you going to do?"

"Who knows? Get a cortisone shot, do something about this hair, maybe rent a movie."

"You're being smart."

"I'm being smart," I repeated.

I dropped his hand and hauled the almost empty picnic basket to the new rental. I unlocked the doors and got inside. Before I could close the door, Tex yelled to me. "Hey Night?"

"Yes?"

He pointed a finger at me. "You need anything, you call."

I smiled but knew I'd already made my one gratuitous phone call for help.

I drove home and picked up Rocky from the neighbor, then drove to the studio. I'd been half-joking to Tex when I mentioned bankruptcy, but in all honesty the bills were exceeding the cash flow and mine wasn't the type of business that bounced back quickly from setbacks. I didn't have any jobs lined up at the moment and there seemed to be no better time than the present to do something about that.

I let myself in through the back door and turned on a couple of lights. I patted the back cushion of a white rectangular sofa and a layer of dust particles flitted through the air. If nothing else, I could use the time to give the studio a once over.

I flipped the Closed sign to Open and started cleaning. A small portable Rat Pack-era bachelor's bar stood by the front door, stocked with a variety of green cleaning supplies. I pulled out a yellow chamois cloth and a bottle of Murphy's Oil and set to work polishing the wooden chairs, table legs and bars. Next I used a feather duster to knock the slight layer dust off of the crevices of each lamp, clock, object d'art, and knickknack in the room. The sun streamed through the front windows, glistening off airborne particles. I'd neglected my business for too long and it felt good to clean. It felt as though I was clearing the cobwebs from the life I had before the murders started.

I put the cleaning fluids and rags into a bucket and lugged them to the office. I wheeled a Dyson out of the closet by the back door and waved the extension wand in the air to suck up the floating filaments of dust. When I reached the corner where the arc lamp had stood I clipped the attachments onto the hose and got down on my hands and knees, working at the carpet pile to eliminate any signs of the rectangular marble base that had sat there before Rocky knocked it over. Something touched my left shoulder and I screamed.

A man stood, bent at the waist, his hand inches from me. I whipped the hose of the vacuum cleaner toward him like the barrel of a shotgun, my eyes wide with terror. He put his hands up in the air and stepped back, almost colliding with a woman with shaggy jet black hair and black cat's eye sunglasses. The man's lips moved, but I couldn't understand him over the din of the vacuum. I used my right hand to leverage myself up to a standing position, and switched off the machine.

"Who are you?" I demanded.

"We're the Duncans."

"The who?"

"Ned and Connie Duncan. We left you a message about our house?"

I looked around the office. "When, today?"

"Ned, let's go," said the woman, tugging at the sleeve of his madras plaid shirt.

"No, no, I'm sorry, I'm a little jumpy," I said. They looked at me like I belonged in a psych ward. *Good going, Madison. That's a surefire way to get clients.*

"My dog knocked over a rather large lamp and I'm a little shaky from the crash. Again, I'm sorry," I said in my most professional tone. "I didn't get your message but if you'd like we can meet in my office and discuss what interests you."

They exchanged wary looks but ultimately followed me. When they saw Rocky chewing on his rope bone from the nook in the middle of a lime green beanbag chair, they calmed considerably. Shih Tzu as anti-crazy endorsement. That's a new one.

The couple sat in the chairs in front of my desk and I sat behind it. I placed them in their early thirties.

"Now, what did you have in mind?" I asked.

Ned spoke first. "I think we should be honest. We have pretty strong ideas of what we like: all the classics. Saarinen, Nelson, Wright, you know. . . we were thinking about doing it ourselves. Well, us and Design Within Reach."

Internally I cringed at the mention of the retailer famous for reissues of classic mid-century designs, even though I knew their mere presence and success validated my own efforts.

"You bought a mid-century house?"

"Yes."

"Well, I admire your interest in keeping the interior true to the exterior. That's my business. And you can certainly go the direction you mentioned, with reissues, but I prefer a more honest approach. Actual items, some restored, from the era. Originals mixed in with a little kitsch."

"Can you show us your work?" asked the woman. Her sunglasses had the kind of lenses that darkened with sun and now, in the comfort of my office, had faded to clear.

"Of course." I pulled two large photo albums from the bookcase behind me and set one in front of them. "These are all rooms that I've done, and a few close-ups of restored pieces. Let me give you a couple of minutes to go through them and talk. I'd really like to put that vacuum cleaner away," I said with a smile.

I left them alone with my portfolio and Rocky, the best one-two punch I could come up with on short notice. When I returned to the office, they were all smiles. We discussed room dimensions, my fee, and when I could come to see their new house and take interior pictures and measurements. It felt good to focus on something else for a change, something that usually was the single most important part of my life.

Close to two hours later, I walked the Duncans to the door and returned to the office. I wanted to start a file on them while the creative juices were still flowing. Getting the details down while they were fresh in my mind would serve to make me look like a detail-oriented genius in time. Rocky slept in the corner while my fingers flew over the keyboard.

I typed up several pages of notes, referencing items in the storage unit and items I'd seen in the market place. I had a pretty good idea what direction to go to please them, and when

I was done with my pitch, they'd seemed more pleased than when they'd walked in, although, considering they'd been held at vacuum-point, it wasn't a stretch to know things could only get better.

When I shut down the Word document, I launched the Internet and checked my emails. Digests from my MCM Yahoo loop had been filtered directly to their folders. A couple of automated eBay reminders peppered my inbox along with an announcement from a dealer looking to liquidate a surplus of Danish modern furniture. And in the middle of them all was a note from Susan at AFFER with the subject line: *Call John Phillips*.

Hours earlier, I would have made that call. Before finding the threat. Before talking to Tex. Before moving on with my life. I moved the email to the trash bin without reading it. I shut down the computer and locked up the office.

I drove the Explorer to Old Towne, a strip mall off of Mockingbird. It had been left behind in the age of newly renovated luxury malls, but at the moment it held everything I needed: a no appointment necessary hair salon and a used DVD store. If a doctor with cortisone shots on demand happened to open an office in the vicinity, it would have been perfect.

There wasn't much the teenaged stylist could do to my hair. The jagged edges I'd been left with after hacking off my ponytail had created layers too short to blend. The long, smooth cascade of blond hair I'd once had would take months, maybe a year, to grow back. Forty-five minutes later my hair was layered around my face, pouffy with the humidity and volumizing mousse that had been used. It was shorter than I liked, but that was life. It would give me an excuse to dive into my hat collection for a couple of months.

I walked a few doors down to the DVD store and went straight to the comedies and looked up P. There it was: a copy of *Pillow Talk*, mine for a mere seven dollars. Ironically, it was one of the few Doris movies I didn't own, thanks to my generous lending habit. I left the store and walked Rocky to the car. My cell phone buzzed from inside my handbag. *Private Number.* I expected it to be from the Duncans. It wasn't uncommon for new clients to follow up a first meeting with a phone call. I answered with the name of the store.

"Mad for Mod, Madison Night speaking."

"Night, where are you?" asked Tex. "It's important."

"I know this can't be about the case because you specifically asked me—"

"Not now, Night. Where can I find Hudson James?"

"Hudson? I don't know," I answered, confused by his no-nonsense tone. "Why?"

"Because we just issued a warrant for his arrest."

Twenty-Three

"I need to know where I can find him," said Tex.

"Hudson is not the man you're looking for."

"Night, you don't know what you're talking about. We found evidence that doesn't put him in a good light and that's all I'm going to say."

"What evidence?"

Hudson had explained away every single thing that had come up and I didn't believe he'd been lying. It didn't fit. "Something isn't right. You're trying to jam a square peg into a round hole."

"No, I'm trying to solve a homicide."

"You're looking for the wrong man."

"Night, I don't know where these misplaced loyalties toward James are coming from but listen to me. He's dangerous. He's a killer. And if I find out you know where he is and you're not telling me, I swear I'll arrest you for obstruction of justice."

"What? What could you possibly have on Hudson aside from gossip and innuendo?"

Tex disconnected the call.

I didn't believe for a second that Hudson was guilty but I was a little scared about Tex's threat. Hudson had been at my apartment only last night and Tex knew it, only he didn't know I knew he knew it. Keeping the men in my life straight would have been like a comical mix-up in any one of Doris's sex comedies if it weren't for the severity of my situation. I had to get home and find out if Hudson had returned to the building.

This time I kept my eyes alert for signs of Hudson's pickup truck. I didn't see it. The access to the parking lot was simple: pull in the driveway on the south side and exit through the driveway on the north side. The driveways and the lot made a U around the building.

I pulled into the long narrow driveway that led to the lot in the back and eased the new Explorer into my space. The driver's side door scraped against the metal frame that held up the aluminum covering. One more expense I didn't need. My Mexican neighbors loitered around their lot with a case of Tecate torn open, partially distributed amongst them. I nodded hello and pulled Rocky away from their group and into the back door. From four steps away I could see a note taped to the front of my apartment.

Even before I reached the door I knew who it was from. My heart skipped a beat. I looked up and down the hallway, for what I wasn't sure. And then I read it.

Madison, I'm involved more than I should be and that could become a problem for you. I'm sorry for the trouble I've caused. I'm also sorry about the trouble you'll find on the other side of this door but I didn't know who else to trust. Yours, H.

Everything about the note terrified me. Unlocking the door terrified me. I glanced out the window and saw a police cruiser turn into the exit driveway of my building. It stopped midway through the driveway, before it reached the lot. I didn't know what they were doing there, but if no other cars attempted to leave, they could park in one of the open spaces and be up to my apartment in about three minutes.

Carlos Montana, my next door neighbor, came out of his apartment and stared out the back window. "What are those pigs doing now?" he asked angrily.

Carlos was a retired mechanic. He was never late on his rent, changed my oil for free, and made a mean enchilada. He also maintained a dislike for cops. "Don't they know nothing?" He let off a string of Spanish words that didn't sound like compliments.

"Can you go tell them they can't come in that way?" I asked.

"Sure. I'll stick it to them." He tore off down the stairs and crossed the lot to his El Camino. I watched long enough to see him pull up head to head with the cruiser, honk his horn and engage in a yelling battle. God bless Carlos. I'd have to cut him a break on the rent next month.

I turned the key in the lock and slowly pushed the door in. Rocky bounded a few feet inside, yipping happily. Before I could hit the light switch I heard a hiss. Then a whimper. Then Rocky returned to my side. I shut the door behind me and put on the chain, then felt around for the knob on the atomic lamp. I twisted it and almost tripped over a cat carrier.

Mortiboy was in the house.

For once, Rocky kept his distance. I picked up the blue-grey plastic carrier warily, not sure if the cat and I were on much better terms than he was with Rocky. He crouched low on his paws, with his tail fat and his back arched, and let loose another hiss in my direction. A low, angry yowl emanated from the back of his throat. I leaned down toward the little grated door and stuck a finger between the metal. He took a swipe at me and one of his claws connected. Before I could say or do anything, there was a knock on my front door.

I picked up the cage and carried it into my bedroom. "Just a minute!" I called out.

When I returned and looked through the peephole, I found Officer Nast and Officer Clark standing in front of my door. I opened it but left the chain on.

"Hi, Officers," I said tentatively.

"Madison, is everything okay in there?" asked Officer Nast. She leaned in to peer through the narrow opening, her green eyes darting from side to side, taking in my living room.

"Everything's fine."

"It sounded like we heard a yell. Are you alone?"

"Yes, I am. I . . ." I looked behind me, unsure if I really was. I hadn't had a chance to see if Hudson was in the apartment, like last night. "I had a kitchen accident. Cut my finger. You must have heard me."

I held up my index finger. Mortiboy's claw had punctured the tip, producing a trickle of blood that spidered its way around the knuckle. It looked worse than it was. Unless the furry devil had given me cat scratch fever.

"You need to get that under cold water, ma'am," said Officer Clark.

"I was just about to do that when you knocked."

Officer Nast pushed a hand against my front door. "Are you sure you're okay in there? Nobody else around?"

"Just me," I said innocently. Then we all heard a crash from my hallway.

"Ms. Night, I'm going to need you to open that door."

Rocky, in his fear-slash-enthusiasm over Mortiboy's presence, had knocked over another lamp. When the officers and I reached the pile of broken ceramic, this time formerly in the shape of a Chinese man, it was with more relief than concern.

"My dog has developed an unseemly habit of knocking over lamps."

Rocky crept out from the bathroom, front paws barely on the carpet of the hallway, back paws securely on the pink tiled floor, both head and tail low. He knew he'd done wrong.

"Come here, you," I said, making a big show of picking him up and cradling him, all the while talking to him like he was a very bad dog. The officers looked uncomfortable with my maternal show of doggie affection, exactly what I'd hoped for.

"Sorry to have bothered you. Keep an eye on that little guy," said Officer Clark. He reached out and ruffled Rocky's fur.

"Will do."

I followed the officers to the hallway. Before descending the stairs, Officer Nast turned back to face me. "Madison, from one woman to another, don't let your emotions get you involved in something you shouldn't be. Once you start listening to your emotions, you're burnt."

I wondered if she was talking about Hudson or Tex. Either way I nodded my agreement and smiled.

Despite the afternoon hour, I donned white silk pajamas and crawled into bed in the middle of the day. Rocky curled up next my left leg and Mortiboy sat on the corner of the right side of the bed—the closest he'd come to actual contact that didn't involve bloodshed. I put the new DVD into the player and relaxed back against aqua and pink seersucker pillow shams.

Pillow Talk was the reason I became a decorator. I was born on April third just like Doris Day, which made me an Aries. I first discovered the actress's canon of movies when I was thirteen, but as time went on, I recognized pieces of myself in every role she ever played: strong, confident, independent, determined to do everything on my own. Where other people dismissed her body of work as light airy fare, I found it to be effervescent and bubbly in an uplifting manner. I wanted to be a modern day version of her. Capable of accomplishing anything, not needing a man to take care of me, getting by on my talents and intellect. And when I looked at the sets, I lusted to live in a world that looked like that.

Growing up, I watched her movies over and over, learning the dialogue, idolizing Rock Hudson and James Garner, decorating and redecorating my bedroom to match what I saw, wondering when my own personal romantic mix-up was going to happen. It's how I first got interested in mid-century decorating, and by studying her vast array of movies down to the smallest details, I'd developed an expert eye for accuracy. Eventually, I literally made it my business to bring the look of her movies to other people who felt the same way I did. I loved this movie. I loved *all* of Doris Day's movies.

But somewhere out there was a person who didn't.

I paused in the middle of the Roly Poly song and dug John Phillips' phone number out of my handbag. A gruff male voice answered midway through the first ring.

"Could I speak to Mr. John Phillips, please?"

"Who's calling?"

"Madison Night, from the Mummy Theater in Dallas? Is this Mr. Phillips?"

"About time you called."

"Do you have a minute to talk?"

"It's late. I've been waiting for your call all day. So, what did Susan tell you?"

"Not much. She said AFFER received a letter about Doris Day movies?"

"That's just the tip of the iceberg. I always thought that letter would have been funny if it wasn't so disturbing."

"I'm a little lost."

"After we got the letter we thought it would be funny to watch a bunch of Doris Day movies, you know, stir the pot. We got into the second reel of *Pillow Talk* and, let me just say, everybody in that audience got more than they bargained for."

I dropped my voice. "So it's true?"

"What's true?"

"A dirty movie? With *her*?"

"Listen. The woman looked like Doris Day and dressed like Doris Day, but I can tell you for certain that was no Doris Day."

"What did you do?"

"The only thing we could do. Turned off the projector, apologized to the audience, and packed it up. The plan was to go back and try to figure out what happened but we never had a chance."

"Why not? What happened to the film reel?"

"Didn't Susan tell you? Wait, that's right, she doesn't know. I might as well tell you, since you're in the middle of this thing. The day after we showed the movie there was a break in at the AFFER warehouse. The temperature gauges were tampered with, which destroyed about a third of our inventory, but only one thing was missing. Our copy of *Pillow Talk*."

Twenty-Four

"How did AFFER recover from the loss of inventory?" I asked.

"Beneficiaries. People who care about what we do. We replaced most of the movies through donations from the Hollywood community. There are a lot of people out here who are interested in preserving our cinematic history and we were fortunate that they saw value in what we were doing. It took some time, but we built our inventory back up. Never caught the bastards who did it, either. And I still say it had something to do with that letter."

"I'm sorry to bring this back to Doris Day, but Susan said you had a beautiful copy of *Pillow Talk*. Was she wrong?"

"No, she was right, we do now. Didn't for a long time. Some grass-roots renovation team was working on an old theater in Cincinnati and found a beautiful print in the basement. Probably hadn't been shown for fifty years. I'm telling you, this business is amazing. You never know what's going to show up when some newcomers take over a theater and organize their inventory."

I wasn't sure what to say to John to keep him talking, but I wasn't satisfied that I knew all I had to know.

"Mr. Phillips, do you think the letter is related to the break-in or the murders in Dallas?"

"It would almost have to be. The gist of it is that this guy wanted us to destroy all of Doris Day's movies."

"Are you quoting that or is that what you remember?"

"You want to read it for yourself? Give me your address and I'll drop a copy in the mail."

"Can you fax it?"

There was a long pause. Susan had told me that John was retired and in his seventies. I wanted to see these letters but I didn't know how interested he would be in going out of his way to get them from Hollywood to Dallas on a quick timetable.

"Tell you what I'll do. You got email?"

"Sure,"

"I'll scan them in and email them as an attachment. You can print out your own copies."

"Perfect," I said.

He took down my email address and we disconnected. I spent half an hour obsessively clicking the refresh icon in my inbox before changing out of my pajamas and back into my aqua and white tunic and aqua jersey pants. I took Rocky out for a sprinkle and gave John time to do what he'd promised.

When I returned inside, I filled a hollow rubber toy with peanut butter for Rocky and tossed it into the living room to occupy him while I sat at the computer. There was one unread email in my inbox. *Letter re: Doris Day movies* from John Phillips. Rocky made little snorting noises in the background while I read the words of a Doris Hater.

Dear American Film Rentals,

Your work in the realm of preserving cinematic history is to be commended. Too many filmgoers are being educated by the likes of Bruce Willis, Will Farrell, and Adam Sandler, unaware that a vast array of movies prior to these created an art form to be revered. While I admire your efforts to continually educate your audiences on the importance of the films in your inventory, I must recommend that you take immediate action against those movies that are a cancer on the landscape of American Cinema, namely, the fluff of Doris Day. As an educated filmgoer, I believe that the ultimate destruction of this kind of nonsense will serve to highlight the greater cinematic achievements that were created during this notoriously otherwise lush window of moviemaking. I believe it is the only responsible action for AFFER to take.

May I suggest that you are in the valuable position of changing the way people view movies forever, and by destroying the existence of this blemish on our country's cannon of film, you will rewrite history in the eyes of future film aficionados? I see it as irresponsible for you to continue to preserve these movies, because their very presence forever alters the way film is viewed from a historical perspective.

This is more than a suggestion. It is your obligation as a patron of the arts.

Sincerely,

A Concerned Moviegoer

It was quite a letter: well written, well argued, and the kind of thing that would have been kept in a file and pulled out each year at the office holiday party if it hadn't led to an act of vandalism.

Another email from John Phillips popped into my inbox. *News about the break-in* was the subject. I opened the second attachment and stared at a newspaper clipping. The action described undermined the humor of the letter. I toggled back to the letter and printed off a copy. Somebody had to have looked into the letter and connected the two. I called John back.

"John? You said 'he'."

"I said what?"

"He. You referred to the writer as 'he'. But I'm sitting here reading this letter and there's no signature."

"Well sure I said he. That's what ties the whole thing together. There was a name on the return address of the envelope and I don't know a lot of women named Richard Goode."

Richard Goode, I kept telling myself, was a common name. I didn't want to think that there was a bigger reason for the murder at the theater, that the man responsible for our programming, the man who dealt with stress with a bag of mary-jane, the man whose chair I had occupied not even ten hours ago, was involved in this, but pieces of what I knew fit. He had access to the pillows in my trunk, and had fought me on the Doris Day film festival. But other pieces of the puzzle remained unconnected to him, not making sense.

I held the letter in my hand and grew angry. People's lives were at stake. Their futures. And I doubted that Richard had told the police about his anti-Doris Day stance. I called the Mummy and left a message on his voicemail for him to call me back. His home number was at the studio and I'd promised Tex—I'd promised Tex nothing. We were beyond promises of me minding my own business. We were officially in "I'm involved" mode. I looked up Richard's home address.

The addition of Mortiboy to the family unit presented a couple of unforeseen problems, not the least of which was what to do with the two of them while I was gone. So I did the unimaginable. I let the two of them have free reign of the apartment and I left.

Richard Goode lived in east Dallas, in a neighborhood not very far from the Mummy. More flat roads, many of them unpaved. It was on the way to Garland, and the further you drove in that direction the more you got into the part of Texas people thought of when they never lived here: flat, dusty, less cosmopolitan, more folksy. The real estate was cheaper than in

Dallas county or Collin county, which put the smarter, more frugal folks out that way instead of in the higher profile areas like the forever burgeoning downtown. Richard hadn't gone far enough in that direction to really benefit. He was frugal-adjacent.

Prior to today, I'd been to Richard's place one time, and I relied on memory and instinct more than the address on the piece of paper, made two wrong turns, but eventually drove down the alley that led to his house. There were no cars in the driveway. I parked the white Explorer along the curb and caught the tail of my tunic in the door when I shut it. The fabric tore when I tried to yank it free.

I approached the front door and rang the bell. No answer. I knocked for good measure, waited a couple of minutes, and headed around back. The street was deserted. No children playing, no people lounging on their front porch. Unusual for a residential neighborhood.

The back door was preempted by a screen door that hung from one broken hinge. I pulled it open and knocked on the door between. Unexpectedly, the door swung open.

"Hello? Richard? Are you home?" I called through the hallway. No voices met my question. "Richard?" I called one last time.

Common sense, courtesy, and general intellect told me to leave. But instinct, coupled with questions about why the back door was open if no one was home, why the neighborhood was noticeably quiet, and why Richard Goode's name was signed to a letter sent to AFFER years ago, trumped common sense. And if answers were on the other side of the floor that separated me from the rest of the house, then I was going in.

I tiptoed across the worn floor, a poorly measured and cut piece of linoleum roll made to look like tile. The seams by the bottom of the cabinets were not lined up and grime had since discolored the gap. As a decorator, I had a knack for assessing a room quickly, picking out the pieces that made up the personality of the person. It was a necessary skill in being able to design a new room for people who wanted to feel at home in it, not feel like they'd walked into a stranger's house.

At first glance Richard's living room was a study in post-college dorm room. Mismatched bookcases lined three walls. A futon, unfolded, faced the flat screen TV, probably worth more than all of the furniture combined. An empty wine bottle sat on the makeshift coffee table. Even though the bottle was empty, he'd shoved the rubber cork back into the neck.

"Richard?" I called again, answered only with more silence. I scanned the bookcase. The shelves were packed, upright and then covered with books on their sides. Books on filmmaking. Directors. Producers. Script Supervisors. How to break into Hollywood. How to make it in the movies. How to do anything and everything I could imagine relating to the industry.

I didn't know what I was looking for. Richard had a computer set up on a small table by the front door and a tiered bookcase next to it. I moved forward, no longer aware that I was trespassing in another person's house. The shelves of this bookcase were full, too, this time with scripts. Shelf after shelf of scripts. I slid one out of its space on the shelf. *The Monkey Conspiracy by Richard Goode*. I slid it back in and pulled out another. *Venom and Intimacy by R. Godenov*. A third: *Freak Show Superhero by Ricardo Godinsky*. I got the feeling he'd been experimenting with pen-names that never quite worked.

I pulled another script off of the bottom shelf. *Raging Bull*. Next, *Taxi Driver*. Next: *Fitzcarraldo*. He kept his own assortment of unsold screenplays on the shelves by those of works that he respected. I knew he respected them. He'd pitched some of these very same movies to the Dallas Independent Group for Movies over the past year and I'd been there to hear it. There was no surprise in finding proof of Richard's passion for film; you didn't become the director of a film society that presented only old movies on the big screen if you didn't like—no, love—that kind of thing. Yet was this an interest, a passion, or an obsession? Before I'd read that letter I would have thought the former. Seeing this, coupled with the declarations he made in the letter, I wasn't sure.

A car turned into the cul de sac. I had more questions now than I'd arrived with, but there was no time to search for answers. I had to get out of there. I ran out the back door and pulled the door shut behind me. Two steps away I doubled back and tried the knob. It was locked. The handbrake clicked on a car out front and I hurried down the stairs and around the side of the house. A green sedan sat in Richard's neighbor's driveway.

I remoted the doors to the SUV and hopped in, flipping the visor down and shielding my face with my hand while passing the neighbors. I drove to the theater. Two blocks away, as I sped through an intersection, I passed a black Jeep on a side street. The next thing I knew, I'd picked up a tail.

Two traffic lights and three stop signs later, I pulled over. Tex parked his jeep in front of me. So much for faking him out and making a clean getaway.

He approached my car and draped his tanned forearms over my open window. "What are you doing in this neck of the woods?"

"I was looking for someone," I said, shielding my eyes from the sun.

"Anyone I know?"

"How long have you been following me?"

"Who said I was following you? I saw you blow through that intersection and thought I'd see what you were up to."

"Move your car, please," I demanded.

"I don't think so, Night."

My fists balled up and I punched the steering wheel. "I could report you for harassment if I wanted. You have no right—*no right!*—to question me about my comings and goings!"

187

"You might have a point. Go where you're going. I'll follow. If you want, I'll drive and save you the gas."

I threw him a curve ball. "Fine. I have a lead on your case and you can drive me. It'll save us both time."

"You're going to see Hudson?"

"No. I'm going to the Mummy."

"Forget the Mummy. Carrie Coburn's murder was a mistake. The Mummy isn't involved in this."

"That's where you're wrong, Cowboy." He took a half a step backwards. "You can't even connect all four murders with Hudson. You have twenty-year-old unproven allegations and the current murder of the previous victim's mother. You say Carrie Coburn's murder was a mistake? What about Pamela Ritter's? What does she have to do with Hudson? Try as you want, you can't wrap it all up into one neat package. There's no connection."

"Night, I didn't want to be the one to tell you this, but you're wrong. We found our connection between Hudson James and Pamela Ritter."

Twenty-Five

"What connection?" I asked. My foot relaxed against the brake and the truck glided forward, tapping the back bumper of Tex's Jeep. I threw it into park and turned off the ignition.

"You don't know?"

"They dated?" I blurted out before I could self-edit.

"What? No, well, I don't know about that." He looked at me oddly, as if he was assessing why I'd jumped to that conclusion. "He did some contract work for her. Staging, I think it's called. Hired him to come into a couple of the houses she was selling and fix stuff up so it fit the fifties look." He paused for a couple of seconds, and watched my expression.

For no good reason, I felt betrayed, but fought to keep that from showing on my face.

"And if that's not enough for you, it seems Thelma Johnson had a yard sale a couple of weeks ago. Pamela bought a couple of pieces of furniture and hired Hudson James to fix them up. But she never paid him, for that job, or for a couple of others. We found the invoices, a couple of them with handwritten notes."

"Hudson wouldn't kill someone over unpaid invoices," I said. My eyes broke contact with Tex's, which I instantly regretted. He continued to stare at me, making me feel all the more self-conscious. "How much?"

"Enough to make him confront her."

My eyes flitted around while I thought, not settling on any one thing in particular. I was trying to piece this together. So she owed him money. And he'd sent invoices, that wasn't too big of a surprise, it was standard in the industry. And he'd included a couple of notes? Well, that was just polite. But why hadn't he told me? Staging was more the job of a decorator than a handyman. When we'd talked about the murders, why hadn't he mentioned he had a relationship with Pamela, or that he'd recently worked on furniture that came from Thelma Johnson's house? Those two omissions troubled me more than I cared to admit to Tex.

"Okay. So you have a connection between Hudson and Pamela. Considering his skill set, it's not such an odd connection. That can't be enough to give you a warrant for his arrest."

"It wasn't."

"There's more?"

"I'm not going to throw the case to prove to you I did my job."

"And I'm not going to let you use me as bait to catch an innocent man."

"Damn it, Madison! Don't you think this job is hard enough without me having to keep you out of trouble, too?"

"Then stop it! Stop following me! Stop watching me! Leave me out of it!" I turned the key and threw the car in reverse. I hit the gas. I peeled out, narrowly missing the left bumper of Tex's Jeep. Three blocks later there was still no sight of him in my rearview mirror.

If Tex wanted to find me, he would, because I drove directly to the theater like I told him I was going to. But even after I parked the car and sat in the lot for five minutes collecting scattered thoughts and wits, he didn't show up. Whether he had a better lead on Hudson than following me around or not, it seemed as though, for the time being, I'd shaken my tail.

I went to the Mummy for one reason: Richard. The theater was his home away from home and maybe, just maybe, I'd learn something else if I spent some time looking at things through his eyes.

I went in through the back door. The air was mingled with the scent of dust and stale popcorn. We popped fresh popcorn for all of our events but often kept the leftovers in large plastic bags in the back room, for after hours viewings and donations to local shelters. One of the bags sat by the back door, never having been couriered to its next stop. The plastic had split and a stream of kernels was strewn across the floor in a diagonal pattern. Several kernels had been flattened by the sole of a shoe. I placed my foot next to the footprint. It was almost double the size of my yellow canvas sneaker. A man's shoe.

I crossed through the kitchen and turned into the office. It was empty. No sign of Richard or anyone else. In fact, there were no signs the theater had ever reopened at all.

I sat in Richard's chair and looked around the room. What did he see when he sat here? What made this *his* office versus the office of a different manager?

The bookcases, unlike his bookcases at home, were bare. Shelves held knickknacks like ceramic popcorn bags, empty film reels, and the kind of fake Oscar statues popular at Academy Awards parties around the country. Nothing seemed out of the norm. Nothing looked like it represented anyone other than the twenty-eight year old who operated the theater. We all knew his contacts in the industry had landed him here, contacts he'd made getting his Masters of Fine Arts. He'd been, to the city of Dallas, an example of what could be accomplished with passion and networking skills. But add that letter into the mix and suddenly he wasn't the person I knew. Suddenly he was a stranger.

Footsteps. Over my head. Clear creaking of the boards in the balcony, making the kind of noise that can only come from a person advancing across the floor. I'd left everything of mine in the car except for the keys. They were on the desk, somewhere. Frantically, I padded my palms over the piles of paper that covered the scratched wooden surface, looking for the metal lump. When my left palm landed on them I knocked the papers aside and saw my name written in block letters. *TELL MADISON—*

I pushed more of the papers aside. Tell me what? Was this what I was looking for?

TELL MADISON SHE'S NEXT.

The handwriting matched the handwriting of the other threats. And it matched 'anonymous,' the signer of the letter that John Phillips had faxed me. I had my proof, my connection. But I still didn't know what it all meant. I couldn't begin to fathom what Richard's hatred of Doris Day's movies had to do with the murders of four different women, but what it didn't relate to was Hudson. It was something for me to take to the homicide division to make them rethink their one track investigation.

I pushed the rolling chair away from the desk and stood. My right shoelace caught in the wheel of the chair and I fell, slamming my left kneecap into the ground. Even painkillers couldn't mask the explosion of nerve endings that caused me to cry out.

"Madison?"

I heard behind me. I struggled to get up, to get out of there.

"Madison, wait!"

I fought unsuccessfully to free my shoelace from the chair's wheel. The casters bobbled while I kicked my foot back and forth. I removed the shoe with the toe of the other foot and pulled myself from the floor. The chair crashed into a stack of metal film reels, a cacophony of noise echoing around the room. Worse, Richard stood in the doorway, blocking my exit.

Twenty-Six

"What are you doing here?" he asked.

I stood facing him, balanced on my bare right foot. My hand had closed around one of the metal film reels and I held it in front of me like a shield of protection. My left knee pounded with pain. In seconds I assessed the situation: I was hurt, but he was unarmed. In fact, he was disheveled, with a couple of days beard growth, and he didn't smell altogether fresh. He took a step toward me and I pushed the metal reel out.

"Stop!" I yelled.

"You're hurt. Sit down. I want to help you."

"Stay where you are."

"Madison, what's going on? Are you the one who's after me?" he asked.

"After you? You just came after me! I know you're the one who's been leaving me threatening notes. And I know about the letter to AFFER, so back off and let me call the cops."

"No!" he hollered.

My hand rested on the receiver of the phone, and quite frankly the last person in the world I wanted to call was Tex, except that I kind of did want to call him because here I was

194

face to face with a person who was somehow tied to the murders. Only Tex didn't believe me and I didn't know how to make him understand without more information.

"Stay back!" I shouted, still clutching the reel.

"Madison, what happened? Did they get to you, too? What is going on?"

"Did who get to me?"

"I don't know who. The people who are doing this."

"Richard, you're not making any sense. You have a lot of questions to answer before I tell you anything."

"I'll answer anything. Just please, stop acting crazy."

"I'm not acting crazy," I said, and readjusted my grip on the metal wheel.

"You look like you might decapitate me with that film spool."

I looked down at my hands, holding the metal reel like a Frisbee. "Sit down. Over there."

"You're not going to hurt me, are you?" he asked, the whites of his eyes wide with fear.

"Sit down, Richard."

He collapsed into a red molded plastic chair, like a balloon with a slow leak. All of the air, the bravado, fizzled out of him. His rumpled clothes and unshaven face hid a grey pallor that was borderline unhealthy. I knew I wasn't going to hurt him— probably wasn't capable either physically or mentally of hurting him unless he came after me—but I wasn't about to tell him that before finding out a few things. He wasn't acting like a murderer, but what he was doing could be just that—an act. And I wasn't going to fall for it.

"Why are you threatening me?"

"I've never threatened you."

I pushed the papers around the desk and held up the sheet of paper.

"You thought those were threats?"

"How do they sound to you?"

"I was brainstorming potential titles for your film festival."

"That sounds like a convenient cover story."

"Come on, 'Your Days Are Numbered.' The title for a Doris Day film festival? Considering you know I don't even like the idea, you have to give me credit for a good event name. Can you please put that thing down?"

I lowered the film spool to the desk and rested my hand on it. The pressure I put on my palm offset the weight on my right leg, still holding me up. Despite the pain in my leg, I stood, not willing to trade my position of power.

"Tell me about the letter you wrote."

"What letter?"

"The letter about Doris Day movies being a cancer on the landscape of American Cinema."

"How do *you* know about that?"

"Never mind how. I want to know why you wrote it."

"That letter is the biggest buzzkill ever. I can't believe it's going to haunt me after all these years."

"So you admit you wrote it?" I asked, wishing for a second I had a tape recorder.

"Of course I wrote it. It was my entrance essay for the MFA program at the University."

"Keep talking."

Richard slumped down in the red plastic chair, his shoulders hunched, his spine curved in the way a mother would immediately correct. He kicked his feet out in front of him and pulled on a raffia cord that was tied around his left wrist.

"There were only five spots for the advanced program's admissions, and I wanted to get in. We had to write a letter to an industry professional to prove we were hungry, that we wanted to be there. Show our passion for the art of film and cinematic history, man. I thought it would stand out from my classmates and give me an edge. I didn't want to take the chance of sounding like a kiss-up like everyone else."

"Did you get in?"

"Yeah. But what's the big deal? It was an entrance essay. The only people who saw it were on the deciding committee."

"It that's true, then how did it end up at AFFER?"

"It went to AFFER? Why didn't anybody say anything?" he asked. He sat forward, the fear that had crumpled him now replaced with an interested expression. He was suddenly alert and his eyes danced around the room. "That's fantastic! What did they say?"

"Richard, focus. If you didn't send the letter, who did?"

"Why do you care? So I wrote a letter about destroying Doris Day's movies. It's not like I actually meant it. Wait a minute. You think I meant it? You think I have some kind of Doris Day vendetta?" He jumped up from the chair and it flipped over backwards. "You think this has something to do with the women who were murdered around here, don't you? You think I'm a murderer?"

It was hard to admit to his face that I did. If I really did think he was a murderer I'd done a lot of stupid things in the past couple of hours. Like go to his house, leave him messages on his phone, corner him at the theater....

"Richard, why are you camping out at the theater?"

"Because someone's after me and I don't know where else to hide." He righted the chair and sat back down. His shoulders raised and fell, shuddering unevenly a couple of times. Theatrics or not, the man was clearly shaken up.

"Someone's been leaving notes under my windshield. About not letting you organize the Doris Day film festival. At first I thought it was a joke. I told the other people from the committee we'd end up doing your idea unless one of them could come up with something better. I wrote that note to myself when nobody came up with any other suggestions. 'Tell Madison she's next.' I didn't want us to go down that path of fluff. No disrespect," he added.

"None taken."

"I tossed the notes but they kept coming. *Don't let her get away with it. Make her stop or I will.* It would have been funny if it hadn't started freaking me out. Then the notes started showing up at my house. They were all sort of the same tone. I didn't know how to deal with them. Who did I know who knew where I lived, knew where I worked, who wouldn't come to me directly?"

"Did you tell the cops about this?"

"I'm not about to invite the fuzz into my personal business, if you catch my drift. I know how they work. I tell them about those note and they bust me for possession. The only reason I'm involved at all is that Carrie was killed at the theater. I used up a whole can of air freshener that day."

"Richard, who had access to your entrance essay?"

"My professor and roommate. My parents. My ex-girlfriend. The deciding committee."

"That's a lot of people. Can you give me a list of names?"

"You don't actually think one of them is involved, do you?"

"Maybe, maybe not. But it's too weird that someone sent your letter to AFFER. Whatever your motivation for writing it, somebody out there thought it was a good idea to send it. And they didn't bother taking credit for it, which means maybe they didn't want anyone to know what they were up to."

I encouraged Richard to go home. If nothing else, he needed a shower and a meal other than stale popcorn. He left and I stayed, straightening up the mess from where the stack of film spools had crashed. I told him I had last minute business, not entirely untrue. I wanted to look around a bit. Richard's explanation was sufficient, but I still felt he was hiding something. I walked up the stairs to the balcony to see his makeshift sleeping quarters. And there, in the corner of the projection room, next to a couple of sheets that had been pushed aside in a pile on the floor, lay two small, round, velvet pillows like the ones that had been used to kill Pamela, Sheila, Thelma, and Carrie.

Twenty-Seven

I broke a few traffic laws driving home. While stuck at the third of five red lights I flipped through the recent callers on my cell phone and found Hudson's number. I didn't know where he was, but he needed to know what I had discovered. If he was on the run, not sure what was going on here, then maybe what I'd learned would make him come back and look less guilty.

He didn't answer after four rings. I hung up and called again in case he was screening. When he didn't pick up on the second call I left a message.

"Hudson, it's Madison. I found something that might matter. Call me back." I flipped the phone shut and tossed it in the cup holder. At the last red light I dialed him a third time. Call waiting beeped while it was ringing. I punched the button to take the call without looking at the display.

"Hello?"

"Night? What are you trying to do?" It was Tex.

"I can't talk right now, I'm waiting for an important call."

"From Hudson? I warned you to stay out of this." Despite his accuracy, I bristled at his tone.

"Why do you think I'm waiting for a call from Hudson?" I asked.

"Because his cell phone is sitting on my desk and you just blew it up with a bunch of calls. You want to tell me what's so important?"

"Why do you have his cell phone?"

"It turned up at the theater after Carrie Coburn's murder."

"You never told me that."

"I don't have to tell you that," he said. "It's part of the investigation."

"How's that?"

"Remember that text message you got telling you to go to the theater? The one you didn't get because you were busy being mad at me?" he asked.

I didn't like where he was going. "Yes?"

"You didn't think we forgot about that, did you?"

I didn't answer, but my hand started to shake because where he was going had just gotten worse.

"We got the phone company to pull the records. That text message came from his phone."

My cell phone fell to the floor mat of the explorer. I bent down and fished around for it and put it on speaker.

"Night? Are you there? Night? *Night!*"

"I'm here."

"Let me ask you a question. Did Hudson have access to the trunk of your car?"

I closed my eyes and took the first of several deep breaths. I was hyperventilating. I needed Tex to spell it out.

"He did, didn't he? C'mon, Night, I know you're not stupid. Why is it so hard for you to see that Hudson James is trying to kill you?"

After I hung up on Tex, I pulled into the driveway and swung around the parking lot. I backed into my space, no longer worried about avoiding damages to the rental car.

The building was dark. I wanted to go inside, to shower for an hour and crawl under pink four-hundred thread count sheets trimmed with daisies and eyelet, to fall asleep to the innocent nuance of a Doris Day movie, but life wasn't that simple anymore. Until five minutes ago I had been sure—beyond the shadow of a doubt—that Hudson was innocent. Yet what Tex had just said scared me. The idea that I'd spent last night with Hudson in a vacant apartment, feeling safe just because he was with me, shook me up. I wasn't that naive, I wasn't that trusting. Not anymore.

I was cautious as I entered the building, tension mounting from deep within me, like bubbles of boiling tomato sauce that creep up from the bottom of a vat of marinara. I hesitated outside my apartment. It was silent. I inserted the key in the lock, telling myself I'd come home alone a thousand times and aside from once, no one had ever been waiting for me on the other side. Had it been better to be in the dark about how easy it would be to get to me?

I turned the key and pushed the door open. There was a crash from the bedroom. I didn't hesitate. I pulled the door shut behind me and ran as fast as my knee would allow down the back staircase, over worn blue carpeting, to the parking lot. I would have welcomed the sight of the tailgaters in the lot next to mine, but I was alone.

I pulled out of the lot with a screech of wheels and the near-miss of an oncoming sedan. The driver laid on his horn. I spun the SUV in a dangerously tight left turn onto Gaston and hit the gas, eager to put distance between me and the only place that felt like home. Within seconds, red and blue lights pierced my rearview mirror.

I continued driving until I got to the parking lot that led into Lakewood Plaza, where other cars and other people created the illusion of safety in numbers. The cop pulled into the space next to me. I didn't recognize him.

"License and registration, ma'am," he said.

I was unaccustomed to being pulled over for minor traffic violations, but that wasn't the least of what was bothering me.

"Officer, I live back there. I'm sorry for speeding but I wanted to get away."

"Don't we all? License and registration."

My hands clamped down on my wallet and I nervously pulled out my library card and Visa before landing on my license. I held them out the window to the young man. He took it without a word.

"Officer, you don't understand," I started.

"Registration?" he prompted.

I stared at the glove box for a couple of seconds, wondering if I needed a key or not to open it. I yanked on the handle, but it didn't move. I turned off the ignition and tried the key. The glove box popped open and a flood of AAA maps fell to the floor.

"I'm sorry, it's a rental and I don't know how it works."

"You should always be familiar with your vehicle, ma'am," he instructed, still holding a penlight over my license, staring at the information on the small plastic card.

"Is this really you?" he asked.

"Of course it's me. Why would I have a fake license?"

"Wait here."

Before I could dig out the registration, he walked away from the truck. I put the key back into the ignition, rolled the window up, and cranked the air conditioning. I turned to watch the officer. He opened the door to access his radio and held the small mouthpiece in front of his face. A curly cord connected the small black box to his car. I couldn't hear what he said. He stared down the street in the direction from where I'd driven. He never once turned back to face me.

After several minutes he sat in his car and pulled the door shut. His head was bent down. I imagined him writing me up for some traffic violation I'd committed while getting away. It occurred to me if I backed the car up and fled while he was giving me a ticket, he'd be forced to follow me, and maybe even take me into the station. Surely that would provide some kind of escape from the situation I found myself in now, wouldn't it? But if I was taken away, then there would be no one to check on Rocky.

Rocky. In my apartment. With Mortiboy.

Crap. Double crap.

I knew who had caused that crash. I had to get home.

I used the driver's remote to roll down the passenger side window. "Officer, are you almost done? I have to get home."

"I thought you were trying to get away?" he asked without looking up. They must teach a class on sarcasm at the academy.

"I think I made a mistake."

"We're not going to take any chances. I'll follow you back to the apartment and go inside with you. If there's a threat, I'll take care of it."

And if Hudson's there, he won't have a chance, I thought, realizing why the young officer had stared so intently at my license. He'd called Tex. He'd been given instructions to see me home. For all I knew, the cops were already at my building.

The young cop returned to my window and handed my identification back. "Let's go."

I drove home at a steady thirty-five miles an hour, adhering to every traffic law I remembered. The cop followed too closely for me to back into the space and I ended up parking slightly crooked. My neighbor would have a hard time getting her car into her space if I didn't fix that when we finished.

We walked to the back door and up the stairs. I turned the key in the lock, not sure what I'd find. The officer was on my heels, close enough that he'd see everything I saw the second the door was open. I leaned in and took a half-step, blocking his path, feeling around for the atomic lamp. The lamp wasn't there. I took a few more steps in, my eyes adjusting to the darkness. The cop clicked his penlight and flashed it around the room.

"Damn," he said.

"What?"

"Ma'am, I think you've been robbed."

Twenty-Eight

I took a few steps into the room and tripped over something. Something that hadn't been there when I left. My hands flailed through the air to break my fall. They landed on the arm of the sofa. My balance lost, I fell forward, head first into a cushion.

"Nice view. I've never been a fan of polyester knit until now," said Tex from behind me.

I used my hands to turn myself over and push myself back up until I was standing again.

"Where'd you come from?"

"I was in the neighborhood," he answered. "Are you going to turn on the lights?"

"The light isn't where it used to be. Flip the switch in the kitchen." My eyes adjusted to the darkness and I saw my pink atomic floor lamp laying on the floor. I kicked it under the sofa, out of the way.

The younger cop rounded the corner. "What the—shit."

Tex ran to the kitchen and hit the light switch. The young officer leaned against the counter, balanced on one foot. There was a smushed pile of dog poo on the floor. I handed the officer a roll of paper towels.

"Night, where's your dog?" Tex asked.

"Rocky?" I called out. "Rocky?"

"Wait here," commanded Tex. He moved into the hallway and flipped on the light. I followed him despite his instructions. The bedroom was torn apart, the closet open, clothes in a pile on the floor. "Is this normal?"

"No, it's not normal. I don't keep my house like this."

"So what do you think happened here?"

"I don't know."

I looked around the bedroom. The lamp on the nightstand was on the floor, the bulb shattered. The comforter was pulled off the bed. A piece of caramel colored fur peeked out from under the bed.

It twitched.

I stooped down and lifted the comforter. Rocky sat curled in a ball, staring at me with big, sorrowful eyes. There was no graceful way for me to get him out, but I didn't care. I leaned forward, with my butt in the air, and reached for his front paw. He resisted my efforts at first, but I won, pulling him forward until I could reach around his body and hold him close to me. There was a scratch on his face by his nose and I suspected I knew the bully who had swiped at him, even though there was no sign of the black cat.

Rocky cowered in my arms. He was as scared now as when I took him to the groomers.

Tex hadn't said a word while I was down on all fours. He stood in front of me stroking Rocky's head. "Scared little fella, isn't he?"

"Rocky: four, lamps: zero."

The young officer walked out of the kitchen, his shoe in a clear plastic bag in his hand. He fiddled around with the locks on my front door. "Lieutenant? There's no sign of a forced entry on this door."

Tex joined him by the door and conducted the same fiddling. I held Rocky close, his racing heart beat pounding against my own.

"Lieutenant, I don't think this was a break-in," I said.

"You're not going to tell me he did this, are you?" Tex asked, petting Rocky.

Despite my urgent need to believe in Hudson's innocence, it was getting harder to refute the facts.

"I'm not going to tell you he did this," I confirmed. "Let's move into the living room. We need to talk."

I tidied up a bit while Tex spoke to the young officer. Rocky sat in his crate. Not because I was punishing him, but because I didn't want him to be underfoot while I righted lamps, folded blankets, and rehung most of my wardrobe. There was a chance that indeed he'd had a hand in the mess, or rather a paw, but I couldn't see him accomplishing this kind of an interior redesign on his own. And still, I wanted to find Mortiboy. His absence troubled me more than I wanted to admit.

Tex saw the other officer to the door and closed it behind him. When he returned to the living room I gestured toward the sofa. "I can offer you a glass of white wine or tap water. It's grocery time. You want anything?"

"I want to know what you want to tell me. You're stalling."

"Fine. Have a seat."

He sat down on the end of the sofa. I could have sat next to him but instead I took the green chair that faced him, with the low boomerang coffee table between us. I balanced on the edge of the cushion, leaning forward, not allowing myself to get comfortable. That had been my mistake too many times before.

"Remember when you told me to stay out of this and let you do your job?" I asked.

"Yes."

"I didn't completely follow your instructions."

I waited for him to either reprimand me or explode. He did neither. He leaned against the back of the sofa and rested his left arm on the silver metal frame. His light brown hair was slicked back today, away from his face. He was generally rumpled, his white button down collar shirt creased from the time he'd spent sitting in his Jeep, I guessed, his faded jeans marked with dirt along the hems. Light gleamed off of the face of his Swiss army watch, flashing in my eyes, causing me to squint.

"And?" he prompted.

"And I have new evidence."

"So do I."

"What's yours?" I asked.

He was silent.

"Oh, right, ladies first and all that."

More silence. His light eyes bore into me like frozen blue Otter Pops, and gave me the chills.

"You're not going to lecture me?"

"I want to know what you know."

"Hudson was here. A couple of nights ago. He was waiting for me inside the apartment after you dropped me off. He didn't attack me, if that's what you're thinking, but he needed a place to stay."

The look on Tex's face told me he wasn't just listening as a cop.

"I have a vacancy in the building and I let him stay in the empty apartment." I didn't tell him how I'd spent the night in the apartment with him or the nature of our conversation. It felt too personal, but it also felt like a stupid thing to have done.

"He didn't return the keys, did he?" Tex asked.

"No, he didn't." Silence draped over us like a throw blanket on a dying fire.

"Night, are you okay?"

I snapped my head up. "I'm fine."

"Your leg is bouncing like it's been hooked up to a generator."

I looked at my leg, hammering a rhythm against the floor. I couldn't stop it if I tried. "There's more."

He leaned forward.

"Richard Goode. You have to talk to him."

Tex sat very still, watching me, nodding his head. He was taking me seriously.

Surprised, I kept talking. "He's involved, but I don't know how much or why. He's anti Doris Day, and even you can't deny how frequently Doris Day keeps popping up in the middle of your investigation."

He didn't react.

"Anyway, Richard wrote a threatening letter to a film rental company several years ago, an aggressive letter telling them to destroy their Doris Day movies. At first AFFER thought it was a joke, until someone broke into their warehouse, assaulted a security guard, and stole a bunch of movies. There was sabotage, I don't know the details, but a lot of their inventory was ruined."

"AFFER?" he asked.

"American Film Rentals. Listen, are you hearing me? This is a pretty strong connection. Don't you want to write some of this down?"

"I have a pretty powerful memory," he said. "Keep going."

The more I spoke, the sillier I felt, and if it wasn't for the pieces of the puzzle I'd put together that afternoon, or for the pillows I'd seen in Richard's makeshift sleeping quarters, I would have stopped talking altogether.

"Night, where did the pillows in your trunk come from?"

"An estate sale."

"When?"

"About a month ago."

Tex's face was unreadable, but I could tell he was paying close attention. I didn't know what it all meant myself, but with what he knew that he wasn't telling me, maybe pieced together with what I had found out for myself, the key to unlocking this thing might appear and the idea of ending the nightmare might exist.

"Tex, the thing is, Richard acted scared. I think he's involved more, but I don't know how."

Tex leaned back against the sofa cushions. "We talked to Richard. He's cooperating with us. But what I don't get is where Hudson comes into this? What's their connection?" Tex asked.

"What connection?"

"Between Richard and Hudson. That's what you're giving me, isn't it? The goods on Hudson James."

"You're not listening to me! I'm telling you about Richard! I went upstairs to the balcony of the Mummy after he left and I found a couple of those velvet pillows you saw from my trunk. And he told me, the day after Carrie Coburn was murdered, that he had been in my trunk without me knowing. Those same pillows are your murder weapon in four different homicides. Aren't you going to check it out?"

"I checked out Richard Goode myself. Aside from the facts that he doesn't like your favorite actress and he's a recreational pot smoker, he's clean." He leaned forward and rubbed his palms over the front of his faded blue jeans.

"No, you aren't getting it. Richard has a zillion scripts, he's acting! He even told me once he acted in college, and that's when the letter was sent, and even if he says he didn't send it, there was the deciding committee who had access to it and one of them might have been working with him. This has to do with cinematic connections, not Hudson!"

"Night, forget it. Richard Goode came to us and gave us those names. We already checked them out. There's no motive.

The sci-fi expert lives in Hollywood. The documentarian was a—"

"Documentary filmmaker," I corrected.

"What?"

"It's 'Documentary filmmaker', not 'documentarian'."

"Whatever. He was a freakin' astronaut. And the pop culture expert wrote her dissertation on Doris Day. Besides, Richard Goode was the one who found Hudson's phone outside of the theater. I thought you were going to give me evidence that they were working together but you just proved to me that Goode's on our side."

"How can you be so sure?" I asked.

"How can you not be?" he asked. "Hudson James skipped town. He's been around every time a dead body that matches this profile has turned up—from twenty years ago until today. Richard Good was eight years old when the first murder happened. Hudson's got no alibi, and we have hard evidence connecting him to every one of the victims. Including you, though somehow despite my caution you continue to put yourself directly in his path."

"You're missing something, Tex. I don't know what it is, but I can feel it."

"Listen, Night, I didn't want to tell you this but you're going to see it in the newspaper tomorrow morning. We got a warrant and searched Hudson's house. Those round velvet pillows you're so fond of? We found a couple of them on his sofa."

"His sofa is orange tweed—" I started but Tex put his hand out to silence me.

"We opened them up. They've been re-upholstered."

Twenty-Nine

The article came out at the worst possible time. *Arrest Warrant Issued for the Pillow Stalker* read the title. Numbness shot through my arms and my legs, and my silk pajamas were suddenly not enough to keep the chill at bay. I sat in my kitchen, drinking a cup of coffee, flipping through the morning newspaper. I wanted to shut it, to crumple it up, or use it to line Rocky's cage, but I had to face the reality of what Tex had been telling me all along. I had to force myself to read the article, to see in print what concrete evidence had led to this moment in time.

The journalist had done his research, digging up much of what had been written about Sheila Murphy's murder two decades earlier. To be fair, he printed Hudson's story of picking up the young woman, offering his shirt and a ride to her apartment. He also printed the statements of the neighbors who identified Hudson's truck, the dry cleaning label that identified his shirt, and all of the other details that Hudson had explained to me personally. None of that was a surprise. But when I continued to read, it became clear that the journalist had camped out in front of Hudson's house in order to get this story. Was he the one who had attacked me? It seemed unlikely.

He had watched the handyman's comings and goings, watched him throw a packed bag into the back of his truck and set a cat carrier on the passenger seat. He knew Hudson was planning to leave town. He went through his trash, looked into his windows, and cooperated with the cops when it came time to tell what he'd seen.

It sickened me, this invasion of Hudson's privacy, yet if he was a killer who had been living with his freedom for the past twenty years, then that privacy was undeserved. I thought about the people I watched on crime TV, people who have been living in the open for decades before DNA evidence caught up to them. People who thought they got away with murder. Is that what Hudson had done? It certainly was what the article implied, and it would be a hard detail for people to ignore a second time around.

Richard's name had been kept out of the article, but I recognized his actions as that of the confidential source. He'd discovered a cell phone on the edge of the Mummy property and thought nothing of it at first. It sat in the lost and found until the battery wore low, beeping a caution, and alerting him to its presence. It was then he realized it might be a clue and turned it over to the cops.

I shut the paper. It would still be here when I returned from swimming. At last, they'd reopened Crestwood, letting me get in my much needed morning workout. I could clear my head in the water. I could let the rest of the world seep away, if only for an hour, and be at peace. It was the only place for me to take the edge off.

I stuffed my towel, cap, and goggles into a nylon shoulder bag, pulled on a bathing suit and zipped into a terrycloth dress. Rocky had been nervous all last night and this morning and I wasn't about to leave him alone again. I held him close to me and walked into the kitchen to find a

Milk Bone biscuit. I opened and shut three drawers before I found them. When I shut the last one, I heard a yelp.

I looked at Rocky. He looked at me. The sound that I'd heard wasn't a sound he normally made.

I opened the last drawer again and shut it. Another yelp.

I set Rocky on the floor and armed myself with a wooden mallet, the kind you use to pound chicken. I stood as far away as possible and maneuvered a black plastic two-pronged spaghetti fork around the pink ceramic knob of the cabinet, easing it open. I looked inside. An angry black cat sat at the very back corner of the cabinet, wedged between my silver colander and a large white serving dish that only came out for Thanksgiving.

"Mortiboy!" I said, dropping my utensil weapons. I reached in for him. He swiped at me and left four small punctures on my left hand. I put on oven mitts and tried again, this time pulling him out by the scruff of his neck. As soon as he saw sunlight he wriggled free from my grip, dropped to the floor, and shot like a cannon into the bedroom. Rocky took off after him, as though they were playing.

I followed them. Rocky stood outside of my closet. Mortiboy clung by his nails to a turquoise and white tennis outfit that I'd rescued from Thelma Johnson's closet the day I went by myself to her house. There was a series of holes in the polyester, indicating that this wasn't the first time the outfit had been climbed.

I pulled Mortiboy off the now ruined outfit. He wriggled around but this time I was prepared. I carried him into the bathroom, dropped him on the carpet and shut the door behind me. Yowls of protest followed me into the hallway.

I went back into the bedroom and looked around. How had I missed that? The fact that the clothes in piles on the floor were all by the closet. That they had small puncture marks through them, the size of cat's claws. That the top

214

shelf of my closet, normally filled with tidy stacks of round hat boxes, was in disarray, with my belongings pushed aside at odd angles, revealing the faded pink and white floral wallpaper I'd never replaced when I first moved in? I'd been right the first time. Mortiboy was the guilty party who had trashed my apartment, not Hudson, as Tex had implied. That's what I got for leaving the two animals unattended.

I'd ignored the details, the rational explanation. I violated Hudson's confidence. I gave Tex fuel for his fire of tracking down Hudson and left him with no doubt that my former contractor was a killer. I didn't know which was worse—that I'd allowed myself to think Hudson was a killer or that after all of my declarations of his innocence, I'd helped the cops go after him.

It was too wild of a theory not to test. I opened the bathroom door and let Mortiboy out. He ventured into the hallway, hissed and swatted at Rocky who had trotted his direction, and took off into the bedroom. Up the polyester tennis outfit, onto the ledge where my hatboxes sat, squeezed behind a Styrofoam head that held an old Halloween wig. The top box tipped precariously, then spilled. A red felt beanie fell to the floor, landing on top of the pile of clothes that had been torn from the hangers. It looked like a cherry planted on top of an ice cream sundae. All this mess at the paws of an angry cat.

I slid the closet door shut. If Mortiboy was capable of this much damage, he needed to be contained. Besides, he'd already shown a preference for dark spaces.

"Come on, Rocky, leave the cat alone. Let's go to the pool."

Rocky led the way to the white Explorer and hopped up the step on the outside, onto the floorboards and then into the driver's seat. He stepped over the center console to the passenger side and stood on his hind legs, front paws on the window. My neighbors stacked paint cans into the back of a pickup truck. They smiled at Rocky's interest.

I drove to Crestwood, wondering if there would be signs of the yellow crime scene tape lingering by the parking lot. My car should be cleared any day now, and life could start getting back to normal, if there was such a thing. Only, it couldn't. Because despite what Tex had told me, and what I'd told him, and what it seemed was the reality of the situation, my life would never be normal again.

Somewhere along the way my hard shell had broken, and I had become involved with two very different men. Hudson's story, his alienation from many of the people who lived in Dallas and always thought of him as guilty, had followed him around for the past twenty years, and I saw what that had done to him. But Tex—Tex had a hard exterior like mine, and I felt his cracking, too. His flirtatious nature, his sarcasm, his jokes to the other officers showcased a one-dimensional man. But after spending time with him, I knew that was far from accurate.

Tex believed Hudson was guilty. But that was based on so many things that could have been misinterpreted. Twenty years ago Hudson had avoided being convicted for the murder of Sheila Murphy. This time he might not be so lucky. And it was entirely possible, though I wasn't willing to admit it to myself, that he was involved.

It was all too much. Too much danger, terror, and murder for me to deal with. I needed a release. Even the idea of work held no interest for me. It was as if my life was stuck on a moment in time, like I was a glob of fruit suspended in the middle of Jell-O.

I turned the white Explorer onto the winding gravel driveway that led to the pool. Trees, plus the occasional large rock, lined each side of the road, keeping it mostly secluded from the street. The yellow tape was gone. So was my car. But a few familiar vehicles were parked in their usual spots. I wasn't the only slave to routine around here. It would be nice to see the whole gang again. Even old Mr. Popov.

Rocky seemed as happy to be back at Crestwood as I was. I knotted his leash around the metal handrail at the end of a small set of bleachers, where I could keep an eye on him between laps. He turned around twice, figuring out his boundaries. I ducked into the locker room and put my clothes in one of the top lockers, then carried my cap and goggles to the edge of the pool. Alice and Jessica sat on the deck, tucking their hair under thick rubber caps. Jessica's buttoned under her chin. I waved to the two of them and dug a kickboard out of the metal bin that held the pool supplies.

"Madison! I wasn't sure we were going to see you today," called Alice.

"Why's that?"

"After what happened at the swim club, nobody would blame you if you took a couple of days off. Sixty degree water! That's crazy!"

I shrugged. "I'm fine now. It was probably the best thing for my knee," I said and pointed to the swollen joint. "Like taking an ice bath."

"You're lucky you're in such good shape. That kind of shock to your system could have been very bad. I don't think I would have recovered so quickly at my age," she said.

Jessica joined in. "None of us would have. In a way, it's a blessing it was you." She placed a frail hand on my upper arm. "Take it easy today, dear," she said. "We're all glad to be back, but it feels different now that Pamela is gone."

I nodded but didn't say a word. I was happy to be back at the pool, happy to have an outlet for my mind and my body, but she was right. I didn't want to think about what had happened the last time we were all here. I still couldn't accept how much my life had changed in a matter of days.

I leaned over and ran my fingertips through the water. It was the right temperature. After tucking my short hair under the swim cap and pulling on my goggles, I eased myself into the shallow end and pushed off. Lap after lap I swam. By the seventh lap I was back in my zone.

I used to think as long as I was in a pool, I was safe, but after the cold water at the swim club, that was no longer true. Yet it felt good to be in a secluded tank of chlorinated water, without Tex, without Hudson, without Doris Day movies and angry film students. My worries dissolved into the bubbles around me and I kept going. As long as I didn't stop, I was fine.

My mind sifted through bits of information and I realized I'd never asked Tex about his personal involvement with Sheila Murphy. It would be a hard subject to bring up, and it wasn't really my place to do so. But they'd been at that costume party together.

There must be something that he knew, something that he wasn't sharing, that would shed light on what had happened to her later that night. I understood that there were details I'd never know, not from an investigation standpoint, but it was possible that, outside of his statement, he'd never had an opportunity to vent. And by keeping it all bottled up inside of him, he'd created an emotional prison he might never escape.

I stopped by the end of the pool and rested against the blue tiles. Other swimmers occupied the pool, regulars and a couple of new ones. Whether it was the curiosity of the murder or the incident at the swim club, I didn't know, but it had created a cross-pollination of the lap swimming public. I liked it better when it was just the people I knew. Our little family.

"You make it look so easy, Madison," said Alice. She sat on the pool deck dangling her ankles in the water. Even though she was into her eighties, as she kicked her heels against the tiles in a childlike manner, with her hair tucked away under a swim cap, I could see a glimpse of the younger woman she once had been.

"Alice, I hope when I'm your age I'm still swimming laps," I replied. "You're a smart lady to keep this up."

"Ah, yes, but that's just me clinging to a bit of my youth. I'm an old lady now but the pool does make me feel younger."

"You're not that old," I interjected.

"Madison, please. I'm eighty-four. My best years are behind me. They were good years, and I wouldn't trade them for anything. I just wish my memory was as good as it once was so I could cherish all of the experiences I had."

I put a wet hand on top of hers. "You keep telling me you're going to share those stories someday." I patted her hand.

"That's right, I will." She leaned down close to me. "And I'll start with the ones from the time Thelma Johnson and I worked together on a Doris Day movie right here in Dallas."

"Alice! All these years we've been swimming together and you never once told me about that?" My mind started to race. "When was this? Which movie?" I hoisted myself out of the pool and landed on the deck with a splat.

"Are you gals swimming or gossiping?" asked Andy. "Cause if I'm taking you to the breakfast buffet I want to get there before the eggs get overcooked." He zipped up the front of his jogging suit and walked up behind Alice.

"Andy, leave us alone. I was just about to tell Madison about the time I met Doris Day," Alice said.

"There's too much talk about her these days. You keep your mouth shut about that, Alice, or that crazy killer who's obsessed with her might come after you. Now get dressed and let's get some food"

"What's this about breakfast?" I asked.

Alice pulled her ankles out of the water and spun herself around. "He's so nice, that Andy. Do you know he came over to my house yesterday and worked in the garden with me? Poor thing got all scratched up from the rose bushes. I offered to take him to breakfast to thank him but he insisted it would be his treat."

"How long are you going to make him wait?" I joked.

"I can always swim tomorrow. Today, I'll take the morning off and enjoy a breakfast buffet with a nice man who seems to enjoy my company." She smiled and leaned back down toward me. "Madison, don't spend all of your free time alone in the pool. Sure, the water can make you feel good about yourself, but sometimes a man can do that, too." She winked at me and walked to the locker room.

Not half a minute later I heard her scream.

Thirty

"Alice! Alice!" I yelled, pulling myself out of the water as quickly as I could. Andy and Jessica and a few of the others beat me to the locker room. Rocky yipped at the commotion from the sidelines. A scattering of strangers stood about on the deck, unsure what to make of the chaos at their new swimming venue.

When I entered the locker room I found Alice sitting on a wooden bench in the middle of the room. She was white. Water from her wet ankles had created a small puddle beneath her. Jessica sat beside her, with an arm around her petite frame, and Andy stood in front of her, clutching a scrap of torn paper.

"That's it. We're not going to breakfast, we're getting you out of Dallas."

"What? What is it?" I asked the sea of faces.

Jessica snatched the paper out of Andy's fingers and pushed it toward me. It said: *YOU'RE NEXT.*

"Where did this come from?" I asked no one in particular.

"It was on my tote bag, sitting right on top of my towel. Is it from the killer? Is this what happened to Pamela?"

"It doesn't make any sense," I said half-to myself.

"It makes a lot of sense if you ask me," said Andy.

221

"How?"

"She's part of the Doris Day connection all over the news. She just said so. The serial killer is out to get women who look like Doris Day and she fits the bill."

I knelt down in front of Alice who was still shaken up. "Alice, you need to give this to the cops and tell them about your connection to Doris Day. Can you do that if I make the call?"

"The hell she has to do that. What Alice has to do is to get out of here before your boyfriend can come back and do her in. I saw him snooping around here this morning. For all I know he's been hiding by the pool, waiting for us to come back."

"My boyfriend? What boyfriend?" I asked.

"The one in the beat up truck. It's not the first time I saw him hanging around here either. He's at the heart of this. I'm getting Alice out of town now."

He leaned down and put an arm around her and gently helped her stand up. Her towel was loosely draped over her shoulders and she looked down, not willing to make eye contact.

"I don't think I should just leave, Andy," she said.

"I don't think you should, either, ma'am," said a voice from out front.

I was actually happy to hear it.

"Everybody decent? I'm coming in." Tex walked into the ladies locker room. He didn't look happy. "Everybody clear out of here, but wait out front. I want to talk to Ms. Sweet alone."

"Who called you?" I asked. "Shouldn't Officer Nast be here?"

"I called him," said Andy. "He was here the morning your boyfriend got Pamela. He's the one who's going to catch the bastard."

My eyes shifted back and forth between Andy and Tex.

"Can Madison stay? And Andy?" Alice asked tentatively.

With the slightest of movements, Tex shook his head no.

"Alice, I have to check on Rocky." I turned to face Tex. "I'll be right back."

When I returned to the locker room Andy and Alice were sitting side by side on the wooden bench and Tex was facing them, perched on top of a folding metal chair with a misshapen frame. Andy's arm was still around Alice, comforting her.

"And that's where I found the note, Lieutenant."

"Ms. Sweet, I think I have everything I need."

"I'm taking her out of town for a couple of days," Andy said. "She needs to get away from here. She needs to be safe."

"I think that's okay," said Tex.

Rocky strained against his leash, trying to get closer to his new friend, but I kept him in check. Tex wasn't reacting the way I thought he'd react and I wondered what was going through his head. Whatever it was, it was masked below the kind of poker face that probably won a lot of hands.

"You need to reach her, you call me. Here's my number," the old man rattled off a phone number that Tex jotted down in his notepad. "Alice, let's get that breakfast."

"I think you're forgetting something, Andy," I interjected. "She needs time to change out of her bathing suit and that means the two of you have to go."

I waited in the locker room while Alice showered and dressed. Her yellow cotton blouse and matching skirt were more festive than the mood of the morning. She must have been looking forward to that breakfast. I didn't say anything while she primped but noticed that her hands were shaking as she patted her curls into place.

"Madison, what did Andy mean when he said he saw your boyfriend here?" she asked.

"I don't know, Alice."

"Be careful. Don't let your guard down. I don't want to be next but I don't want you to be next, either." She hugged me tightly and left.

The chlorinated water had dried on my skin. I wasn't in the mood to shower and change at the pool anymore; I wanted to go home. I spun the dial on the padlock that secured my locker and jumped when Tex's voice sounded behind me.

"You decent, Night?"

"What do you want now?" I asked.

He entered the locker room and swept it with a broad gaze. "Why are you standing there?"

"I'm trying to unlock my locker. I want to get my stuff and go home."

"Which one's your locker?"

"The one with my hands on it."

"Night, I'm not kidding. Is that yours?" he pointed to the blue metal door.

"Yes. Watch this and I'll prove it to you." I spun the dial to the left and back to the right, hitting the combination on the first attempt, and popped it open. A small corner of torn white paper fluttered down to the floor.

"Shit." Tex picked the scrap up and measured it against the note Alice had found on top of her towel.

"What?" Even from where I sat I could see that the two edges of paper were a perfect fit.

"Your locker was directly above where the old lady's bag sat. That note wasn't meant for her, Night, it was meant for you."

"Shit."

Tex followed me back to my apartment. I asked him to wait in the parking lot with Rocky while I showered and dressed. He didn't ask me why. It was just a matter of time before he discovered I was watching Hudson's cat, but for the moment I wanted to keep that to myself. If there was one innocent party in all of this, it was Mortiboy. And without me, the black ball of fur had no one to look after him.

It looked like there was no way out of Tex's companionship now, even if I wanted to shake him. And the way things were going, I wasn't so sure that was still the goal.

When I emerged from the back of the apartment building it was in crisp blue jeans that were cuffed to mid-calf, black penny loafers, and a red and white gingham checked cotton shirt. I tied a red and white bandana in my hair to keep my short hair off my face.

Rocky sat on the hood of Tex's Jeep, swatting at the lieutenant's hand. Tex scanned me from head to toe and let off a low whistle. "Even when you're butch you're sexy."

"I'm going to ignore that."

"Let's get out of here. I think I make your neighbors nervous."

I glanced across the parking lot to the Mexicans. They were rearranging paint cans in the bed of their truck, not making eye contact. I blew off the opportunity to make a joke at both Tex's and their expense.

"Let's go to the Metro and get some breakfast. Hop in."

"Rocky can't go into a diner, and I don't feel good about leaving him tied up outside. Hold on," I said and carried the little dog back into the building. Effie agreed to puppy sit while I went about my day.

The scenery, grey buildings and green lawns, blurred past my window as Tex drove us to the diner. Silence carried us from his Jeep to the interior of the diner, to a booth between a couple of high school kids and a family of five. Tex shook his head and gestured toward a more secluded booth along the back wall. The waitress dropped a couple of menus and two plastic tumblers of water on our table. The silence remained until she walked away.

"So Night, I'm only going to ask you this once. Why are you covering for Hudson?"

225

I slapped the plastic menu down on the table. "You're only going to ask me that once? Funny. Because that's the fifth time you've only asked me that once."

"If you'd just work with me instead of against me this could all be over."

"I tried that. Remember? And look what happened. How about you answer some of my questions instead?"

"We've been over this," he said in a low voice.

"I'm not talking about your investigation, which you're not even supposed to be conducting. Why don't you tell me about the Halloween party? What you and Sheila Murphy fought about before she ran off and got herself killed?"

The words popped out of my mouth unedited. Tex's eyes bore holes into me, but I matched his stare with the same intensity. I would not allow him to manipulate me into feeling guilty for asking about that night, not after the way he'd used me to try to catch Hudson.

Abruptly, he stood. The plastic tumbler on the table bounced and water sloshed onto the menu. He strode toward the front door, leaving me alone. I wasn't worried. His code of honor was too great to leave me behind.

The waitress came back to the table. I ordered two cups of coffee and two blue plate specials. Eggs, toast, bacon, sausage, and potatoes. Enough food to distract an angry cop if he returned to the table. Enough to feed a small dog and cat in my apartment if I ended up taking it to go.

The food arrived on the table before Tex came back. I waited for half a minute, letting it cool down while I wondered if it would be rude to start. Hunger dictated the answer. I bit into a piece of bacon then followed it with a forkful of scrambled eggs.

"Damn, Night, you got a hell of an appetite."

I turned around and looked up at him. He snatched a triangle of toast from the small ceramic plate, then slid back onto his side of the booth.

I wasn't sure if his return required words on my part. He speared a sausage link and bit into it, while I nibbled on a second piece of bacon, pinched between my fingers. We finished three quarters of our food in silence. He seemed to have picked up on my theory of us getting along better when we didn't talk. When the waitress came by with our check, he snatched it before I had a chance to reach out.

"What's my share?"

"It's on me."

"No, I'll pay my half. This isn't a date, Tex."

"You think I don't know this isn't a date? It stopped being a date the minute you brought up my ex-girlfriend." He pulled a couple of bills out of a well-worn leather wallet and tucked them under the sugar shaker. "Besides, when we go on a date, it's not going to be to a diner and you're going to wear one of your little cotton numbers."

" 'When'?"

"I don't know when. Soon."

"No, I'm not asking when. I'm questioning your choice of 'when' versus 'if'."

"Oh, it's a when. But there's a couple of things we have to figure out before I get around to asking. I don't like having this thing between us. Let's get out of here. We gotta talk."

"Lieutenant, if you think a greasy meal at a diner is going to make me turn against a friend, then you're mistaken."

"I wasn't talking about you, I was talking about me. It's time I talked to someone outside of the force about what happened with Sheila that night."

Thirty-One

"**G**o to my studio. We can talk there," I instructed. We were close enough that it was a good idea and Tex knew it.

He parked the Jeep behind the storefront. I climbed out and a beam of pain shot through my knee when my feet hit the ground. I stopped for a second, closed my eyes, and fought to get the pulsating intervals under control before I continued moving. Tex headed to the building without me. When he reached the back door I stood straight up and followed. Even though he knew about my torn ACL, I fought the pain. It had become a matter of pride to hide my injury from the lieutenant even though we both knew it had happened.

I unlocked the doors and we went inside and sat down on a long, low turquoise and lime green chenille sofa that was framed in silver chrome. It was nine feet long and I was able to put my leg up on the cushions and face Tex without coming close to touching him. I waited. He wanted to talk and he knew I wanted to listen. It was his responsibility to start.

"I've been over that night so many times I don't know where to begin. I'm missing something, I know that much. But it doesn't make sense."

He rubbed his thumb and index finger along his forehead just below the front of his hair. He'd taken to wearing the cowboy hat while driving his Jeep and his hand knocked the brim back, like James Dean in a thousand promotional photographs. The only things missing were the reed of straw between his teeth and the devil-may-care attitude.

"Who knows? You might see what I'm missing."

His words surprised me. With that one sentence, he gave me respect. He was no longer a cop looking out for a potential victim, and whether or not I wanted to see it that way, that was the relationship we had. But the way he related to me now, sitting in my studio, thinking back over a night that had set into motion a chain of events that couldn't have been, still couldn't be predicted, he was letting me into his thought process, his memories. He was hoping I'd see things more clearly than he did. He was treating me like an equal.

"I'll try, but I can't help if you don't start."

"Okay. We were kids. I was in the academy. She and I'd been dating for a couple of months."

"Exclusively?" I asked, instantly regretting the interjection.

He looked up and focused his eyes on me for a moment. "Yes."

I nodded. "Sorry. Keep going."

"We went to a costume party at a house by the lake. A couple of friends of hers threw the party and wanted people to come as their favorite movie couple. She wanted to go as Rock Hudson and Doris Day. I guess her mom was an extra in a Doris Day movie once and had a lot of clothes that fit the bill. Sheila ransacked the closet and put together an outfit. All I had to do was put some black stuff in my hair and wear a suit and skinny tie and we were set. I picked her up at her mom's house but she was in a bad mood when we left. She said she and her mom fought about the costume, about her taking things from her mom's closet without asking. When we got to the party Sheila went straight for the bar."

"I'm sorry to interrupt again, but did you know Thelma Johnson? Did they have a good relationship?"

"I met her a few times but I was a twenty-year old kid. I wasn't into hanging out with parents. Sheila was a bit of a wild child, so her mom liked the idea of her dating me, you know, since I was in the academy. Thought she was safer that way."

I didn't comment on the elephant in the room, the fact that it was on his watch that she was murdered.

"So she hit the bottle pretty hard as soon as we got to the party. I tried to tell her to slow down and she got pissed. She told me she didn't need another parent. She started flirting with the other guys, which made it an awkward scene since everyone there was half of a couple. I didn't want to stick around and be humiliated but I didn't want to leave her there in that condition. She wasn't making good decisions. The last time I saw her we fought on the front porch of the house. She said we were through. She went out back with another guy, someone I'd never met. That's it. That's the last time I saw her alive."

"You left?"

"Some of the guys started up a poker game and I stuck around for awhile. It wouldn't have been a good idea for me to get in a car and drive. Half of me thought it would blow over, like it always did. We had a volatile relationship. Heat. Fire. Passion." He shrugged. "When you're young that seems like all you need." He stared into his hands.

I didn't say anything. I watched him press his right thumb into the center of his left hand. He cupped his hand around the thumb, closing in on it. It was like he was trying to make something fit, to find a pressure point that would erase the memories that spilled out of him. The clarity with which he spoke defined how often he'd been over this same memory himself. Just like Hudson. Tex was fighting against a different emotional jail cell. I'd do what I could to help him break free, but again I felt pulled in two directions.

"Go back to when you drove her to the party. She must have said something about the fight between her and her mom?"

"They're women. They fought about clothes."

"I resent that."

"If you had a daughter who went into your closet and took some of your clothes for a costume party, how would that make you feel?"

"Hard to say. I don't know what it would be like to have to relate to a daughter."

We stared at each other, now both aware of the holes in each other's lives. I broke the silence.

"I like to think that someone would ask first whether they're related or not. Just seems polite. I also like to think a fight over borrowed clothes might be a fight over something bigger than borrowed clothes, because that seems a little petty."

"Sheila was mad at her mom because of the man she was dating. Sheila's dad had passed away when she was thirteen. She didn't have a father figure, and as soon as she could, she sought out male attention. Her mom started dating when Sheila started dating and I don't think that was a great thing for either one of them."

"Did she say anything specific about the fight? She must have."

"When she came downstairs, her mom almost passed out. She asked Sheila where she got the outfit. Sheila said it came from her wardrobe. Thelma grabbed her wrist and dragged her into the next room, the one with the green and blue floral wallpaper. I think she didn't want me to hear what she said."

"Did you?"

"Stupid stuff. Lecturing a child. She said she had something valuable in her wardrobe and she couldn't take a chance—" Tex's answer was cut off by his pager buzzing from his hip. He unclipped it and looked at the small display, then glanced at the yellow donut phone on my desk.

"Use it if you need to. It works," I offered.

"I'm not sure I can conduct police business on that phone."

"Do what you have to do."

He picked up the top half of the circle that made up the donut and dialed the number from his pager.

"Allen. You paged?" He paused for a moment. "I'm in the neighborhood. Be right there."

He put the phone back on the cradle and walked out of the room. I wasn't sure if he expected me to follow or not. A few seconds later he came back to the door.

"You coming?"

"Where are we going?"

"Thelma Johnson's house. There's been a break-in."

Thelma Johnson's neighbors were aware of the break-in long before Tex and I arrived on the scene. Three cop cars with lights in full swing were parked in front. Two along the sidewalk and one in the driveway. Kids and parents stood in their front lawns at a couple of neighboring houses, watching the action with interest. I had to admit, I was interested, too. Tex's story was incomplete, but something was nagging at the back of my mind. I just wasn't sure what it was.

Tex hopped out of his Jeep and approached the front door where the uniformed officers stood in a group. One of the cops was Officer Nast.

I hesitated. I didn't know my place here, arriving in Tex's car, whether I was a trophy or a decoy. Could be I was neither. The suspicious nature of my thoughts indicated I might want to learn a thing or two about how normal people relate to each other when this was all over.

"Night! Get over here," Tex called to me. His invitation, née command, clarified a few things. I walked up to the group of cops.

"Hi officers," I said, trying to be friendly. "Nice to see you again."

"It's not a party, Night. Listen," Tex shoved the cowboy hat back on his head. "When's the last time you were here?"

I waited a couple of seconds before answering, not sure if he expected me to lie. Too much was at stake for that.

"A couple of days ago."

"How did you get in?" asked Officer Nast.

"I found a spare set of keys in the back under the Dracaena tree in the blue pot."

"You still have them?" Tex asked.

"No. I left them here the day I ran out."

"So the place has been unlocked for days? Good job," said Officer Nast. Her attitude toward me had eroded since our first meeting.

"Listen," I said, taking a half a step forward and positioning myself directly in front of her. "I thought I was here legitimately, conducting my business. It's while I was here that I discovered someone was hiding in the attic. I fled because I was instructed to flee by your superior, Lieutenant Allen. If the Dallas Police Department was aware that someone was here, then the Dallas Police Department should have followed up with that and made sure the perpetrator was found. That is not my fault. As far as I can tell, you're the officer in charge of this investigation, and if you intend to imply that I somehow interrupted the rather sloppy job that you're conducting, then I'll be sure to clarify that when I speak to your police chief."

"Nice little spitfire you got yourself, Lieutenant," she said, and stepped away from the group.

The men stood around, looking at their shoes and their watches and anything but me and Tex, both collectively and individually. Before I had a chance to consider if an apology was in order, Tex put a hand on the back of my elbow and propelled me away from the group.

"Nice scene."

"I'm sorry. I was out of line. But I told you already that I don't intend to be made a fool of by you and whatever it is you want people to think about us."

"So you're allowing for there to be an Us. That's progress."

"Lieutenant!"

"Seriously, that was great. Nobody's ever stood up to Nasty like that. The uniform scares a lot of people into behaving. I didn't know you had that in you."

"Why am I here?" I asked.

"I want you inside."

I raised an eyebrow.

"Like you said, you were one of the last people here. You went over the house with that decorator's eye of yours. You're probably better than a lot of my men at figuring out if anything looks out of place, if anything's been taken."

"You really want my help?"

"I might as well make full use of you as long as you're in a cooperating kind of mood."

I was just as curious as Tex to get inside and see what had been taken from Thelma Johnson's estate. I'd cleaned out as much as I was capable of doing on my previous trip, but Tex had brought it back. Boxes and bags of knickknacks lined the wall just inside the house; Tex hadn't bothered trying to put things back where they went.

As we walked through the house, it became evident that someone had been here since me, someone who didn't believe mid-century furniture was a work of art. Somebody who'd been willing to flip the floral chair in the sitting room and slash through the fabric. Wads of stuffing were scattered across the rug.

"I didn't leave the place like this."

"So someone was looking for something. Did they find it?"

"Not here. The bedroom."

The fake Steve Johnson entered the room while my words hung in the air. Tex looked at him, then back at me, then back at him.

"It's not what you think," Tex said to him.

"Go to the bedroom." I commanded. Tex took the stairs two at a time with fake Steve right behind him. I ascended the staircase, too, as fast as I could, but my knee put me at a disadvantage. When I reached the room that only days ago had been filled with lemon yellow sunlight bouncing off floral wallpaper, hitting the beautiful walnut dresser that had been overflowing with vintage lingerie, scarves, silk stockings, and ribbon tied letters that Thelma Johnson had thought to keep for so long, I gasped.

The dresser had been smashed. Splinters of wood stuck out at corrupted angles, contrary to the simple ninety-degree angles of the original piece. Three of the legs were on the bottom of the dresser, snapped. The fourth sat alone, on the floor, on a monogrammed white cotton handkerchief. The doors that had at one time folded, accordion-like, over the front of the piece now hung from their hinges. Empty drawers had been thrown on the carpet and smashed. There was no repairing it.

"Why did they have to ruin the wardrobe?" I asked.

Tex stopped in front of the broken wood and slowly turned around.

"What did you just say?"

"It was a beautiful piece of furniture. Not worth that much, really, but it was in great condition. You can't find things like that anymore. The lines of it, the wood, the right angles, they were calming. I've always found right angles calming. And now it's scrap wood."

"No, not that. You called it a wardrobe."

"Dresser, wardrobe, some people might have called it an armoire, but they'd be wrong. Why?"

"That's what Sheila and Thelma fought about that night. Her wardrobe. She said she had something valuable..." his voice trailed off while he followed his memory back to that night.

"Did she say she had something valuable in her closet or her wardrobe?"

"Wardrobe. She said wardrobe."

We stared at the destroyed pile of wood. The room was hot and my gingham shirt stuck to my back. I fanned myself with a hand, but it made no difference.

"Sheila was found in her underwear. Someone took her clothes. What if what we're looking for wasn't in her wardrobe," I waved my hands in circles over the dresser, "but was in her wardrobe?" I waved my hands up and down the length of my outfit. "As in, her clothes?"

Tex had a faraway look in his eyes. He processed my question, running my take on his story against what he'd already concluded.

"You took more than what I returned to the house, didn't you?"

I nodded.

"And I bet the first thing you went for was the closet."

I nodded again.

"That's it, Night. You have whatever it is this killer is trying to find. It's somewhere in *your* wardrobe now. I'll get a warrant if I have to, but you don't really have a choice."

"A choice in what?"

"Looks like I'm going to be getting into your drawers after all."

236

Thirty-Two

I couldn't begin to count the number of reasons I didn't want Tex to drive me back to my apartment. They started with the notion that I had something worth murdering for and ended with the furry ball of terror trapped in my closet. I couldn't readily explain Mortiboy's presence without tipping my hand to how much I knew about Hudson's leave.

Hudson. From the minute my mind processed the broken dresser and the one single wooden leg that had been snapped off and laid delicately on the pristine white handkerchief, I knew he'd been there. He remembered what I said about the table legs and he'd set this one off to the side as a message to me. He was out there, somewhere, trying to figure this out, too, so he could move on with his life, away from the accusations, the arrest warrant, the gossip, the lies, and the innuendo. But he probably didn't know what Tex and I had figured out. He was operating on his own without the same amount of information. And that put him in danger.

I followed Tex halfway back to the Jeep before making up an excuse to go return to the inside the house.

"I have to go to the bathroom."

"Night, we're going to your apartment. Can't you wait?"

"No, I can't. And if you were a gentleman you'd not make this any more embarrassing than it is. I'll be right back," I said, and headed into the house.

"Not by yourself, you're not. Nasty!" he hollered.

I didn't wait to see if he was really going to direct her to babysit me. I went as fast as my knee would allow me up the stairs and into the bedroom.

The curtains blew into the room with a slight breeze. I moved to the open window and looked out at the row of dogwood trees that defined the property line.

That's when I saw him. Wearing a black T-shirt and jeans, with a red bandana that matched my own tied over his head. Hudson's hair curled against his tanned neck just like it had when I watched him in the garage, working on the table legs. He looked up at me and our eyes connected. My hand reached out, as did his, and although two stories and one withering vegetable garden separated us, it was like we were touching.

"What the hell do you think you're doing up here?" said a female voice behind me.

"I was going to go to the bathroom."

"Funny detour you're taking," Officer Nast said. She pushed me out of the way of the window and looked around. "What's that?" She pointed at the lawn.

I held my breath, hoping she wasn't pointing to Hudson, hoping he'd gotten away before she had the chance to identify him.

"What? What's what?" I asked innocently.

She picked up her radio and pushed down a button on the side. "Lieutenant Allen, there's something tacked to a tree behind the house. Can you check it out?" She turned to me. "You done yet?"

"I'm done."

"Let's go."

I followed her down the stairs. When we reached the back yard, Tex stood by the row of dogwoods with a piece of paper in his hands.

"What's that?" I asked.

"You tell me," said Nasty. "I think she threw it out the window when she was upstairs."

"I did not!" I exclaimed.

He handed the paper to me. Written on it in familiar handwriting was a new threat. *IT ENDS AT THE MUMMY.*

"Where was that?" I asked. When I'd looked out the window at Hudson, there'd been nothing of the sort in my line of vision.

"It was pinned to this tree. With this." She held up a hat pin. It was the one Hudson carried around with him to remind him of his grandmother.

"Night, where did that hat pin come from? And don't lie to me. I can tell you recognize it. You might as well tell me now because I can make a guess and I'm probably right."

"Whoever the owner of the hat pin is, it doesn't mean he left the note. It could have been stolen from him."

Too late, I realized I'd as much as fingered Hudson with a simple choice of pronoun.

"Take me to my apartment." I turned and walked away, leaving Tex and Officer Nast behind.

I didn't talk on the drive back to Gaston. It wasn't because I didn't have anything to say, but more that I couldn't figure out which thought to start with. Too much connected Hudson to the murder, that I knew. Why did I believe in his innocence more than his suspected guilt? What was it about me that wanted—no, needed—to help find a way to allow him to move on from the net of memory?

It was because I was trapped in the net of memory myself. Since leaving Pennsylvania, leaving a bad relationship, leaving behind a life I thought I was happy with and starting over, I'd spent so much time looking forward I never justified the past.

But through everything I was living now, the memories were pushing against the surface.

I wasn't born yesterday. Just because my business was relatively new didn't meant I didn't have the battle scars gained from forty-seven years of life. I saw those same battle scars in Hudson and Tex. How their lives had been changed because of all of this. And focusing on this murder investigation had made it become my problem. It had taken the focus away from me and the problems I already had. Not trusting people. Not letting people in. Not seeing reality. Not willing to open up enough to allow myself to get hurt that badly again.

Tex pulled into my apartment building and backed into an open space by the dumpster. He left the engine on.

"Night, you are one crazy woman. I can't begin to figure you out and on some days that is an incredible turn on, but on other days it makes my job very hard to do."

"Lieutenant—"

He held up a finger to my lips, shutting me up with both the unexpected intimacy of his gesture and the heat coming off of his hand.

"I keep telling you I think Hudson is guilty and you keep covering for him. But think about this. If you're right, and he's not guilty, he's in a lot of danger. He's closer to this thing than even you are and the best way for you to protect him, which is what I think you've been trying to do, is to let homicide do their job."

"Homicide wants to arrest him."

"Homicide wants to solve the crime and catch the bad guy. Right now, everything points to him."

"And if it didn't? If I could make you see things see things differently, what would you do?"

"How are you planning to do that?"

"That's my problem, not yours."

"*You* are my problem, Night. Like it or not, until this case is solved, I'm sticking to you like glue."

The sun had dipped below the tree line and the dumpster and a shadow fell across the hood of both the Jeep and Tex's face. The heat was still in effect. I reached a hand up and adjusted the bandana that held my hair back. It would have been cooler to have my hair in a ponytail but necessity had eliminated that option. Now, my hairline, damp with sweat, created sticky tendrils that had snuck loose.

"I'm your only link to the investigation, aren't I? The only reason you're here, carting me around Dallas, layering on your inappropriate come-ons and your man-about-town persona is because you need me."

I expected him to deny it, or to say something flip, but he didn't. He reached a hand around the back of my neck and pulled me close to him. Our lips met in a crush of a kiss, powerful and unexpected. At first I fought him, but something inside me, a flicker of passion I thought had been turned off forever, lit and I kissed him back with equal intensity.

My heart pounded when we pulled apart. We stared at each other. I didn't know what to say, whether I should be embarrassed or flattered or both.

"Night, I hate to break it to you, but you got your facts all wrong," he said, his voice husky and low. My eyes dropped to his T-shirt, where they lingered. I was afraid to make eye contact again. I was afraid of what that kiss had meant.

"I'm going inside now."

"Are you going to invite me in?"

I raised my eyebrows. I wasn't sure what kind of an invitation he was looking for, and after that kiss I certainly wasn't thinking clearly.

"Glue, Night. Whether I'm in there or out here, I'm not leaving. If Hudson James is your kind of guy, that's your business. But if he wants to find you tonight, I'm going to know about it."

"You better make yourself comfortable, Tex," I said, and climbed down from the side of the Jeep. I took a few steps toward the back of the building and turned around.

He was watching me; he'd been expecting me to change my mind.

"If it makes a difference, I'll bring you a pillow."

He didn't respond.

I turned around again and went into the building.

I hadn't thought about romance since Brad. I thought that closet door was shut and locked. But I'd kissed two different men in two days, and whether I wanted to face it, the door was unlocked and open. And on top of everything else, I had to wonder what was so wrong with that anyway.

I kicked my shoes off by the sofa, then called Effie to let her know to bring Rocky by. I glanced at my email. Buried between Fourth of July offers from Bed Bath and Beyond, Sears, and eBay was one from Susan at AFFER.

There was a knock on my door. Susan would have to wait. I was eager to see my cuddly little fellow. I peered through the peephole and opened the door to Effie, with Rocky cradled in her arms.

"Thanks again for watching him all day. How's he been?"

"He's been a doll, as usual, but he keeps sniffing around like he's looking for someone."

I draped his leash around my neck and cradled him in my arms. "Probably just wanted to play with a particular toy, that's all." I buried my face in the fur on the top of his head. "You said someone," I commented.

"What?"

"You said he was looking for some*one*, not some*thing*."

"Well, I know you've had a couple of, um, friends over lately and I thought maybe he was looking for one of them."

"Oh?"

"No offense, Madison, but I don't think I ever saw three different men come by your apartment in the same week!" She giggled.

The smile on my face froze like it had been hit with liquid nitrogen but I fought to hold it in place. Something didn't compute. She'd seen Hudson at my apartment. And she'd been there when Tex came over, too. But three?

"I think you counted Lieutenant Allen twice. He does occasionally like to pretend he's someone he's not."

"No, I can recognize the Lieutenant by now. I meant him, the handyman, and the Russian."

Thirty-Three

A chill shot through me like a bolt of electricity. I put my hand on the desk to steady myself. "Effie, can you do me one more favor?" I asked, and reached for a pen. "The lieutenant is out back in his Jeep. He's parked next to the dumpster. Can you take this to him?"

Before she could answer, I grabbed a piece of paper from my desk and scribbled on the back of the paper *Who is the Russian?* I folded it in half and half again and held it out in a gesture of expectation, not giving her the chance to turn down my request.

"Is he here on cop business or personal business?"

I smiled enough of a smile for her to assume the answer she wanted to believe. Her eyes flicked back and forth between mine, bouncing from the left to the right, checking if I was pulling her leg or if I was serious. The gravity of the situation kept the smile from returning to my face. She made a silent O with her mouth and left me in the hallway.

"Sure, I'll deliver your love note." She patted Rocky on the head and looked back up at me. "He's cute, Madison. Lucky you," she said.

244

I waited until I heard the back door close before I entered my apartment. I turned on lights, a lot of lights. Lights in the living room, the hallway, the bathroom, and the bedroom. Enough lights to flood the parking lot with clues that I was inside.

Nothing was out of order, but I suspected there was one angry cat in my closet. I pulled on a pair of oven mitts and headed into the bedroom, ready to face Hudson's little devil. Somewhere during my pep talk to myself, there was another knock on the door. I pulled off the mitts and peered through the peephole. Effie stared back at me.

I pulled the chain off the door and turned the knob. "That was fast!" I said before the door was all the way open. That's why I didn't see the black-gloved hand come at me, covering my mouth, pushing me back into my apartment.

Richard stood in front of me, his eyes wild. He had a firm grip on Effie's upper arm. She looked terrified. He pushed her away, down the hall. "Get out of here. Now."

Rocky, caught up in the excitement of unexpected visitors, bounded back and forth on his hind legs, front paws on our kneecaps, looking for his own bit of attention in the melee. His barking was lost in the white noise of the apartment and the sound of fear ringing in my ears. Richard kicked at him and pushed me against the bookcase.

"Where is it? Madison, where did you hide it?" His fingers bit into my biceps and he shook me. "He's going to kill me if he doesn't get it. You started this whole thing, you have to finish it. I can't hide anymore."

"Richard? What's going on? What are you doing here?" I tried to stall.

Effie had come back too soon. She hadn't had a chance to deliver the note to Tex. And I'd seen the look on her face before she ran to her apartment, and it was one of fear. Not of fighting, or standing up to a bully, or taking control of the

245

situation. If I was lucky, she would call 911 and Tex would get alerted by way of dispatch.

Richard pushed me out of the way, against a wall, and kicked the front door shut. My feet sought footing and I wished I was wearing my shoes instead of being barefoot. I felt something under my heel, crushed glass from the bulb of the lamp Rocky had broken earlier. Small shards stuck into my foot. Richard pushed me to the side and looked at my bookcase. Like a crazy man his eyes scanned the shelves, until he tipped the whole thing over, scattering volumes of decorating magazines and reference material across the floor. Even if someone did show up and try to come in, the door would be blocked.

The lights were on and if I could get Richard into the bedroom, Tex might see his shadow backlit from the light in the room. He'd know I wasn't home alone. He wouldn't know who was with me, but that didn't matter. Nothing mattered except getting help.

"What are you looking for?"

"Don't play stupid with me, Madison. The film? The stolen reel? You think I don't know you have it now? He tracked it to you and he's after me to get it back. After all these years, it's come down to this. You couldn't leave well enough alone. You wouldn't get scared, and now he's going to kill us both. I don't even know how you ended up with it, but I've already gone through too much to lose it all." His eyes darted around the apartment.

He wasn't making any sense, but he wasn't acting like a killer. He was acting like a very, very scared man who had a very real threat pressing down around him.

"Richard, are you Russian?" I asked. He glared at me for a second before he opened my hall closet and started pulling down large rubber tubs of personal belongings that had been packed away. Stale mildew-laced air wafted from storage bins. Blankets and dolls and vintage clothes that needed mending spilled into the hallway. He shook his foot to get a green tweed dress off the toe of his heavy black shoe.

"It's not because I'm Russian. It's because of the application. He would have found me whether I had Russian parents or not. I changed my name so I could disappear and start over. And you've ruined that for me. Killing me won't bother him, he's already killed four people!"

"Richard! What are you talking about?"

He looked into my eyes with an intensity that scared me more than anything else that I'd seen. He kicked at the clothes between us. I took a step backward. He advanced until I was pressed up against the wall in the hallway. His face was inches from my own. His hands pushed against the wall on either side of my head, creating a cage of limbs.

"The film reel. I need the film reel." The lights had solved the biggest problem that Richard had, which was being able to clearly see what I owned and where I kept it. "Where did you hide it?"

"I don't have any film reel!"

There was a knock on the door. Richard clamped a hand over my open mouth, black wool fingers jutting between my lips, triggering a gag reflex.

"Quiet," he hissed. "It's him."

I couldn't speak or yell if I wanted to and I really, really wanted to. I wanted to throw something at the window to make it break, to shower the parking lot with a glass shard cry for help. I wanted Rocky to create the biggest ruckus he'd ever made.

Rocky.

Where was Rocky?

He'd gotten out. When Richard had forced himself in, Rocky had taken off. He was a dog, a little dog, a little defenseless dog who liked people and attention and cars and didn't know any better when it came to traffic when he wasn't on his leash. And despite the threat against me, tears stung my face as I thought about little furry Rocky outside, alone, in the dark, in the night.

The knocking continued. *Come in come in come in* hammered against my brain, willing any of my neighbors to show up at my door. From the hallway where Richard was pressed against me, I could see the shadow of two feet by the front door. *Come in come in come in,* I thought again. *This is no time for politeness. Come in. You heard something or you know something, or you found my dog, but just come in. Try the knob and come in.*

"Madison? Are you in there?" asked a male voice. "Madison, I found Rocky running down Gaston. His address is on the tag on his collar." There was another knock on the door. "Are you in there? I thought I heard you."

It took me a second to place the voice. I looked at Richard and shook my head rapidly to get his hand away from my mouth. "It's okay, I know who it is. He's from the pool where I swim. Be human, Richard. I'll help you find whatever you need but let me answer the door and get my dog back."

Richard pulled away from me and wiped the sweat from his forehead with the back of his arm. It was still hot, too hot to be wearing a sweatshirt. He pulled it over his head, exposing a black T-shirt with a picture of Klaus Kinski on the front.

"Thank you," I said, and stepped over the mounds of clothes to the front door. The knob turned before I got to it and the door hit the resistance of the books on the floor.

"Hold on just a second, Mr. Popov, I mean Andy," I said and kicked the books away from the door.

Mr. Popov.

With a force I didn't know he had, he shoved a foot in the opening and pushed against the door, crushing magazines behind it. He did not hold my dog.

"*Volpa jenshiva,* you stupid little girl," he said. His face twisted, his wrinkles etched deep into angry lines on his forehead, by his eyes, and on either side of his down-turned mouth. "You couldn't leave it alone, could you?" He walked toward me and again I found myself retreating. I looked around but didn't see Richard anywhere.

"That reel of film cost me my career. I thought I took care of it, but I didn't count on Thelma Johnson or her daughter. That kid was no good, she caught me searching her mom's house and tried to blackmail me. She wouldn't let it go. I had to shut her up, for good. And your friend the good Samaritan came along and made it all perfect. I convinced her mom he was the killer and she never once suspected me. But I couldn't find the reel. I thought I'd bide my time, wait until I found it and get her to give it to me. It wasn't until she said she sold a bunch of stuff at a yard sale that I realized it might be gone. I freaked and she realized the truth. And even after I took care of both of them I didn't count on you."

His face twisted into an angry knot. His words were laced with an accent normally kept under wraps at the pool.

"Where is it, girly?" he demanded.

"Where's my dog?" I demanded back. I couldn't stop to think about the danger I was in because I still couldn't wrap my brain around what was going on. But Rocky's life depended on every move I made.

"Stupid little mutt, just like you. I took care of him. He's in the dumpster." A maniacal sound erupted from his throat and triggered a volcano of rage inside me. I stepped forward and brought my knee up to his groin, hoping to catch him by surprise.

He anticipated the move and caught my knee. With his bare hands he twisted my shin far enough to the left to let me know he'd been paying attention all of those mornings at the pool where I'd favored my left leg. The pain grew steadily stronger, until I was all but incapacitated.

I heard the snap before I felt the pain. As a kaleidoscope of colors burst in my head, blotting out my vision and my common sense, I lost both balance and the ability to fight back. I collapsed onto the floor.

Thirty-Four

When I came to, I was on the sofa. Richard pressed a bag of ice against my kneecap. I pulled away, on alert. I couldn't feel my leg. I was scared, more scared than I'd ever been. And the pain rivaled the pain of the skiing accident still fresh in my memory.

"Madison, I'm sorry I scared you. Andreev's been after me for a while. He thinks I have a reel of a Doris Day movie he stole from AFFER. But it's not *Pillow Talk*, it's something else. Something he hid decades ago."

"Richard?" I uttered.

His voice dropped to an urgent whisper. "Where is it, Madison? Where did you hide it?"

"I don't know what you're talking about. Any of it."

"He knows you have it. If you just tell him where it is, he might go away and not hurt us."

Sounds of someone tossing my kitchen like a Waldorf salad filled the background. Richard was more gullible than I took him for. Four murders, countless attacks, threats, breaking and entering? Popov wasn't going to let us go no matter what he found in my cabinets, and I still didn't understand exactly what he thought I had.

251

"Richard, listen to me. There's a cop, out back, sitting in a Jeep next to the dumpster."

"No there's not, Madison. I saw him on my way in. I knew he would stick around if I couldn't get rid of him."

"What did you do?"

"I told him Hudson James was at The Elbow Room getting drunk. He thanked me and took off. That's how Popov got past him."

I stared at the ceiling, not wanting to believe Richard. Catching Hudson was the one thing more important to Tex than my safety. Tears stung my eyes, and I fought to sit up.

"Listen to me, Richard. That man is not going to let us go. We have to get out of here and I can't walk."

"Please, Madison, tell him where you hid the film reel."

"I don't have a film reel. I didn't hide anything. I don't know what you think I have, but I don't have anything you don't see."

"Think. Thelma Johnson had it and you are the only person to take anything from her house. You must have taken it, even if you don't know that you took it."

Pans crashed against the linoleum floor. My downstairs neighbor would hear that if anyone was home. Where were the rest of my tenants? Why wasn't anyone coming to check on the noise coming from my apartment?

Popov came out of the kitchen. "Are you sure you don't want to save me the trouble of searching the apartment, missy? If you just give it to me, I'll get out of here. Get in my car and get to the airport and on the next flight back to Russia. I could have been home years ago but first them, then you. You were more stubborn than everybody else. The rest of them got scared. You lived like you had nothing to lose."

"What is so important that you were willing to kill four people?"

"My reputation in my country. My Russian citizenship. My life. Here I'm an old man. There, I was an astronaut. A legend.

252

I stole the evidence they had of my infidelity to my country. Thelma Johnson—she screwed everything up, she thought it really was *Pillow Talk*, thought it had a scene with her in the background. When she found out the truth, that the only interest I had in her was in the film reel, that I had killed her daughter over it, she came after me with a knife. I should have destroyed the film when I had the chance. But that woman hid it. She knew its value to me and how dangerous I was. A man without a country. Because of the mission to Mars, because of what I knew, because of what I told. It's the only evidence that I sold secrets of our space program, that I sacrificed the Soviet strategy for money. They'll have no proof I'm a spy and they'll have to let me back into my country, to formally apologize, to celebrate me as a hero once more."

Andreev Popov was crazy. He was not going to allow either one of us to walk out of there alive, even if I had been able to walk at the moment.

"I'll tell you where it is if you let Richard go," I said boldly.

"Madison, no!"

"That's the arrangement you made with him, years ago, when you approved his application to film school, right? When you first saw the letter campaigning to destroy all Doris Day movies? You knew somehow you could use him. You thought you'd create an ally, even an even an unwitting one. You sent his letter to AFFER. You even mailed it with his name on the envelope, so he'd be under suspicion if anything happened to *Pillow Talk*."

"He wanted to cooperate at first."

I looked at Richard. The bravado had left him and all that was left was the shell of man in a grimy sweaty rumpled T-shirt. Even Klaus Kinski's Nosferatu looked less threatening than he had earlier.

"It was a highly competitive program and I wanted an edge," Richard said. "That's why I wrote the letter in the first place. And when Mr. Popov taught my class on documentaries he asked for volunteers to help with a project. I wanted a good grade. I thought it would make a difference, you know, have a solid reference on my resume. He was supposed to be teaching us how to get good footage, how to get past the people that try to keep you away from the truth. How to get inside, you know?"

"The kid did good, too. I gave him an A," the Russian said with a laugh. "I could have assembled an army on the power of a grade in those days."

I still didn't know where this supposed film reel would be, and I'd just offered to give it up to save Richard. Running through my head, along with the fear and the pulsating rush of blood, were snippets of conversation that Hudson and Tex had shared with me independently. *It was in her wardrobe.* But I'd seen the wardrobe. It had been destroyed. The table leg, sitting off to the side, told me Hudson had been there. Hudson needed to find the film reel, too, to show that there was a clear motive for murder between someone else and Sheila Murphy, between someone else and Thelma Johnson.

But the fact remained that Popov thought I had it. And what if I did? What if the best items I'd taken from Thelma Johnson's wardrobe included whatever we were looking for? That whatever we were all looking for was now in my wardrobe? Was it possible that between polyester pant suits and vintage cotton dresses hung proof of a Soviet espionage ring, secrets that people would kill for?

I tried to stand, but pain shot through my leg. I collapsed back onto the sofa. I was dizzy and nauseous. And then I remembered Mortiboy.

"Popov, it's in the closet. On the top shelf."

"Madison!" cried Richard.

Popov moved like a mountain lion stalking prey in the wild. His shoulders hunched and his sleeves, pushed up to expose the hair on his forearms, tensed with muscles that had never atrophied under his eighty-year old skin. I realized he'd been at the pool so many times but had never been in a bathing suit. I'd never seen his physique, never knew he was a solid and menacing mass of muscle, now coated in the stink of desperation.

I pushed at Richard. "Get out of here. Now!"

"I can't leave you with him."

"Get help. Fast." I could only speak in short words, the pain interrupting my ability to breathe. Richard stood up and looked in the bedroom. Popov was bent over, moving the piles of shredded laundry that Mortiboy had left on the floor after yesterday's climbing session. He would soon turn his attention to the closet. Mortiboy had been trapped in the closet for almost a day. He would be one pissed off cat. At least, that's what I was counting on.

Popov didn't notice Richard move toward the front door. He flung the sliding closet doors aside in a grand gesture. Mortiboy jumped out of the closet at him, clawing his face, his neck, his arms. Popov screamed.

I pulled the bandana off my head and wound it around my knee. While Popov wrestled with Mortiboy, I pulled the metal rod of the broken pink and brass lamp from under the sofa and angled it like a cane.

And then I heard the crash.

I looked in the bedroom. Popov was on his knees, holding his face. Streaks of blood on his cheeks indicated Mortiboy's damage. But as he knelt on a pile of clothes, with blood-covered hands pressed against the wounds on his face, a stack of hatboxes settled into a pile on the floor in front of him.

And it wasn't the turquoise felt trilby that caught my attention. It wasn't the brown and white rabbit fur cap that buttoned under the chin. I hadn't looked at either since buying them years ago and tucking them away on the top shelf of my closet, where I'd stacked the hat boxes I'd brought home from Thelma Johnson's house.

It was a reel of film that fell out of the bottom box and landed by Popov's knees. A reel of film that Thelma Johnson had hidden in a hatbox years ago.

Popov grabbed the reel with bloody fingertips. I stood, balanced on one foot, and stared at him. I had to get out of there while I had the chance, but I couldn't walk. Popov tore a pillowcase from its case and threw the reel into it, then held it shut the way a miser would clutch at a bag of gold coins.

"You stupid girl. You had it all along. So many people dead. So much wasted time."

He moved toward me, a sharp kitchen knife in his hand, his eyes bloodshot with fury. His hair, a comb-over, stood on end and fell down longer on one side than the other. I put the weight of my bad knee on the pole of the lamp and mustered up the strength to fight him, yet even if I had two good knees I couldn't win this battle. I couldn't run away, could barely stand. Mortiboy had been my ace in the hole and he'd done his best, but now, like so much of my life, I was on my own. I was about to become victim number five.

My fingers closed around the pink metal pole. I pressed my back against the wall of the living room, hearing Popov's footsteps getting closer. I could smell the rancid odor coming from his t-shirt as he approached. Just as I saw the toe of his shoe, I yelled as loud as I could and swung the broken lamp with all of my might. The weight of the lamp caused it to arc low, knocking the knife from his hand. The metal connected with his kneecap. He fell onto all fours and cursed in hard, guttural words.

He crawled toward me like an animal.

"This ends here, Popov," I said, and tried to move backward.

"You're right, missy, it does."

He grabbed at my knees, forcing them to buckle. I lost balance and fell to the floor. My head ricocheted off the corner of the low wooden coffee table but I fought to stay in the moment. He knelt down on top of me, his kneecaps piercing my thighs, pinning me to the floor. His breath, hot and spicy, blasted my face. My leg was underneath me, bent at an unnatural angle. Popov set the reel next to my elbow and reached behind him for a pillow from the sofa. He pushed it into my face. The last thing I saw were his white knuckles.

My scream was lost in the fabric.

Thirty-Five

The blood pumping through my ears drowned any sounds
from outside. I couldn't get air. I felt my hands along the
rug, searching for something, anything. My fingers
threaded through the metal film reel. I pushed it over my head
and hoisted it, then slammed it down. Popov's body went limp
on top of me.

I pushed him off me and gasped for breath, huge gulps of
air that did little to calm me down. I blinked several times to
clear my vision and pushed at his body, kicked at him with my
right foot, trying to get out from under him before he started to
move.

That's when I heard my name.

My reaction to Tex was less than graceful. Tears clouded
my vision, streamed down my face. My nose was running.
Blood ran from an opening on my hand. I didn't know I'd cut it
when I picked up the broken lamp. Tex pulled me up onto the
sofa and put his arms around me. I cried into the soft fabric of
his shirt. And then I heard barking.

Sloppy wet kisses covered my cheek. Rocky wriggled next to
me on the bed, trying his best to elicit a response. When I

moved and reached out to him, he yelped with the happy announcement that I was awake. I looked around, trying to figure out where I was. The walls were white, the bed was white, the unfamiliar nightgown I wore was white.

This wasn't home.

People in scrubs, moved around a white room with peach and green paintings framed in white-washed wood. A man I didn't know sat in a folding chair next to the door. He flipped through a dog-eared golf magazine.

"She's awake," he announced to whoever was listening from the hallway.

Tex came into the room. For a moment he stood by the foot of the bed and looked at me.

"Night, you sure know how to prove a point."

Rocky snuggled into the nook of my arm. His nose prodded the right side of my ribs. I curled my arm around him until he was against me like a teddy bear might have been for a child.

Tex sat on the edge of the bed and put a hand on Rocky's head. "I should have been there like I said I would."

"It's not your fault."

"It's my fault that it got as out of hand as it did."

"Popov..." my voice trailed off as I auditioned the different questions I had against the priority of how to start.

"Popov isn't a threat to you anymore."

"He's dead?"

"He's in jail, and based on what we know and what I think we'll find out after talking to you, he'll be convicted of four murders, along with whatever is on that spool of film. And after the home run you hit against his kneecap, I doubt he'll be able to go anywhere."

Ironic, I thought.

"I don't get it. He's been after that spool of film for twenty, thirty years?"

"The preliminary info is still coming in, but we know that Andreev Popov was an astronaut in Russia while the MIR

259

space station was still operating. He was convicted of selling secrets to other countries. He compromised his country for money. The proof is on that footage."

"But how does it all tie in with Doris Day?"

"That's the weird part. He actually showed some promise as a filmmaker while he was working on the space program and had contacts in the States. He arranged for someone to send American movies to their mission base. It made him popular, important. The guy who could procure entertainment from behind the Iron Curtain back when very little was getting there. We weren't racing to partner with Russia, and Russia wasn't racing to cooperate with us. The only race anybody knew about was part two of the race for space."

"The race for space was in the late sixties and Popov isn't that old. I'm not following."

"He had movies sent in to his camp. Doris Day movies were easy to come by. It was the mid-eighties, and people were fascinated with movies of the sixties. He arranged to see *Pillow Talk* and *The Glass Bottom Boat*."

"What does this have to do with anything?" I asked.

"Scenes were filmed outside of NASA in *The Glass Bottom Boat*. That's when he got the idea, a way to send secrets out of Russia. He spliced footage from his own camera into a reel of the movie loaned to them, and sent it back. This reel is from *Pillow Talk*. Only, it isn't *Pillow Talk*. It's footage from the Buran space program. Photos, schematics, plans. Projections. Timetables and formulas."

"But I heard that movie reel was a little," I sought the best word, "provocative."

"It is. Aside from the information about the Buran missile, it also shows a young Andreev Popov having sex with a blonde secretary in a restricted office. That's what made this particular reel so valuable. It wasn't just footage of their mission. It was the footage that ID'd him as the spy."

"And that copy of *Pillow Talk* ended up at AFFER. Are you telling me that Popov came to the states and has been looking for it since he left Russia?"

"The woman came forward. Told her story to the media, told what he was doing. He denied any involvement in the spy scandal. His cover story was that someone stole his camera and made the footage inside the space station. The Russian media didn't believe him, so he fled, but he knew he had to find that film and destroy it if he ever wanted to return. Once in the States, he made a name for himself as a," he paused for a second, "documentary filmmaker, all the while searching for that reel of film."

He tipped his head to the side and stared out the window. "He knew what he was doing when it came to filmmaking. Russia had no proof he was the spy, unless they came into the possession of this reel, but they were unforgiving. His career was over. He knew this reel of film was in the US so he went about finding it. Madison, he's not a dopey old man. He's a spy. A successful spy, who sold his country's secrets for money. He was smart. But he was vain, too. He used his charm and his wits to get into the beds of women along the way—Thelma Johnson being one of them, and in the end, that was his undoing."

"You found the connection between Popov and Thelma Johnson."

"From what we can determine, Thelma Johnson knew she had something very valuable in that film reel. We'll never know if she knew what it was, but she realized early on that as long as she had it and told no one where it was, she was safe from Popov's rage. He wouldn't dare hurt her without knowing where she'd hid it."

"What about Sheila?"

"We're still working on that."

"I think I can help you out." I told Tex what Popov had said, about Sheila finding him searching the house. Tex had known she was a wild child, but he hadn't realized she was capable of blackmail.

"After Sheila died, Popov must have convinced her mom that Hudson was guilty. She never considered anything else, until one day twenty years of bottled up rage and frustration over the fact that he still hadn't found the reel caused Popov to snap. Thelma must have realized he killed her daughter. Before she could do anything, he killed her, too."

"What about Hudson?" I asked.

"He's not involved."

"Does he know you know that?"

"If he doesn't, he will soon enough."

"You should have listened to me."

"Night, don't go there."

The funny thing was, despite what Tex thought, I didn't want to go there either. Too many what ifs fluttered around us: what if he'd stayed at my apartment building instead of going on Richard's wild goose chase after Hudson? What if I'd been better at asking for help? What if Hudson had cooperated with Tex long ago instead of hiding? What if Popov had had a few more seconds to hold that pillow down over my face?

Tex moved his hand from Rocky's head to my thigh and I didn't push it away. It reminded me of how long it had been since I'd let someone touch me. And it wasn't just physical touching I craved.

I put my hand on top of his. "Where'd you find Rocky?"

"In the dumpster. I wasn't the one who found him. It was Donna."

"Who's Donna?"

"Officer Nast." He said her name differently than before, softer. "She's the one who gave him a bath. He didn't smell so good when we fished him out. Someone in your building likes tuna. Or doesn't, considering how much we found in the dumpster."

"And the cat?"

"We found a black cat in your kitchen cabinet, next to an old popcorn popper. You never told me you had a cat."

"I don't. I'm watching him for a friend who had to get lost for a couple of days."

This time Tex was silent.

"So it's over," I said.

"Mostly," he answered.

"Mostly?"

"There are still a couple of loose ends."

"Like what?" I asked.

"Rest, Night. We had a guy look at your knee, and you're going to need surgery, most likely, though you've proven me wrong before. Anyway, we'll get into the other stuff later."

Officer Nast came to the doorway. Her long brown hair was loose. Soft waves framed her face and hung off to one side. She was out of uniform, and dressed the way Pamela used to dress when she wasn't posing for a real estate flyer. Thin white T-shirt, low-rise jeans, hoop earrings. She tossed her hair behind her shoulders.

"Allen, you coming?" she asked. Her green eyes sparked from across the room. I looked at him then her, and tried to figure out what had changed, and when.

He sat on the bed, our fingers entwined. An IV was hooked up to my arm, and the liquid from a pain-killing drip made tiny plinking noises. Otherwise the room was silent.

"Go. It's easier this way," I whispered.

He avoided eye contact and I knew. I knew neither one of us was in the right place to take on a challenge.

He took two steps toward the door, then turned back around, his blue eyes clouded. He was going to move on, and I almost didn't blame him.

"It's easier this way," I repeated.

"Maybe it's time I stopped taking the easy way." He walked out of the hospital room and left me alone with my puppy.

A week later I was out of the hospital. My knee was still my knee. A replacement might be in my future but as long as they could make do with what God had given me, I wasn't going to fight it. They wanted me to use a cane. I didn't. They won. Taking Rocky for a walk was trickier now that one hand had to stay on the wooden prop.

For the time being, my apartment was a household of three. Rocky, Mortiboy, and me, though I knew Hudson would soon come to collect his charge. He sent me a letter, explaining he had to go away for a while, but would be back. I knew he had sent a similar letter to Tex because the lieutenant told me, though I hoped the tone of that letter differed slightly from the tone of mine. But each day, when I got up to feed the cat and take Rocky for his morning walk, I looked up and down the street for a heavily primered blue pickup truck.

Speaking of cars, my Alfa Romeo was returned, neatly backed into my space. I didn't ask who had driven it over. The driver would have needed a ride getting home and there was a good chance that this was one project Officer Nast could do with Tex. It bothered me that the idea of them together bothered me. It made me think I was starting to feel things again, and that bothered me most of all.

Rocky was out front, peeing on the lawn, when Tex's Jeep pulled up and parked along the curb in front of the no parking zone. The perks of being a cop, I guess.

"Night, we have to talk."

"I didn't know our relationship had progressed to the point where that sentence was due," I said, and immediately wondered about the casual manner with which I'd said 'relationship'.

He seemed not to notice, to be preoccupied with something else.

"How's your schedule today?"

"Mostly open. I have an appointment with a new client at two and I'm doing a walk through with the Duncans at four-thirty, but other than that, nothing. Why?"

He stopped about ten feet away from me and stood there, his face taut. I could see his teeth clenching, not because they were bared but by the subtle movement of his jaw.

"What's wrong, Lieutenant?"

"Remember when we searched your car?"

I nodded.

"We found something. I couldn't say anything until we figured out what it meant. Turns out it didn't have anything to do with Popov or the Doris Day murders."

The Doris Day Murders. That's what the press had been calling Popov's killing streak. The Doris Day Murders committed by The Space Case, as the disgraced Russian had been labeled. It represented the fundamental flaw with creative license, that when it came to things like murder, there should be a journalistic rule against being too clever.

"So why are you telling me? My part is done. I sacrificed my knee to help you stop a killer," I said, trying, and failing, to keep my voice light.

"Can you come with me? Now?" he asked, ignoring my tone.

"Sure. Come inside and I'll get my things."

Tex was more in emotional lockdown than he'd been since I met him. I wondered what had caused this shift. Was it Officer Nast? Or had all of the flirtation, all of his attention, really been about the murders? Had I simply been a means to an end?

Inside the apartment I put Rocky in his crate and lifted my white wicker handbag. My uniform post injury had been a full skirt, boat neck T-shirt, and ballerina flats and today was no different. The fabric of the skirt swirled around my knees, covering the black Velcro brace I'd taken to wearing 24/7.

I followed Tex to the Jeep and got inside. He drove up Gaston, continued up around the bend and turned left again on Lakeshore Drive. Two miles later he swung the Jeep into the Mummy parking lot. I looked at him, no words spoken, but questions evident in my expression.

"We found something hidden by your spare tire. Did you put anything there, keep anything there?"

"No." The hair on the back of my neck bristled. "What did you find?"

"One of our forensic guys found a reel of film when he went over your car. About six minutes' worth. We thought it had something to do with Pamela Ritter's murder."

"How did she get a reel of film into my trunk?"

"She didn't. It's been there for awhile.

"You've known about this all along? What's on it? I mean, you watched it, right?"

He looked away. "Yes, I had to. It turned up before we connected Pamela's murder to Sheila's. I was still on the case, and I had every reason to believe it was part of my investigation."

"But I'm guessing it didn't, and I'm guessing it had something to do with me. That's why I'm here, right? I can tell you I didn't hide any film in my car, for what it's worth, and I hope by now my word counts for something."

It seemed a pretty minor thing, a random loose end for him to use to visit me. Especially after the way I'd seen him interact with Officer Nast in the hospital. And it dawned on me, what this was. An excuse to see me.

"Damn it, Lieutenant, you didn't have to try so hard. Life isn't really like a sixties sex comedy where you have to create an elaborate ruse to get my attention. If you wanted to come see me, just come see me."

"Let's go inside."

He got out of the Jeep and came around to my door, helping me get out. A week ago, I would have shaken off his assistance. With effort, I anchored the cane in the dirty driveway.

We walked, slowly, into the theater. "Go inside and take a seat. I'll be with you in a second."

"Tex?" I asked, wanting some kind of reassurance. He had no words to offer.

The lobby was empty. So was the theater.

"Take a seat, Ms. Night," said an unfamiliar voice.

I looked around, side to side, then up to the balcony. A short man in a rumpled coat stood by the projector.

"This is for your viewing only. Technically what you are about to see belongs to the Pennsylvania police department, but Lieutenant Allen informs me that it pertains to you, so, as a courtesy, we will show you this footage. Once. It is his assumption you have not yet seen it."

"What's this all about?" I asked.

"Take a seat, Ms. Night," said the booming voice again.

I felt like Dorothy, commanded by the invisible Wizard of Oz. Tex stood next to the white-haired stranger and nodded at me. I slid into the end seat of the sixth row of the theater.

A grainy image filled the screen. At first I didn't know what I was watching. And then his face came into focus, staring into the camera, sitting in a brown leather chair that had at one time been my favorite chair. Leaning forward, elbows on his knees, converse sneakers with his navy blue windowpane suit and light blue polo shirt.

Brad Turlington.

The married man I left behind in Pennsylvania.

As his voice fed through the theater's speaker system, my stomach turned with the cruel humor of making me watch him, larger than life on a twenty-foot screen. I wanted to get up and run out of the theater, but on so many levels, I couldn't. I was paralyzed—no, crippled—both emotionally and physically, and this was the person who'd inflicted the deepest pain of all.

Hudson had come face to face with his past, and Tex had his resolution, too. Maybe, just maybe, it was time for me to face my own demons.

"Madison, I'm sorry. I'm so sorry. I can't believe I lost you over this. You're the only woman I've loved, honestly, truly. I've never known a woman like you. I wanted to tell you, tell you everything. I wanted to be honest with you from the minute I we got back together but you were too perfect and I was in too deep. I was afraid to jeopardize everything."

The film crackled and every couple of frames it faded to orange but it was more riveting than a blockbuster. As much as I'd wanted to run only seconds before, now I was caught in the tractor beam of Brad's charisma.

"I'm sorry I lied to you. I wanted to tell you the truth so many times. I was going to tell you at the top of the mountain. But I saw them—they were there. When we went to the Poconos, when we got out of town, I thought we were safe. I told you I wanted us to get away from it all, and I meant it. I didn't know they'd followed me. Us. And I knew if I told you, I'd bring you into it. I couldn't do that to you. You were, are, the only thing that mattered. The only person that mattered."

He'd said these words before, but they were tainted. Tainted with the knowledge I wasn't his one true love. His wife was. He'd said as much right before I'd skied away from him and the limited engagement he offered me. It had taken every ounce of self respect to leave behind the one person who made me feel complete, but I was not willing to be a part of the relationship equivalent of a time share.

He held his head in his hands. His shiny black hair, gelled into place with Top Brass, barely moved. He took his square glasses off and turned them over and over in his hands. It was a nervous gesture I'd seen him do before.

I'd denied him the opportunity to apologize to me when I left. I'd cut off all contact with him. These were great lengths he'd gone to, to communicate his apologies on a piece of film he'd hidden in my car. It was selfish on his part to inflict this on me after I'd fought so hard to get over him.

He put the glasses back on and stared directly into the camera. "Madison, listen to me carefully, because I can only say this once. I am not married. I never was. But I got myself involved with some bad people. I had to keep you safe. When I saw them at the top of that ski slope I knew they would come after you if they knew how important you were to me. Lying to you was the hardest thing I've ever done but it was the only way to drive you away. I knew it would take you out of my life. I didn't know you would hit that tree. It almost killed me not to be able to console you while you were in the hospital. But it was the only way—"

His head snapped up suddenly, to the right of the camera. "No, NO!" he said to someone off-screen. He held his hands up as a defense mechanism. "Don't do this!" he yelled. The camera tipped over and the screen went black.

Four shots fired in rapid succession. *Bang. Bang. Bang. Bang.* The end of the film spun through the spool, slapping the take-up reel.

"He's—he's dead? It's over?" I asked the darkness, looking for answers.

"Depends on your definition of over," said Tex. He jerked a thumb over his shoulder, to the balcony and the man in the projection booth. "According to him, your Brad Turlington is very much alive."

About the Author

Diane Vallere is a textbook Capricorn who writes mysteries and loves clothes. She also writes the Style & Error Mystery Series, featuring fashionista Samantha Kidd. She launched her own detective agency at age ten and has maintained a passion for shoes, clues, and clothes ever since.

Visit her at www.dianevallere.com.

From the Author

Unlike Madison Night, I didn't grow up watching Doris Day movies. I discovered them when I was going through a rough time in my life. It was during that time I lived in·a small apartment in Dallas, Texas. While I tried to remain true to the Lakewood/White Rock Lake area, I fictionalized businesses and locations to create Madison's world. I'm sure parts of what I remember fondly no longer exist, but in my memory, they always will.

If you enjoyed this book, you might
enjoy these other mysteries:

DESIGNER DIRTY LAUNDRY

Samantha Kidd, ex-buyer turned Trend Specialist, designed her future with couture precision, but finding the Fashion Director's corpse on day one leaves her hanging by a thread. When the killer fabricates evidence that puts the cops on her hemline, Samantha's new life begins to unravel. She trades high fashion for dirty laundry and reveals a cast of designers out for blood. Now this flatfoot in heels must keep pace with a diabolical designer before she gets marked down for murder.

A Style and Error Mystery by Diane Vallere
More details at www.PolyesterPress.com
June 2012

OTHER PEOPLE'S BAGGAGE

Three Interconnected Mystery Novellas

Baggage claim can be terminal. This is what happened after a computer glitch mislabeled identical vintage suitcases and three women with a knack for solving mysteries each grabbed the wrong bag.

MIDNIGHT ICE
A Mad for Mod Prequel by Diane Vallere
When interior decorator Madison Night crosses the country to distance herself from a recent breakup, she learns it's harder to escape her past than she thought, and diamonds are rarely a girl's best friend.

SWITCH BACK
An Elliott Lisbon Prequel by Kendel Lynn
Ballantyne Foundation director Elliott Lisbon travels to Texas after inheriting an entire town, but when she learns the donor was murdered, she has to unlock the small town's big secrets or she'll never get out alive.

FOOL'S GOLD
A Jaya Jones Treasure Hunt Prequel by Gigi Pandian
When a world-famous chess set is stolen from a locked room during the Edinburgh Fringe Festival, historian Jaya Jones and her magician best friend must outwit actresses and alchemists to solve the baffling crime.

More details at www.HeneryPress.com
December 2012

CPSIA information can be obtained at www.ICGtesting.com
Printed in the USA
LVOW062153221012

303942LV00008B/20/P

9 780984 965328